ANTHONY

SYDNEY LANDON

1

ANTHONY

I lean my hip against the second-floor balcony and glare at the dark-haired woman below. "What in the fuck is she doing?" I snap to my club manager, Jax Hudson.

Jax shrugs his shoulders indifferently. "Don't know for sure, boss. Seems like a weird place to hold a job interview, but that's what it looks like. She's got people filling out paperwork, and hell, there's even a pen stuck in her hair. She's hot, though, so maybe I should apply for whatever this position is. I've always had a thing for the nerdy accountant look." He licks his lips in a way that makes me want to punch his face. "That's smoking."

Rolling my eyes, I then shake my head in resignation. If I've learned nothing else in my time as the owner of one of the hottest clubs in town, it's that people are basically nuts. I'm rarely surprised anymore, but seeing the woman below collecting papers from the group of men surrounding her table is a first. But she's vaguely familiar. Her slim build and the curve of her neck stir something in my conscience, but I can't place what. My body is reacting to her, which is downright insane. Scantily dressed women surround me every night, and most of them throw themselves at me regularly. So why in the fuck would I look twice at some uptight broad who's obviously picked a bad place to conduct whatever business she has? "Go see what's going on. Her little enterprise is blocking the entrance to the bar."

Jax straightens away from the banister, saying, "You got it, boss."

I remain where I am out of curiosity as he reaches the bottom floor and approaches the table in question. He weaves his way through the group of men and leans down to speak in the woman's ear. She nods a few times, then looks up. Her eyes search the area before locking on mine, and I hiss. *Holy fucking shit.*

Jacey. The hair is different, but I know the face. It's haunted my dreams for longer than I care to admit. Powerless to stop it, my mind drifts to the day we met. I was helping my friend, and the man I consider a brother, Lee Jacks, deal with the man known as the father-in-law from hell. Luckily, the monster in question is dead, and there is one less piece of shit in the world thanks to the woman below.

Jacey Wrenn, sister of Lee's wife and former assistant, Jade, killed her father that day in a move that surprised us all. And considering the men in the room, that was no easy feat. Fuck, my cousin, Marco Moretti, still speaks of her in a voice filled with awe—*and lust.* At every mention of her name in the past eleven months or so, I've wanted to kick his ass.

After discovering their mother was murdered by their dad and didn't die in a car accident as the police record had shown, Jacey had lost it. She'd spent most of her life believing one thing only to find out it was a complete fabrication. And her father made the mistake of gloating. The bastard had also bragged about having my father, Draco Moretti, killed along with his business partner and best friend, Victor Falco. *The kill should have been mine.* Every man in that room acknowledged the unspoken rule. *Revenge.* The Morettis lived by a code. And even though I've distanced myself from the daily operations of the family, I'll never completely be free of them—nor do I want to be. I'd played with Wrenn, letting his ego write checks that his body couldn't possibly cash. His admission caught me by surprise. How he managed to cover his involvement in my father's death was astounding. I still believe someone within the family was paid off to look the other way, and eventually, I'll find out who. But for now, Jacey has my sole focus.

The delicate, beautiful vixen who shot and killed her father before passing out in my arms.

I took her home with me that night. She stayed for a few weeks before she walked out when I refused to give her what she wanted. I knew she wasn't ready for what she was asking me for. Truthfully, I'm not sure she'll ever be. I have no idea exactly what she did as the right hand of her father, but I have a sick feeling that it was more than she could physically and emotionally deal with. Add in murdering her father in cold blood, and you get one colossal, fucked-up mess. And she's been in denial about pretty much all of it. She smiles at the right moments, acts rationally, and appears normal. All of which is bullshit. She is anything but.

I've seen her at family gatherings over the past year thanks to my friendship with Lee. But she's largely ignored me. One of my guys keeps an eye on her. Even dead, a man like Wrenn could still have enemies, and Jacey is an enticing target as the head of Wrenn Corp. She sold off a lot of holdings since taking over the company, but that means nothing to those harboring grudges. I also fear she has a death wish, and given she makes zero effort to keep a low profile and doesn't have security of her own suggests I'm right. Sadly, that's left me in the position of protecting her from not only unknown enemies but from herself as well.

I half expected her to go wild—regressing into teenage rebellion with her father gone—but that didn't happen. Even though I wouldn't have liked that scenario, I would have at least understood it to a degree. People deprived of a decent childhood often attempted to recreate it later in life. But instead, she threw herself into the family business as if nothing else existed. Maybe she's still trying to prove her worth to her old man, even though she put him in the ground. Bottling your shit up isn't healthy, I can attest to that. Eventually, you need an outlet, and if you don't find one, your body will force the issue. Jacey has been a ticking time bomb since the day she pulled the trigger, and I've been doing my best to stay close so I can put the pieces back together if she explodes.

Who would guess that Tony Moretti is such a noble guy? *Fuck that.*

I'm no one's knight in shining armor or even close. But she's been under my skin for longer than I care to admit. Hell, since before I ever laid eyes on her. Sounds fucking insane, right? In all the time I've been obsessed with the woman below, never once have I imagined how we officially met. Nor have I believed that I'd be in the unfamiliar position of wanting to save her. She has a sister who, although the relationship has never been close, would step in and do anything necessary to help her. So why was I, a virtual stranger, the one enduring the sleepless nights worrying about Jacey Wrenn? *Her father had your father killed.* She was innocent of that crime, but by rights, I should want her dead. Fuck, there are those within the family who desire that very thing. Thank fuck Lee's married to her sister, Jade. There isn't a Moretti brave enough to go after Lee. To touch a single hair on his wife's head would bring down something comparable to the apocalypse, and the family knows it. But if Lee is the devil, then I'm his cousin the Grim Reaper. When I handed down the verdict that neither Wrenn woman be harmed, it became law. Some may not like it, but they fucking know what their disregard of my command brings. *They would burn.*

My relationship with the Moretti organization is complicated. My father, Draco, founded what is now one of the largest crime syndicates in the South. He lavished his family with power and prosperity, thus earning him a type of loyalty that few could imagine. Even years after his death, his name is still revered. I used my inheritance to open my first nightclubs in Asheville, North Carolina, as well as South Carolina, Georgia, and Florida. Even though I'm not active in the daily operations, I'll always be the prince. When I need something, it's granted. My word is law, and every man in the organization will do my bidding without question. It is a strange and complex association, but it works. I'm not a fool. I know there are those within the family who resent the fact I've more or less turned into a law-abiding citizen instead of assuming my rightful place as the head of the Morettis. If it is within my power and influence—and it often is—I take care of my brothers by greasing the right palms and having ties with those in a position to look the other way when needed. The family has grown so large since my father's death that there are some I don't trust. Some who may have helped cover up when Hunter Wrenn killed my father.

A hand on my shoulder has me whirling around and biting back a curse. I must remain vigilant simply because I'm a Moretti, and allowing someone to sneak up behind me could be deadly. Luckily, it's Jax, and the perplexed expression on his face tells me I'm not going to like what he has to say. I raise a brow when he simply shakes his head as if to say, *what the fuck?* "I thought I'd heard it all, boss, but you're not going to believe this shit. The Duchess is holding interviews for a baby daddy. Hell, men are filling out applications and signing waivers for her to obtain their medical records."

What the fuck? To buy some time as I try to process this, I ask distractedly, "The Duchess? She gave you that name?"

He smirks. "We didn't get that far. But she reminds me of that hot Kate Middleton. Isn't she the duchess of something? Plus, she's sitting on that barstool like it's a goddamn throne." His eyes literally roll back in his head when he adds, "She's hot as fuck and smells like a mixture of heaven and sin. What I wouldn't give for a little taste of both."

I snarl before I can stop myself. I bare my teeth at the man I consider a friend as well as a trusted employee and advisor. "That better never happen," I say in what's considered my deadly quiet voice. Anyone who knows me would attest that you'd rather me yell at you anytime. When I'm calm, you run. It's a trait my father also had. He killed men without ever raising his voice.

He throws his hands up and takes a step back. He's been with me since the beginning, so he knows when to back off. "She's yours," he says simply, while looking surprised. *I've staked a claim.* There's always been plenty of pussy to go around. But unlike others, I avoid shitting where I eat, and even though I don't forbid it, I prefer my management team do the same. One-night stands and romantic entanglements are a fucking nightmare in a place that serves booze and a good time. No good can come of it. You're not likely to meet your future wife while she's drunk and grinding against you on a dance floor. But who am I to judge? I certainly don't come from a conventional family, so I'm not the man to make that call. He clears his throat and resumes his place at my side. He leans closer to be heard above the loud beat of the music. "Boss, you catch the part about her hunting for someone to knock her up? That's carrying it a bit far, right?"

And just like that, my calm is gone, and I'm clenching my hands at my sides. I want to march downstairs, throw the Duchess over my shoulder, and take her somewhere to give her what she needs—a spanking. She fucking knows this is my club. Hell, she stayed here with me. Jax has seen her in my apartment—he just didn't recognize her with the dyed hair. I refused to father her child, so she's getting back at me by pulling this stunt right under my nose. Despite the anger humming through my veins, I smile. *You've fucked up, Duchess. Jax is right; that name is perfect for her.* There is a regal bearing in the way she holds herself. Spine ramrod straight. Nose turned up as if no one in the vicinity is worthy of her. She begged the Moretti prince to be the father of her child. *Couldn't get much lower than that, baby.* Without taking my eyes from her, I say, "I heard what you said, Jax, and it'll be taken care of. Just ignore her unless one of her applicants gets out of hand." I glance at my friend before adding, "She won't be back tomorrow. At least not in that capacity."

He nods once before walking off, and my attention returns to her —*always her.* "Just remember, you started this, Duchess," I murmur as she glances up, and her eyes lock onto mine. There's defiance there— which fucking turns me on. But it's the hint of vulnerability that has me wondering if I'm capable of saving her from herself without destroying the last piece of humanity we both possess.

JACEY

This seemed like a good idea earlier—but now I'm not so sure. I knew he was watching me before his manager arrived at my table. Bringing this battle to his doorstep felt like a mistake—a deadly one. But I'm desperate. I need him the way air is necessary to breathe. He is the blood pumping through my veins and the only thing keeping me from falling apart. I didn't want to leave him, but I put it all on the line, and he flatly turned me down. I wasn't a fool; I knew he wanted me—but not in the same way. Otherwise, he wouldn't have been capable of maintaining the tight hold on his control. And God knows, I did everything in my power to make him lose it. If only he simply found me unattractive, that would be easier to deal with. But I'm damaged goods to him. Broken. He thinks eventually I'll shatter into a million pieces—*and I'm terrified he's right.* That very fear was the driving force that made me say such obnoxious things to him when I last saw him. A shudder runs down my spine as I recall my final words to him. "*I might be the daughter of a murdering bastard, but you're the son of a fucking mafia thug. How dare you consider yourself above me? You should be jumping at the chance to father my child instead of passing judgment.*"

He was angry, which was what I wanted, but I didn't count on the other emotion I caught a brief glimpse of before he shut down—hurt. And as crazy as it seems, that bothered me more than killing my father had.

Oh wait—maybe I should start with that. My name is Jacey Wrenn, and a year ago—give or take a few weeks—I gunned down my father when he gloated about murdering my mother and her lover. When I pulled the trigger the first time, it had been pure reflex. A reaction to the lies and years of hell he'd put me through after having taken the only good thing in my life away. The second time, I knew exactly what I was doing. I wanted to ensure he couldn't terrorize my sister and me any longer. *That the power he wielded over us was eradicated.*

I passed out in the arms of Anthony Moretti—Tony. The man whose *father* slept with my mother. By all rights, I should hate him, but I don't. In the short time I stayed with him, he showed me something I hadn't had since my mother died. *Love.* Which is absurd to even think. He was a total stranger to me. We hadn't met before. Yet he held me in his arms when I woke from nightmares screaming. I can still feel the warm press of his lips against my forehead as he murmured words of comfort—promising me that no one would ever hurt me again. Whether he knew it or not, he saved me. If I had been left on my own, I might not have had the strength to face the road ahead. But he sheltered and cared for me until I was ready to carry on. I'm not saying two weeks cured me. Far from it. But I was functional again—more fucked up than ever—but functional. *One step above batshit crazy. Yay me.*

The second week with him, an idea—or a longing—took root that I still haven't shaken. I wanted something of my own. Someone to love. Someone to build a life with and around. The timing might have been odd, considering recent events, but my biological clock had picked that exact moment to go haywire. My inner voice had laughed hysterically, considering how I avoid children like they're the plague. Why on God's earth would I want one of my own? They were messy, smelly, loud, and basically everything I'd never wanted. I'm almost certain they don't make a Prozac dose big enough to deal with all that motherhood entails. So why do I want it so badly? And not with just anyone. It had to be him—Tony. Probably the man least likely to agree to my request. No doubt his views on parenthood are similar to what mine have always been. He is the son of a freaking mobster and owns several nightclubs. Although, from what I observed while staying with him, he rarely slept. That's a plus when you have children. *Isn't it?* What does it matter? I'm after a sperm donor, not a husband. Even if he agreed to *help* me get pregnant, he certainly wouldn't want anything more to do with me after that... *Sadly.*

If he and I are a mess together, then imagine what our child will be? A mixture of the Moretti and Wrenn bloodline. The kid will be all kinds of fucked up. Probably end up in a laboratory somewhere being studied by a team of scientists. And God help us all if it looked anything like Tony. The female population of North Carolina wouldn't stand a chance. Dark, thick hair, sun-darkened skin, stunning gray, perceptive eyes that I sometimes got lost in, and a body that literally makes drool form in my mouth.

Yet even after listing the many reasons it was crazy to consider, I want to have his child more than ever. Hence, this insane stunt I'm pulling right under his nose. *Never corner a wild animal. You'll be sorry... so very sorry. Run...run.* A part of me wonders if it is really a baby I want or simply the feeling of electricity running through my veins at the thought of pushing him too far. He accused me of having a death wish, which might be more accurate than I'm willing to admit. Although I know he'd never physically hurt me, there are other ways to destroy the daughter of the man who murdered his father. If he has a clue how obsessed I've become with him, it would be all the ammunition he needed. I simply didn't have the strength left to survive in a world where Tony Moretti hated me. Right or wrong, he's the reason I get up every morning and is what's kept me moving through the endless hours and days only to repeat the process over again. He's why I'm still here. Before him, I could have given a fuck if I lived or died, and I've felt that way for a long time. I'm loved by no one. I could cease to exist, and not a single person would really care. Sure, my bleeding-heart sister, Jade, might be mildly upset, but she has a life of her own now with a husband who absolutely adores her and a son they both dote on. Her life is a fucking Norman Rockwell painting. And mine is a Stephen King novel. *Because you're a monster. Dress her up—make her pretty. Doesn't change the fact. She's ugly inside. Her soul is black. Who could possibly love such a hideous monster?*

Jax is speaking again. How much of the conversation have I missed during my trip down memory lane? Tony hated it when I zoned out on him. He always wanted to know where I went, so I laughed and made up something silly like a shoe sale. He saw right through me...of course. He knew when the demons were at my door because he's just as haunted as I am. "Listen, lady, as I said, you need to pack up whatever you're doing here and go elsewhere. You're causing a disturbance, and the boss isn't happy about it."

I turn on my barstool and look directly at Jax, who gives me a blank stare before I slowly raise my head and lock eyes with *him*. Even from this distance, I see the shock he's unable to hide. He staggers as if absorbing a blow before the impassive mask falls back into place. "Good to see you again, Jax," I say to the other man without looking away from the figure standing at the balcony above me. *Looking down at the world through those gray eyes. My lone wolf.* The air literally sizzles as awareness shoots through my body. How is it possible to respond like this to a man who is essentially a stranger?

Men are the enemy. They only use and abuse you.

Because Tony lived above the club, I met Jax several times during my two-week stay with his boss. He was always polite and never asked questions in my presence about why I was there. Clearly, he hasn't recognized me yet with the different hair color. His voice is indifferent but curious as he asks, "What's going on?"

Before I can answer, a hand lands on his shoulder as a drunken idiot slurs out, "Hey buddy, wait your turn." He waves a paper in front of Jax's face. "I've got my application ready to turn in." He gives me a leer that has me rolling my eyes in disgust. Licking his lips, he adds, "I'm more than ready to be your baby daddy, sweetheart. No test tube required. The old-fashioned way is much nicer."

Jax blinks a few times as he attempts to process the other man's words. He then grabs the paper from the man's hand and has a nearby security guard escort the man out when he protests loudly. Jax scans the application, and a smile pulls at my lips as his eyes widen. "Are you out of your mind?" he asks incredulously. "You're actually holding interviews in a bar for a man to father your child?" He laughs, shaking his head. "Was McDonald's too crowded?" His eyes run over me appreciatively. "Is this one of those hidden camera shows? You're hot as fuck. There's no way you need to advertise for a man."

I shrug my shoulders, looking the picture of confidence as I pick up a stack of completed applications and slide a paperclip on them. "Can you think of a better place to find eager men?" I glance in the direction of Tony once more before adding, "Now, if you don't mind, others are waiting. And if your boss has a problem with me being here, then please tell him he knows what he can do to stop it." With those words, I turn my back on Jax and wait.

A long moment passes before I hear him laugh—but it contains no humor. Then he says, "You have no idea who you're playing with, lady. If I were you, I'd pack my shit and get out of here while you can."

"Well, you're not me," I toss over my shoulder. "And I'm not afraid of Tony Moretti. You can tell him that, too."

He curses under his breath but leaves. I sag against my chair for a moment, before once again straightening my spine. *The show must go on.* "Next," I croak out through parched lips. Regardless of my brave words to Jax, I'm shaking. I fight the urge to flee. *What will Tony do about this?* But then I remind myself that he can't do anything to me that would be worse than what I've lived through. There is only one way he can hurt me, and that would be to disappear from my life. Anything else is simply another game I'll be forced to play to get what I want. I shake my head at my dramatic thoughts. Who am I kidding? Tony isn't like the others. For the first time, it could be about pleasure—not pain. *Not dominance.* But that's something I hope he never discovers. I know he suspects I did a lot of shady business for my father. In truth, I was mostly kept away from anything illegal. And let's not kid ourselves here; there was a lot of that. Even though he covered his tracks well, I've seen enough since taking over Wrenn to know that a big chunk of his money was dirty. Which is why I've sold off everything questionable. We've taken a big financial hit on some of it, but I'd rather lose money than spend the rest of my life in jail for my father's corrupt ways.

I'm in no way innocent. I sold my body and soul long ago for dear old Dad.

He left me no choice.

My stomach roils as bile threatens to choke me.

Is it any wonder that I'm here now doing something so desperate? Those moments in Tony's arms were the closest I've ever come to feeling like I mattered. And even then, paranoia still lurked. Why would a stranger help the daughter of the man who organized his father's murder? What kind of game was he playing? I waited on pins and needles for days, expecting the retaliation, but it never came. Instead, he put me back together—as much as was possible at least. He made no mention of me leaving. He seemed more than content to let me stay with him. I was the one who walked away when he didn't agree to my demands.

He's not like the others. Maybe he's...good?

I snort as that ludicrous thought fills my head, only to be discounted. I know well that the son of Draco Moretti is far from a choirboy. I'm also aware that I robbed him of his warranted revenge that night. *Does he hate me for that? For taking away something that was rightfully his?* I know enough about the mafia to realize that an eye-for-an-eye is acceptable. Will he forgive me for taking that away from him?

It wasn't premeditated. I have a hard time believing that I pulled the trigger—not once, but twice. And even then, my finger had twitched, wanting to empty the chamber into his black heart. Had I not passed out, I probably would have. *He deserved it—he was the one who destroyed my soul.*

A hand touches my shoulder, and I freeze, feeling some of the energy sucked from the room. I whirl, expecting it to be *him* but blink in surprise when it's not. The eyes are similar. The coloring and build too. This hulk of a man is darkly handsome, and my pulse races even though he's not the one I'm here for. He eyes me leisurely from head to foot without permission or apology. He's not a man used to asking for permission, that much is apparent. Finally, his mouth quirks into a smile, and I see another piece of Tony there. *They must be related.* Either that, or I've officially lost what little sanity I have left, and I'm seeing the object of my obsession in every man now. "I thought that was you, Lucy." His head moves to the side before he adds, "I preferred your hair blond, but this works as well."

Lucy? "Do I know you?" I ask. I assume it's a case of mistaken identity if not for the comment about my hair. On a crazy impulse, I changed my former blond locks to a dark shade of brown. Somehow, it made it easier for me to look at the woman in the mirror. *I hate seeing so much darkness, such a wasted life in front of me. Someone capable of betrayal and murder.* It hasn't changed who I am inside—nothing short of a miracle can do that—but it has made it easier to pretend I'm *not* Jacey Wrenn.

He laughs, and I nearly melt into a puddle in the floor. *This is how Tony would look if he were happy.* But like me, he's more serious and solemn than this man. Were Tony and I ever young and carefree? He places a large hand against his chest in what I hope is a mock gesture of pain. "I can't believe you don't remember me." He glances at the men surrounding us before lowering his head closer to mine. "I've taken care of a lot of details on your behalf. I feel as if that moves us past formality and straight to the friend's level."

I frown as I process his words. Then it hits me. "Marco," I murmur, not needing his nod of confirmation to know I'm right. I heard Tony talking to him more than once, but he wasn't who told me the name of the man before me. That had come from Jade. She and Lee were there *that* horrible day, and when I asked her to fill in the details for me, she mentioned Marco with equal parts trepidation and awe.

He tips his head in agreement, looking at the stack of applications in front of me. Before I can stop him, he picks one up and scans it. I see his mouth twitch as he tosses it back onto the table. "I certainly picked the correct nickname for you."

"Lucy is a nickname? Are we talking the character from *Charlie Brown*?" *I've been called many things, but this is a new one.*

He shakes his head. "Actually, it's after Lucifer. You realize that he was once a fallen angel. And that's what you reminded me of that day— a fallen angel, but no less beautiful for it."

Even though the meaning behind the name isn't exactly flattering, the look in his eyes says he means it as a compliment. Regardless of who I am and what I've done, this man clearly admires me—and desires me. But his desire doesn't make me uncomfortable; quite the opposite. It's almost warm and comforting. I'm not fooling myself, though. He's a Moretti and therefore far more dangerous than I can possibly guess. Yet I'm perfectly at ease with his proximity. *With him.* And while I can appreciate how hot he is, it's different than what I feel for Tony. "I should probably be offended," I toss out, but we both know there's no heat behind my words. This man seems like a friend.

He reaches out to tap my nose as he says, "You know better."

Before I can reply, *he's* there, and all the air *is* sucked out of the room. For a moment, I can't breathe. His lips tighten when he sees the crowd of men still standing near the table. *He's furious.* He refuses to make eye contact with me; instead, he claps Marco on the shoulder, and they do the standard guy half embrace. "Let's go to my office," he clips out before turning on his heel and walking away.

Marco shoots me an amused look as he shakes his head. "You're in trouble, Lucy, and if I'm not mistaken, that's exactly what you were aiming for."

I don't bother to confirm or deny his suspicions. Instead, I give him a blank stare that has him laughing once again. "If I weren't so envious,

I'd feel sorry for my cousin. Because you're bound to make his life a living hell for years to come." He surprises me by dropping an easy kiss onto the top of my head before disappearing in the direction Tony had headed seconds earlier.

Do I have an ally in Marco Moretti?

He may not have put it into words, but killing my father has earned me immense favor in his eyes. And he may have saved my ass tonight. I had no idea what I'd do after Tony knew of my stunt, but now I need to use the distraction of Marco's appearance to retreat. Yes, I wanted a reaction from Tony, but giving him some time and space to cool down might be the smartest move for now. So, I get quickly to my feet and gather the papers I've collected. *They'll be going straight into the trash.* The remaining men protest, but I barely notice as I all but run from Tony's club. I don't relax until I'm locked safely inside my Mercedes driving toward my condominium. I sold the family home as soon as I legally could, having no desire to ever step foot inside those doors again. I took none of the furnishings with me, because I wanted —*needed*—to start over in a place that held no memories of the man I spent my life fearing. *A man who poisoned me with his lies for too long.*

Instead of the usual emptiness I inevitably feel at the end of each day, there's excitement coursing through my veins. How can just thinking about Tony make me feel so alive? *Did I poke the angry bear tonight?* Yes. And who knows how he'll react? But regardless of the outcome, it was the best few hours I've had since I left him months ago. Although that is a sad and true commentary on the state of my life. *He doesn't want me. But any attention from the fierce and potent man is enough...it seems.*

2

ANTHONY

I scowl as Marco drops down into the chair in front of my desk. I was beyond angry when I saw him standing so close to Jacey. *Mine.* Why the fuck does she make me feel so possessive of her? *Because she belongs to you.* Fuck. Not only do I want to kick my cousin's ass over a woman, but I'm also carrying on a silent argument with the voice in my head. I need to get laid and burn off the shitstorm clouding my judgment and keeping me off center. But I know that no amount of pussy is going to cure what ails me. For as much as I consider her mine, I've become hers as well. *How is that possible? You don't even know her.* The strange part is that I do. I only have to look at her and know what she's thinking or feeling. In a weird way, we're connected. And it's fucking unsettling. At times, I wish I could sever that link, and at others, I'm awed that such a thing is even possible. Marco throws his foot onto the edge of my desk, then crosses the other over it. He knows I hate that shit, but his grin says he could give a fuck. I relax as I roll my eyes at the juvenile tactic. I'm closer to him than anyone else in the family, and even when he irritates the hell out of me, I still enjoy his company. "Make yourself at home," I say sarcastically as I mirror his movements on the other side of my desk.

He doesn't waste time with pleasantries but gets straight to the subject at hand. "So, she's back." Then waves a hand in the air. "But what the fuck was that shit about? You're letting her hold some kind of sperm-seeking job fair in your club? I gotta say, brother, you're a lot more open-minded than I believed."

I surprise myself by chuckling at his words. I expected the anger to return, but it's banked for the moment. "She's something else, right? I nearly lost it when Jax told me about her little enterprise."

Marco eyes me suspiciously as if expecting me to shit a unicorn at any moment. Probably thinks I'm drunk or high. Two things I rarely am. "You sound almost proud of her. I mean, I'm the last to judge dysfunctional relationships, because I've been with my share of crazy chicks, but this is a new one for me."

I pull a cigarette from a nearby pack and offer him one before lighting the tip. *I need to stop this nasty shit.* I inhale deeply before releasing the smoke into the air. "A part of me is impressed that after all she's been through, she still has the balls to come into my place and rub my nose into the floor. Do you know a man who would be brave enough to attempt that?"

He shakes his head. "Knew she was special when she took out her old man. She's fucked five ways to Sunday, though, brother. She's all fire and brimstone on the surface, but it's there if you know where to look. And we've both been trained to see what others cannot."

I lean forward to put my cigarette out as I process his words. Marco has always been surprisingly insightful. He's a man who spends a lot of time thinking about the actions of others. He likes to know what drives a person to do the things they do. We've had some deep conversations through the years, especially concerning the death of my father. "I see it too." I sigh, wishing often I wasn't so affected by her. I pinch the bridge of my nose. "I can't be pissed over this fiasco tonight, because it's brought her back into my life. Don't get me wrong. Eventually, I would have gone after her, but…"

"You needed her to come back on her own," he says softly. I incline my head, telling him that, as always, he's right. "Makes sense to me.

Otherwise, you have a woman used to running so that you'll chase her. No good ever comes from that shit."

Marco has no idea, but this stunt tonight wasn't about playing hard to get. If that were the case, I wouldn't be interested. But Jacey isn't like other women. She's not trying to trap me into marriage. Hell, I didn't even expect her to follow me to my office. *That would be far too predictable.*

No, she wants you to father a child.

That desire is so illogical, I've wondered if she had a full-on mental breakdown that night. How else do I explain her insane desire to be a mother? And even if I can wrap my head around that notion, why in God's name does she want me and only me to be the father? Marco continues to speculate on Jacey's motives, but I don't bother to correct him. I don't want to lie to the man I consider a brother, nor am I comfortable sharing something so personal with him. When he pauses, I take the opportunity to change the subject. "Anything new on Tommy?"

A look of distaste crosses Marco's face. Tommy Moretti is a member of the family, but something has always seemed off about him. As Marco and I began digging into the death of my father, even though neither of us found anything that couldn't be explained away, we both shared uneasy feelings about Tommy. And given our instincts have saved both our asses many times before, we know better than to discount them. "He's careful, Tony, almost too much so. He goes to great lengths to cover up family business, which makes no sense to me. Why hide what you're doing from the people who told you to do it in the first place?"

"Because it's become second nature," I interject. "If he did have a part in Dad's and Victor's death, then he's been covering his ass for a long fucking time. Probably doesn't know how to operate any differently at this point."

Marco glances around my office, then leans forward, dropping his voice. I almost point out that my office is soundproof and checked several times a day for bugs. This is who we are. "According to a couple of the guys, he's gotten tight with Frankie Gavino. They were giving him shit about it over dinner a few nights back."

I play devil's advocate as I say dryly, "The Morettis and the Gavinos have a few joint ventures. It's not out of the realm of possibility that they'd be friendly."

Marco snorts, then gives me a roll of his eyes. *Asshole.* "You know that punk has nearly been ex-communicated from the Gavino family a half-dozen times. If it wasn't for his father being a major player, his dumb ass would have ended up in a morgue by now. He's a misfit, but he's just smart enough to think he can pull off something big."

"Like a hit on a Moretti and a Falco," I muse. "It seems almost too obvious, though. Like maybe we're being pointed in that direction. Yet—"

"It feels right as well," Marco finishes. "I've had the same thoughts. Been over it in my head a million times. Hell, he's only a few years older than we are, so would have been a kid at that time. Do you think he could have masterminded a hit of that magnitude? He's not exactly Einstein, so it's a hard sell."

"Plus, Hunter Wrenn confessed to setting the entire thing up. And I can't see him being loyal to a Moretti at that point. Fuck, he'd have gotten off rubbing my face in that shit."

"True," Marco says before adding, "but what if he only thought he'd been the one to pull the proverbial trigger? I don't doubt he paid some junkie to do his dirty work. Sounds about right to me. But let's say that Frankie and Tommy rode in on his coattails, wanting to accomplish the same thing and were more than willing to let Wrenn think he'd done it. Puts things away neatly and gives the family an easy target for retribution."

"That was almost twenty years ago, though. Do we have anything that links Tommy and Frankie together back then? Don't get me wrong, I agree they're both pieces of shit, and on paper, this lines up perfectly. But we're going to need a hell of a lot more than that before we act against them. Like it or not, Tommy is a Moretti, and the family won't sanction anything without a fuckload of proof. Plus, Frankie might be an outcast within his own circle, but if we touch him, we'd damn well better have more than what we do now. Not only would it get us killed, but a war between the Morettis and the Gavinos would be catastrophic, turning the streets into a bloodbath. This city would be turned to ash, and you know it." Even to my own ears, my words sound overly dramatic, but they're anything but. If there were to be a clash between these two powerful families, it would be a nightmare of epic proportions. Even these secret discussions are dangerous.

But I need to know the truth—I must. I've waited long enough.

Marco gets to his feet and begins pacing my office, his brow furrowed in thought. Ever since we were kids, when something bothers him, he's restless like a caged animal. Patience is a trait neither of us was born with. So, the fact that I've waited twenty years to get to this point is nothing short of astounding. "I don't want to believe this," he starts quietly, "but if Tommy and Frankie were involved, then there's someone else. No way those two started this. We know that Wrenn may have inadvertently played a hand, but fuck, there's got to be a Moretti at the helm. It makes me fucking sick to my stomach to say that, but it's there, Tony, you know it is."

I don't bother to confirm or deny his statement; instead, I say firmly, "We have to be careful. You believe we've been covert in our digging so far, but going forward, it's got to be a whole new level of paranoid. Like our lives and everyone connected to us depends on it. Because it's true. Someone at the top of the Moretti food chain may have ordered a hit on my father. And believe me, if they were that fucking brave, then taking us out will be nothing to them. Truthfully, I'm surprised they haven't tried it already just to eliminate any future problems. Probably the only thing that has kept that from happening is my inactivity within the family and the fact that you and I are careful about being seen together. But one of two things could happen with Wrenn's death: the guilty party may relax, thinking he's safe with Wrenn's confession, or he may figure he dodged a bullet and decide to make a clean sweep. All depends largely on one thing."

Marco stops pacing and turns to study me for a moment before nodding slowly. "How much he or they have to lose. If it were only Tommy or even Frankie and Tommy, I wouldn't expect much more than a wait-and-see approach. They're not proactive. They'd rather try to put out a forest fire with a bucket of water, than step on a spark to prevent it from happening."

"Exactly," I say, appreciating once again how easily my cousin and I have always understood each other. Largely because we view life in a similar way. "You need to pass this warning on to Nic. Make sure he watches his back and yours." Nicoli Moretti is a distant cousin, and a man I trust almost as much as Marco. He grew up with us and has never given me any reason to question his loyalty. He's been just as skeptical of the official story of my father's death as I have. And given patience isn't one of his strengths either, he's never been happy about waiting to find answers.

"We know the stakes are high. I'll relay your words to him." Marco's mouth curls into a grin as he says, "I'm fairly certain we could simply release Nic onto Tommy, and he'd be begging for mercy. He hates that bastard with a passion."

I roll my eyes and snort. "Swear to fuck, is he still pissed over the goddamn barbecue competition? Tell him if that's all he's got to obsess over, then I'll buy him a pair of fucking lace panties and we'll change his name to Nicole."

Marco roars with laugher, his big body shaking. "You know he takes everything seriously, including cooking. He swears Tommy paid some famous chef to make the ribs he entered into the contest. Claims they were already almost fully cooked when Tommy put them on the grill."

"Jesus," I hiss. "How have the Morettis managed to intimidate their way through life as Martha Stewart wannabes?" What makes this so amusing is that Nic Moretti is as big or bigger than Marco and doesn't have to open his mouth to scare the hell out of people. To say he's an intimidating fucker is putting it nicely. So, given he's still carrying some crazy grudge over a family cookout from years ago is comical.

Marco flops back into his recently vacated chair, and the wood creaks under his frame. "If we were women, we'd be fighting over clothes, so that's the kind of shit you have to expect when you spend so much time around each other."

I don't bother to point out that he's talking about a family of mobsters, not sorority sisters. "Just pass the warning along."

He looks amused as he remains in his seat instead of preparing to leave. "You seem to be a little impatient. Have somewhere to go, do you? Maybe chasing the hot piece you're so into?" When I narrow my eyes at his choice of words, he grins in triumph. "I'm kidding; you know how I feel about her."

"Who doesn't?" I ask wryly. "I think you've made your affection for her very clear. Fortunately for you, I also know you'd never touch anything of mine—especially a woman."

Looking suddenly serious, he nods solemnly. "That's one concern you needn't ever worry about, brother. I'd never make a move on her, nor would I allow another to get away with harming a hair on her pretty head. She became a Moretti the day you staked your claim. She's a beautiful woman, but she might as well be my sister now." When I cock my head to the side, waiting, he adds, "Okay, my sister with an amazing ass." I flip my middle finger at him, and he chuckles. "Gotta give me that one."

We talk for another half hour before he leaves. I walk to the wall of windows and look at the crowded club below. The two-way mirrored glass is bulletproof and provides complete privacy. It's past midnight. I planned to pay Jacey a visit, but now I'm hesitant. This is too important, and I don't want to make a rash decision I'll regret later. She'd be the first to disagree, but it doesn't change the fact that she's fragile. Fuck, a complicated entanglement is the last thing I need. Not to mention I'd be putting her in the crosshairs of the Moretti family. Hell, if not for Lee and me, the Wrenn offspring would have died along with their father that night. That Jacey pulled the trigger kept her alive.

I run a tired hand through my hair and lean my forehead against the cold glass. *Do I even know what I'm doing anymore?* I'm mentally and physically exhausted. I've never been one to sleep more than five hours a night, but it's gotten worse in the last year. This shit with Hunter Wrenn is a mindfuck. Finding out the truth about my father's murder has become an obsession. And when I can put that aside for a while —*she* is there. I need her—which is insane because I need no one. I worry that she'll snap one day, and I won't be there to pick up the pieces. I *have* to be there if and when that happens, *but I wish I understood why.* I know why she came tonight, and yes, it worked. Jacey Wrenn is very much back in the forefront of my mind.

So fucking tired. I yawn before moving away from the window and walking toward the sofa on the other side of the room. Tomorrow is soon enough to decide, but for tonight, I'll have her in my dreams—just like many nights since I last held her in my arms.

3

JACEY

I'm sitting on the sofa sipping a cup of coffee when the house phone rings. Since it is only used to announce visitors, my heart leaps, and I shoot to my feet. *Damn, it took him long enough.* I grimace as I look at the plain pair of pajamas I'm wearing. *100% cotton—you siren.* I think briefly of changing as I hurry to stop the insistent ringing. Knowing my luck, they'll tell him I'm not home. "Yes," I answer, sounding embarrassingly breathy.

"Mrs. Jacks is here to see you, ma'am." And just like that, I deflate. Not only am I disappointed it's not Tony, but I'm not looking forward to another awkward sisterly visit from Jade. I consider changing as I hurry to grab the phone. They have been known to turn people away if I don't answer quickly enough. Although I really shouldn't complain. I like living in an apartment where security calls to check if they can send someone up.

"Thanks, send her up," I say before ending the call. Even though my past actions say otherwise, I do love my sister. *More than she knows.* And I absolutely worship little Victor. It's Saturday, so she's sure to have him with her. Yet as much as I cherish my nephew, the sight of him also guts me. How can someone that small stir so many emotions within me? The emptiness inside me is at its peak when he's near because I long to be a mother. To be on the receiving end of those wet kisses and adoring looks he tosses so easily at my sister. I *want* to hate her for the life she has now. *But how can I?* I push the bitterness aside as soon as it comes because I made my choices long ago. Choices to keep her safe. Jade is innocent of the wheels set into motion with the death of our mother. Even before then. *You didn't have a choice.* But as that thought enters my head, I know it's not true. *There are always choices.* And maybe that's true, but at what cost? How do you put yourself first and walk away from the carnage you leave behind? Only a monster would do that. *Isn't that exactly what people say you are?* The sound of the buzzer drags me from the inner battle I fight every day. I know I'd choose the same path again to keep her safe, but I still wonder—*what if?*

I open the door without checking the peephole and instinctively check the hallway, looking for little Victor. But there is only Jade, which is for the best. *You're not strong enough today to cuddle that sweet boy knowing you'll have to hand him back when he leaves.*

Will I ever stop feeling this loss? This emptiness?

Jade's smile is the same as always: a touch too big and bright. Forced.

I did that.

Even after nearly twelve months since I killed *him,* nothing has changed between us. There is love in her eyes, but there is also unease. *And why would it be any different? She doesn't know you.* "Good morning," she says softly before holding up a box with the name of the bagel shop down the street on it. *This is serious; she brought food.* After years of unsolicited criticism, for her to come bearing carbs suggests this isn't her usual wellness check. She's left herself wide open for one of my catty insults, but there's no longer any reason for it. The further I kept her at arm's length, the *safer* she was from our father's radar. *Theoretically.* Not believing herself beautiful was a cruel result of my horrid taunts, but it ensured Jade's unassertiveness toward Hunter Wrenn. But now it's strange. She probably needs me to be nasty. She views the shift in my personality as depression, which is exactly what she needs to believe. To explain otherwise would mire her down in guilt. I know my sister—perhaps better than she knows herself—and it will destroy her if she finds out the truth. I will gladly carry it all to my grave. *For her*. My only regret is that we'll never have the relationship we could have had if things were different. But lies build walls, and over time, those become impossible to scale. Even though I want to toss her a ladder, I can't. Our reality was crafted so long ago and can never be undone. *I must remain the ice princess*—the callous bitch with no conscience or soul. *How I hate my father for what he did to us.* The only concession I have made to this image is that I refuse to torment her any longer. I will remain aloof, but I won't verbally hurt her. She doesn't deserve it. *She never did. She* never *deserved the savage diatribe against her.* Plus, there is also the issue of her husband. Any attack against Jade would bring the wrath of Lee Jacks, and I simply don't need his attention focused my way any more than it already is. I know he watches over me—and Wrenn Corp. He'd intercede on his wife's behalf should I be in any harm. I doubt that's even possible because I suspect Tony watches over me as well. She clears her throat loudly and shifts uncomfortably. I realize I've been staring into space and have obviously missed something she said. She appears even more uncomfortable now—and concerned. *Act normal. Be a bitch. She'll expect it.* I shake my head at this notion, which probably makes me look insane. *Can't hurt her anymore. I* won't. "Victor's with Lee doing some male-bonding thing," she tosses out as if she noticed me looking for him earlier.

I force a smile, attempting to put her at ease, and my heart aches at the answering one she throws my way. *I love you, Jadie. I never stopped loving you.* I yawn for her benefit before saying, "Sorry, I'm still half asleep. Let's get a cup of coffee to go with the breakfast you brought. I'm starving." She looks so fucking thrilled I'm not being ugly to her, and if my heart wasn't already in tatters, it would shatter again. Over time, I became so used to playing my role that maybe I've lost sight of how horrible I was. *You had no choice.* I want to throw something as the voice in my head again attempts to placate me. To make excuses for the things I've said and done. She follows me to the kitchen, and I walk to the cabinet and grab a cup for her before refilling my own. I also get cream from the refrigerator, along with a small canister of sugar. Jade has always had a sweet tooth, and I know she prefers her coffee to be more like a latte. The awkwardness returns as we sit at the bar and she looks uncertainly at her cup and the items before her. She's waiting for me to make a biting comment about the calories. But instead, I dump a hefty amount of cream in my cup followed by a couple of heaping teaspoons of sugar. "I need something to get me going this morning." I smile as I nudge the items toward her. She looks at me as if I've grown two heads but proceeds to mirror my movements, and soon we're sipping the hot liquid with sighs of pleasure.

"I got you a cinnamon raisin bagel." She nods toward the box. "You used to like that flavor." Before I can comment, she adds quickly, "I know that was a long time ago, so you probably don't eat them anymore."

Again, she appears shocked when I pull a warm bagel from the bag and sniff appreciatively. "I love these things," I mumble around the bite in my mouth. "Did you get cream cheese?" From the expression on her face, you'd think I asked for crack.

She opens her purse and hesitantly takes a bag from it and places it in front of me. "They only had the regular kind. No reduced fat." When I simply look at her, she adds quickly, "I asked, though."

I want to cry. As unreal as it seems, the desire to have a total meltdown is there, yet knowing that would likely send my sister into a trauma-induced panic attack stops me. A part of me almost wishes I could crawl back into the bitch bubble I've been living in for so many years. The night I killed my father, that ability had all but disappeared along with the blinders I'd been wearing. And the view now is ugly—so fucking ugly. *Was it ever pretty?* I take one of the containers and open it before slathering it on my bagel with the plastic knife they supplied. "I hate that other stuff anyway. It tastes like shit."

I swear, this isn't the Jacey she knows, and clearly, she hasn't a clue what to do next. Probably thinks I'm playing mind games with her. Out of the corner of my eye, I see her spine stiffen, and my first real smile of the day hovers on my lips. *My sister is growing stronger.* But that is quickly wiped away when she says, "So, one of the guys who works at Falco filled out an application to...um...knock you up last night at Tony's club. I assured Lee that there must be some misunderstanding, but Jonathan put a picture of the application on Instagram and showed it to Lee." *Oh fuck.* The next few moments are a disaster as I begin choking on the bite of food in my mouth, then take a huge gulp of my coffee only to spray it all over the bar as the hot liquid scalds my mouth. Jade is whacking me on the back and mopping at the mess I've made. "Sorry—I'm sorry. I shouldn't have just blurted that out. I mean, there's probably some mix-up. Why in the world would you or anyone else do something like that? Isn't that what they have those sperm banks are for? Clearly, Jonathan is delusional. I'll tell Lee that—"

"It's true," I whisper as I wave her away. I'll need medical assistance if she continues to pound on my back. Poor little Victor better have a good chiropractor on speed dial. I put my hand on top of hers, attempting to get her attention. "Jade—I did it. I was at Tony's last night doing exactly what Big Mouth said." *Hadn't exactly counted on being a social media sensation.*

Her eyes go wide as she takes a few steps backward before sitting again. "But...why? I...don't...really? You are asking for strangers to be your...to get you—"

"Pregnant." *Poor Jade didn't see that coming.* "That's right. I'd like to have a baby, and since I'm not in a relationship, I thought it was a good place to start."

I sound like a fucking nut. And only some weird sense of misplaced family loyalty seems to be keeping her from calling a spade a spade. In fact, it's comical when she nods as if understanding me perfectly. "Well, clearly there are a lot of men at places like that. So, I can understand why you'd pick a...er...nightclub. But wouldn't a medical facility be an easier choice? I'm sure they have a thorough screening process. You tell them what you're looking for, and they get you that brand of sperm." She brings her cell phone from her jacket pocket before adding, "Here, I'll google it for you."

Her fingers fly rapidly over the keyboard as she mutters under her breath. There's no help for it; I'm going to have to come clean, or this will only escalate. Before I can second-guess my decision, I say, "Jade, I went to Tony's because I want him to be the father. And considering I have been unsuccessful in even getting him to sleep with me, I thought it might be a way to get his attention."

Silence. Complete and utter silence. She blinks once, followed by a rapid succession of eye movements. It's possibly one of the first times in many, many years that I have spoken with such blunt honesty. No games. No snide or manipulative undertones. Honesty. *And it's no wonder she's at a loss for words.* Finally, she simply says, "I see." Without further comment, she reaches down and pulls her huge purse from the floor and begins digging through it. *Dear God, she could fit a small country in that thing.* Eventually, she comes up with a notebook and pen. She drops the purse to the floor, and it sounds as if a china cabinet is breaking apart inside it. But she appears not to notice. Instead, she opens her notebook and looks at me expectantly. "Okay, so we know what the objective is. And we know what I assume was your first attempt to accomplish that goal." I nod slowly, feeling as if I don't even know the woman in front of me. *You don't.* That last thought hurts, so I push it to the side and focus on my rather surprising sister.

"Now, I don't want you to take this personally, but are you certain Tony is attracted to you? Could he be hesitating to...complete the merger because there's no spark?"

I roll my eyes and laugh. "You realize that's all bullshit, right? Men will use any excuse they can find to keep from being honest. If a man says there's no spark, then he's just too damn lazy or clueless to attempt a seduction. So, if those words ever leave a guy's mouth, you better run because you're going to be doing all the work in bed. You'll be sucking his dick around the clock trying to prove your worth, when all along, he's just a worthless fuck." *Where the hell did that come from?*

By the time I finish with my rant, Jade has her arms folded in front of her, appearing to hang on my every word. She's nodding as if I've just explained a long-time mystery. "I had no idea," she marvels. "You just blew a hole into my rationale for every failed date I ever had. I assumed the spark just wasn't there. But if what you're saying is true, the guy was simply a coward and wanted to avoid confrontation."

I take a sip of my coffee. "You got it. How many men ever want to have the relationship talk? Or if they're not planning to call you after the first date, do they let you know that? No, of course not. Most of the time you leave feeling like things went great, then you're confused when you never hear from them."

Jade blows a wispy piece of hair out of her face. "I haven't been on a lot of dates, but that was pretty much what happened on the ones I did have. At least Lee was honest about the reasons he didn't want a relationship—even if I didn't like it. Sure, he pretended he was unaffected by me, but there are some things you can't hide. Plus, considering he had to see me at the office every day, it was a little tough to avoid me."

I feel a momentary pang of envy at her utter happiness. What would it be like to have that contentment? To know that you're someone's everything? A sharp retort is on the tip of my tongue, but I push it back. I must remember that the disaster that is my life isn't her fault. Instead, I say honestly, "You got lucky. You have a good man." *So lucky.*

Why not me?

She darts me a hesitant look. "Why this sudden urge to have a baby? Or have you felt this way for a while?" She looks at her hands before saying softly, "Shouldn't sisters know stuff like this? There's so much... It's as if we're strangers who share the same parents."

There's no help for this. I can't sugarcoat it. "That's exactly what we are. We're not now, nor will we ever be the big happy family you see in those paintings or on television." A bitter laugh escapes my throat as I add, "After all, our father murdered our mother, and then I killed him. Can't get much more fucked up than that."

I see her flinch and wish I could take the words back—but what would that change? You can tie a big, shiny bow around a pile of dog shit, but that doesn't change the fact that it's still shit. I could have nicely said that both of our parents have passed away, but in the back of our minds, we both *now* know the horrible truth. I read somewhere once that we live in an ugly world with brief moments of prettiness to make it bearable. Yet for me, my world hasn't been pretty since our mother died. Hell, ugly would be a step up to what I've considered it most days. "But we don't have to let it be this way," she pleads softly. "I realize we haven't been close in some time—"

"Try never," I interject bitterly, then wonder why. *She didn't start this.*

"That's not true," she insists stubbornly. "Before Mom...we got along really well. Don't you remember how we used to play together?"

My heart hurts so badly. She's killing me, and she doesn't even have a clue. "Jade, don't," I whisper, wanting nothing more than for her to go away. The pain is more manageable when I'm alone. When there's no one to fool, no masks to hide behind. If I could fall into my go-to bitch mode, this would be easier. There is no longer any good reason for that, though, and I can't hurt her to make things more bearable for me. *You're hurting her now. What do I do? Please leave, Jade. I don't deserve you in my life. Go and never come back. I love you—but I also hate you.*

"Why won't you let me in, Jac? We're all we have left. You can't be happy this way...being alone."

Before I know it, I'm on my feet, my body shaking. "You have everything," I snap, feeling a wave of both rage and self-pity flowing through my veins. "You know nothing, Jade, *nothing* about me. We're not going to be confidants who talk about boys and braid each other's hair. We won't be texting each other at all hours of the day and night to gossip, and if you're going through a tough time, I'm the very last person you think of to call. We are connected by blood only, and there have been days when we've both even questioned that as fact. You have a husband and a child waiting for you at home. You have a life, and it doesn't include me, nor does mine have a place for you." When tears well up in her eyes and she shakes her head in denial, I lower my voice, feeling drained. "We are what our parents created. Too many years have passed, and too much has happened to reinvent our relationship now. I'll attend Victor's birthday parties and even some family events, but we'll never be more than strangers who happen to share blood." Shrugging my shoulders, I add, "We didn't ask for these roles, but they're ours just the same, and we'll play them. Because for us, there is no other option."

I expect more denial, pleading, or an attempt at reasoning with me, but there is none. Instead, she gathers her things together. Only when she reaches the doorway of the kitchen does she look at me again. Her face is blank, but there's no hiding the pain in her eyes. And I wish to God I wasn't so good at reading her. "I've never heard such a load of cowardly bullshit in my whole life. And that's saying something. I refuse to accept we're incapable of change. So, I'm warning you now. Be prepared for some rough waters up ahead, because we're going to be normal sisters, and that's final." My mouth drops open in shock as she turns on her heel and walks away. *Who was that and what just happened?* I drop into my chair, still amazed by the transformation in my sister. It appears that being married to a man such as Lee Jacks has turned Jade from a timid mouse to something resembling a tiger. I was prepared for an epic crying session. She called bullshit on everything I said and slammed the door in my face. I'm a little irritated at her refusal to be rebuffed but reluctantly impressed at her bravado.

It's a shame it won't change anything.

I get to my feet to fix another cup of coffee when the doorbell sounds. Jade either left something behind or has more to say. I consider ignoring her, but I might as well get it over with since my morning has already gone to hell. I stalk through the entryway and open the door with a sigh of exasperation.

"Tony," I murmur as I stare at him in confusion. "How'd you get up here?"

He grins in a way that has my body firing to life. "I own your building," he announces as if he's discussing the weather. "Lucky for me, the doorman has met me before *and* was pleased to hear I have such a... personal relationship with the *lovely tenant* in 10B."

"That bastard hates me," I say dryly. "There's no way he felt anything at your admission other than pity." He doesn't bother to dispute my claim. He simply stands there as if expecting something. "I guess you want to come in," I huff out. "I swear, doesn't anyone call?"

"I saw Jade leaving," he throws out as he puts a hand on my waist and moves me a few steps backward so he can step across the threshold and shut the door. "You two have a sleepover?"

I don't bother to dignify that with a response. He understands enough about my relationship with Jade to know that's not likely. Tony has always been direct with me, so I don't bother with social niceties. "What do you want?"

He pulls a folded piece of paper from the back pocket of his well-worn jeans and extends it to me. "You forgot one last night. Thought I'd drop it by."

I take the paper from him warily, then open it to see one of the applications I passed out the previous evening. A sarcastic retort is on the tip of my tongue—but then I see the name on the first line. I quickly scan the remaining page and am astonished to find the whole thing filled out, right down to the medical history. *What the hell? Is* he *playing with me now?* In black and white, Anthony Moretti has offered to be my baby daddy. This day is totally weird. Wonder if I could start it all over again...but without my sister the lion and the man I'm obsessed with offering me...*himself.* "Er, thanks? But I have more than enough already. But I'll keep your application on file with the others for ninety days, and if a position opens, I'll be sure to let you know." I inwardly wince both at the possible innuendo *and* at the line I've heard recruiters use through the years. If the quirk of his lips is any indication, he picked up on the former and has given the word "position" an X-rated meaning.

But he doesn't comment. Instead, he looks me over before saying, "Go change. We can talk over breakfast."

I turn away, walking toward the living room. "I've already had that with Jade. You're out of luck." I wonder briefly why I'm being so bitchy to him. He's actually here. Wasn't this my plan? *Because he forced you to do something drastic to get his attention. Payback, Mr. Moretti.*

I spin around in shock when he swats my ass. It was nothing more than a playful tap to get my attention—but still. It brings to mind things that I didn't want to dwell on and certainly didn't want to associate with Tony. He sees something on my face that wipes the grin from his. Damn him. He's far too observant. "Please get dressed, Jacey. I haven't eaten since lunch yesterday, and I'm starving. And we need to talk. After the stunt you pulled in my club last night, I'd say that's exactly what you want. Don't throw away this opportunity. I could come to my senses at any moment."

I hate like hell to give in, but we both know he's right. Plus, it would be just like him to walk away to prove a point. I release a long-suffering sigh. "Give me five minutes." Without waiting for a response, I stalk down the hallway and into my bedroom. I quickly pull on an athletic top and a pair of yoga pants. Then sit in a nearby chair and put on socks and tennis shoes. Next, I step into the adjoining bathroom and brush my hair before securing it in a ponytail. I'm still not used to my new reflection in the mirror. Dying my former blond locks dark brown had been an impulse. One I regretted almost immediately. It was as if I thought that by changing my hair, I could also change who I am inside. Yet when the excess dye had been rinsed away, I had still been me. Only now, a paler version. *I look like Morticia Addams. Fuck.*

Tony glances at his watch when I reappear and gives me an approving nod. "A woman who doesn't take hours to get ready. I'm impressed." He waves me in front of him, and when I bend over to pick up my purse from where it had fallen at some point from the entryway table, I hear him groan. "Those fucking pants will be the death of me. I have a love-hate relationship with them."

I glance down, having forgotten for a moment what I'm wearing. "They're just my gym clothes," I mutter crossly, thinking he's making a snide comment on my casual attire.

He lowers his face until it's inches from my own. I fight the urge to step away, not comfortable with anyone being in my personal space—especially a man. "I know what they are, and you look phenomenal in them. I'd like to pull them down with my teeth before kissing, licking, and biting every inch of your sweet ass."

Oh my God.

I've had a strange reaction to Tony since the beginning. Normally, words like these would leave me with a sick feeling in my stomach. But my body hums to life. Desire is a foreign feeling for me, but I recognize it for what it is. Yes, the fear is there as always, but that's secondary to the other things he brings to life. *How far could that excitement take me? Could I be with a man in a normal way?* Or would I still panic at some point and run away? A part of me wonders if he is perhaps my one shot at knowing what it's like for other people. If I can't have that with Tony, then I feel certain it will never happen. Which means that it's either him or one of those sperm banks Jade had been googling earlier. "Whatever," I murmur crossly, but there's no real heat behind it. The only thing that's obvious is my confusion. He is little more than a stranger to me. How can this possibly be? I'm thirty-seven years old. My sexual awakening should have come and gone by now. But with Tony, I'm like some breathy teenager desperate to be noticed by the hot guy in class. *Dear Diary, I just threw up in my mouth.*

Tony steps out into the hallway, and I lock my door behind us. Neither of us speaks on the elevator ride down, but it's a comfortable silence. Each lost in our own thoughts. We pass through the plush lobby and onto the busy street. Without thinking, I go straight for the food truck a few feet away. "Morning, doll," Edna calls out as she leans on the shiny stainless steel counter. Smoke rises behind her as her husband, Mel, cracks eggs directly onto the grill. He gives me a little wave with his spatula before turning back to the grill. Edna's gaze shifts to the man beside me as he clears his throat. She gives me an approving grin. "Well, it's about time you found a fella." She turns to include Mel in the conversation. "Am I not always saying that Miss Jacey needs to find a nice young man?"

I poke Tony in the ribs, whispering, "Well, that would leave you out, wouldn't it?" He retaliates by pinching my butt, causing me to yelp in surprise. Deciding to have a little fun with the ass-obsessed man next to me, I punch him on the shoulder. "Sorry to disappoint you, Edna, but Tony here is like a big brother to me. I don't even remotely think of him in that way." He gives me a look full of amusement until I lean closer to Edna and murmur, "I'm not even sure he bats for the right team, if you know what I mean."

Edna glances at Tony and shakes her head with a sigh. "Figured as much. He's just too pretty. Ain't normal for a guy to be that handsome."

Tony clears his throat and shifts until my back is plastered against his front. His arms slide around me, and I fight the urge to sink into him. *He smells so good. I want...I want.* "Edna, I believe our girl here is having some fun with you." Even though Edna can't see it from her vantage point, Tony pushes his groin against my ass. "I can assure you that I'm completely heterosexual and that I'm captivated by this beauty. As usual, though, she's being difficult. I'd appreciate it if you'd put in a good word for me." I don't need to see his face to know he's giving my friend his most charming smile. There's no way she can resist him. *He's the Pied Piper of horny women.*

"Hmm." Edna appears to mull his words over. She's not throwing in the towel so easily. *I'm impressed.* "You got a job, handsome?"

Tony's voice is amused as he says, "Yes, ma'am, I do. I own several nightclubs."

It's all I can do to hold back my laughter as Edna gives him a blank look. "That mean you like to hang out in bars and drink all night? Then call yourself a businessman instead of a player? I like ritzy hotels. Don't make me a Trump, though."

Instead of being offended, I hear Tony choke back his laughter. "Point taken, ma'am. But in this case, I own these businesses, and I'm not a man to overindulge...on alcohol." The twist of his hips against me once again lets me know what he does want to overindulge in.

"Probably in debt up to your eyeballs, boy. Why'd you think you needed more than one club? Should have got it off the ground and paid it off before branching out. You want to be like those department stores and mega churches that spring up overnight and then go broke?"

"I couldn't agree more," Tony says evenly. "However, my clubs don't operate under loans. My father left me wealthy, and I've made wise investments. My clubs have operated in the black nearly since the beginning."

Instead of lavishing him with compliments, Edna asks, "What'd your daddy do to have all that money? He come from a rich family or work for it?"

Here it is. His weakness. The one thing he can't be truthful about. Or so I think. "My father wasn't the kind of man you'd approve of, Edna. He had his moments of kindness, but his hands and his money were dirty for the most part." *What? Did I just hear that?*

There are a few moments of silence. Edna's expression has softened slightly. She doesn't miss a beat. "You planning on following in his footsteps?"

"No, ma'am," Tony says firmly. "I am my own man. I may have done things you wouldn't approve of, but I'm not my father. Never will be."

Edna nods once before picking up her order pad. "That's all I needed to hear, son. You'll do. Our girl here would run right over a man without some backbone. I had a feeling that wasn't you but just needed to make sure. Now, you two gonna eat, or what? The football players will be here soon, and they're a bunch of hungry savages after practice."

And I am silent. *What. Just. Happened? Edna protected me. Tony claimed me.* I'm so lost that I'm struggling to form an answer. I think I convince Edna that I want a coffee and that despite her huffing and puffing, she's eventually mollified that I have had breakfast. *What I ate of it, anyway.* Given my small frame, I get why she assumes I eat little. *I wish that was the reason why...*

Tony orders an omelet with a side of hash browns, and then we take our tray to a table under a shade tree. For some unknown reason, he indicated we were *something* in front of Edna, but I mentally prepare myself for his next rejection.

TONY

I take my time arranging our food on the small bistro table. It's far from private, but that's probably for the best. Jacey is more likely to relax her guard here than in her apartment. *Fuck, so am I. Those pants, Jesus.* I attempt to gather my thoughts as she sips her coffee. I knew we needed to talk, but I had no clear-cut plan in mind. It might be necessary at times to have a workable script in business, but otherwise, I learned long ago to read the situation and go with my gut. I don't miss the way she keeps darting glances my way. *She's nervous.* So am I. Of what, I have no clue. *You know. You've known since that night.* I take a bite of my omelet, and it tastes amazing. Jacey's lips curve in an amused smile. "Good stuff, right?"

"Yeah, first rate." I nod as I continue to eat. "Wouldn't have pegged you for something so...casual."

She doesn't bother to argue my assumption. Instead, she traces a finger around the top of her cup as she says, "They've...been good to me." She appears almost bewildered as she adds, "They seem to care even though they don't really know me. Why?"

I don't think she's really expecting an answer, but I give it anyway. "Fuck if I know. Been on the receiving end of that a time or two and never quite knew what to make of it. Always looking for a motive. Because in my world, people have an agenda."

"Yeah, mine too," she says solemnly. I see her mentally shake off her moment of vulnerability and am not surprised when her next words are emotionless and flat. "What's this about, Tony? I have things to do, so can we skip the small talk?"

I want to throw the fact that she came to my turf first at her but putting her on the defensive will accomplish nothing. She's too fucking stubborn. *Just like me.* "It's exactly what you wanted, or you wouldn't have put on that little show last night. We both know you have no intention of contacting any of those idiots who were clamoring to get in your panties. Out of curiosity, are we talking the old-fashioned baby making here?"

For a moment, I see what looks like panic in her eyes before they're once again blank. "Hardly. This isn't the dark ages, Tony. Medical science is far more advanced now. I can have a suitable candidate father my child without having to make physical contact." Then she purses her lips before giving me a wink. "Although, for the right guy, I might be willing to consider the traditional route. And there certainly wasn't any shortage of handsome men at your place last night. I put a check mark in the corner of the ones who had the most...potential."

Don't fall for it. She's playing you. Even as I tell myself that, I grab the fucking bait and, no doubt, give her the satisfaction she's looking for. "I'll take anyone apart who touches you. So, if you want that on your conscience, then go ahead and play this little game. Only you will live with the consequences."

I calmly resume eating, letting her process my threat. The air around us is thick and charged although outwardly, few would notice. Finally, she says, "You can't have it both ways, Tony. You know what I want. I came to you first, and you wouldn't even consider it. So, either you father my child, or I'll find someone who will. It's really that simple."

Even though I came to give her exactly what she's demanding, I instinctively want to balk at her ultimatum. No one tells me what to do. I should get the fuck up and walk away once and for all. No good can come of an association between us. And a child? What right do people like us even having reproducing? The kid will be fucked up. Plus, it would tie us together forever—however long that might be. *Isn't that what you want? Haven't you known she was yours since before you met her?* So, for the first time in my life, I let another person dictate my future. This woman before me has the power to do what no one else has. Bring me to my knees. God forbid she ever knows the full scope of her control over me because surely, she'll use it to her advantage even more than she already is. I push my empty plate away and run a hand through my hair. "I have stipulations, Jacey. And you're not going to like them. But you want me to be the father of your child, and no matter what bullshit you've been shoveling, I know you don't want anyone else."

She surprises me by nodding. "You're right. There isn't anyone I want other than you. I made that clear when I asked you. I haven't changed my mind. I will do whatever necessary to have a child, but I hope you won't make me go elsewhere."

I glance around, seeing no one within hearing distance, but I lower my voice just the same. "I don't know who my mother is. I was raised by a series of nannies and whoever else my father saw fit to toss in the mix. My upbringing was...unorthodox at best. I won't allow a child of mine to endure the same." When she opens her mouth to argue, I hold my hand up, effectively silencing her. "This isn't negotiable, Jacey. I won't knock you up, then ride off into the sunset. You wouldn't have asked me if you thought I was that sort of man."

"I handed out applications to strangers in a bar, Tony," she says dryly. "Maybe you're giving me a bit too much credit. I'm a woman who knows what she wants and goes after it. You met me the night I killed my father. Surely, you don't truly believe that a cohesive parental unit is important to me?"

She has a small point. Her look of amusement changes to one of impatience as I deliberately take my time getting comfortable. She hates being kept waiting. *Tough shit, Duchess.* I even go so far as to wipe the table off with one of the spare paper napkins. By now, she's ready to throw something at me. Luckily, her coffee cup is empty. "Yes, I think it's an essential part of your plan. You may have had a father even more fucked up than my own. And a mother who was obviously unhappy while she was alive and then taken from you too soon. You know well how it feels to grow up without what others around you take for granted. You want a child because you need someone to love unconditionally, and you crave that in return. You feel that only an innocent could ever love a woman such as you. You figure that maybe by the time he or she is old enough to know what you did, they will understand you killed him to save yourself." Her eyes are wide, and I know she's struggling with my blunt presentation of the facts. *Yes, I understand you, Duchess.* "Animals are not the only creatures on this earth that do whatever is necessary to survive."

"I killed him because he took my mother from me. It wasn't about survival," she argues. But I don't believe her. The slight trembling in her hand on the table is a dead giveaway.

Eventually, she'll tell me everything, but this isn't the time or place. I'm here so she knows my intent to father her child. *And assume responsibility for her too.* But I'm torn. Is she ready to assume responsibility for a child, though? That's what I don't know. "He wasn't leaving there alive, Jacey. If not you, someone else—"

"You would have done it," she murmurs as she studies me. "Why aren't you angry with me?" She appears almost bewildered now as if this thought has just occurred to her. "I should be behind bars right now or worse, yet you made it all go away. You protected me when I denied you the chance to avenge your father's death." She leans closer, and I inhale the fragrance I've missed. *Honeysuckle.* I have no idea if it's perfume, or simply her, but it's intoxicating. My cock twitches in reaction to her proximity, and I fight the urge to drop my hand and cover the telltale bulge. *Why can't I control myself around her? Like a kid jacked up on hormones.* "Shouldn't the *family* have put out a hit on me by now?"

I grin at the emphasis she places on *family* even though she's closer to the truth than I care to admit. If not for the combined directive from Lee and me, both Jacey and her sister might well have met a similar end to their father. When she and Jade witnessed some of the inner workings of the Moretti family, it put them in danger. The family respects Lee and is leery of his ability to deal a serious blow to their financial empire if provoked. And as the only son of their founder, Draco Moretti, I've always been given carte blanche to give orders. It's not that some in power don't resent it, but they have yet to be stupid enough to act against me. I may have no desire to be an active participant in the daily operations of the family, but I have their back where possible. What none of them are sure of—but probably suspect—is whether Draco kept detailed records of their criminal activity. He was smart enough to know that people were not above biting the hand that fed them. There is enough information to take down the most powerful men in the family. And without them, the rest would eventually fall victim to their own greed and thirst for power. I've been fully prepared to make threats if needed to protect Jacey and Jade, but it hasn't come to that. *Yet*. I reach out and tap her on the end of the nose. "There's nothing to worry about, Duchess. This is the real world. Not make-believe."

"Duchess?" She frowns in confusion. "What's that supposed to mean?"

"Jax says you remind him of Kate Middleton—as in Duchess of Cambridge—with the new hair color, so he's nicknamed you Duchess. It fits as far as nicknames go. You do have that royal air about you."

"Meaning I'm snooty and uptight," she huffs out.

There's no way I'm going there. A smart man knows when to change the subject, and I like to think I'm an expert in survival, so I quickly divert her attention by getting to my feet. "I need to get to the club. Come by tonight, and we'll continue our conversation, okay? See if we can lay out the rest of the ground rules." She surprises me by giving an incline of her head in agreement. I reach down and cup her cheek briefly, rubbing my thumb across the silky skin there before releasing her. I gather the trash from the table and say, "I'll see you later." I briefly make eye contact with one of my guys across the street as I walk to my car. She'd be furious if she knew someone was always guarding her. But there are threats all around us, and I have no idea at this point who's in more danger—her or me. One thing I do know is this: we won't bring a child into this world until that question is answered and dealt with.

What is fucking wrong with me? People like us don't have kids. We are the offspring of monsters and demons. How could we sanction adding more to the mix?

My mood darkens as I acknowledge the truth. I've given her my word, but I'll attempt to drag this out until Jacey comes to her senses and realizes the same thing. *What if she doesn't change her mind? Fuck.* Then God help us both because He's about the only hope our kid will have of being normal.

4

JACEY

I dress in a pair of well-worn Levi's and a floral halter top. I study my reflection in the mirror, deciding it's the right mix of sexy and casual. After the whole "Duchess" comment earlier, I refuse to give him the satisfaction of showing up in a business suit. That comment stung, which is silly considering it's true—*at least on the outside.* My father groomed me from a young age to work alongside him at Wrenn. And he wasn't a man who approved of dressing in trendy clothing. He said more than once that I had to overcome the "handicap of being a woman." *Being the poor replacement for a son chipped away at my heart year after year until there was nothing left to salvage.* No wonder he couldn't marry me off to someone who would have benefited him more. Sadly, that would have probably been a better option for me. Unfortunately, he learned I was more *useful* as a bargaining chip than a giveaway.

Will the burning hate I feel for him ever go away? I've asked myself this question so many times over the past year. He's dead, yet with each month that passes, my anger seems to grow instead of decline. I was on autopilot while he was alive. I hadn't given myself the leeway to feel anything. It was easier to remain blank. But now he's gone, and everything I've kept bottled up inside me is threatening to explode. Going into his office at Wrenn makes my skin crawl so much that I've seriously debated burning the damn building to the ground. Moving the headquarters is the easier answer, but nowhere near as satisfying as watching Dad's pride and joy go up in flames.

I'm not completely out of touch with reality. I know I need help of the professional variety. But even with the patient-doctor confidentiality rule, there's no way I can tell the truth. Murder more than likely voids that rule. And even if it didn't, I'd never trust a stranger with that kind of information. If you can't unburden yourself, then why bother offering a little? Which leaves me where I've been for so very long—on my own.

He's giving you what you want.

I still can't quite believe Tony's giving in this easily. I was prepared for harsh words at the very least over the scene at his club. But he barely made mention of it. *Too easy. Why?* He owes me nothing, least of all something of this magnitude. Yet he sat across from me this morning and calmly stated that if we have a child, we'll raise him or her together. *Isn't that what you've wanted all along?* Of course, I've had the whole white-picket-fence fantasy a few times, but they usually end in laughter. He is the son of mafia royalty, and I certainly won't win anyone's vote for PTA president.

Jade has it all. Why not me? Haven't I paid my dues?

I wonder not for the first time if that's why I want this so badly. *Having a baby won't make you Jade.* No, it won't. Nothing and no one who can take away the things I've done. Nor will a man ever love me in the way Lee does her. Despite his refusal to sleep with me, I know Tony wants me. But I seriously doubt he's capable of that type of devotion. And if he were, it would be for a woman like my sister. One who has lived a normal life and isn't used goods.

If he finds out...

That's the real monster that frightens me. No matter how many times I tell myself that I'm afraid he'll find out before he gives me what I want, I know it's bullshit. I don't understand the connection between us, but I feel like someone when he looks at me. It makes me believe there is hope. That I can find my own happiness.

I attempt to shrug off my melancholy mood as I slip my feet into a pair of low-heeled sandals and pick up my purse. The drive to Tony's club takes a bit longer thanks to the weekend traffic. Asheville is a popular tourist destination, and every year, the crowds increase. I love my beautiful city, though, and can't imagine living anywhere else.

Nyx is packed when I arrive, so I'm grateful they offer valet parking. I hand over my keys to a smiling, muscular guy. He gives me a flirty wink, and I fight the urge to roll my eyes. *I'm old enough to be his...older sister.* He's probably used to scoring big tips by making women feel good. *You're so barking up the wrong tree, kid.* Even knowing this, I still hand him a twenty, and a smile tugs at my lips at his effusive thanks. *When did I become so jaded? The poor guy is probably trying to put himself through college.* Despite being just after nine, a long line already winds down the sidewalk. I stand there uncertainly, not knowing what to do. Tony might be expecting me, but does that give me VIP status here? A few of the women narrow their eyes at me when I don't immediately fall into place behind them. I nearly jump out of my skin when a hand lands on my shoulder. "Hey, Duchess...er...Jacey. Tony told me to look out for you."

"Jax," I say gratefully, recognizing Tony's right-hand man. There are grumbles of irritation as he leads me toward the entrance. "I understand I have you to thank for my new name," I tease as we step inside the dimly lit club. I'm surprised he hears my voice above the loud music, but his laughter tells me that he does.

"What can I say? My sister reads those gossip rags like they're the holy gospel. They're always around her apartment, and I've become quite a fan of the Royal Family. Kate is something else. William is one lucky bastard." I was offended earlier when Tony called me that, but Jax makes me reassess. How can I be pissed off when he clearly admires the other woman?

"So you finally figured out who I am. I guess the hair color threw you off. Plus, it's been a while since I've seen you."

He nods. "That's true. You being in the club taking applications for a baby daddy wasn't something I expected to see. Forgive me for not putting it together on the spot."

We weave our way through the crowd until he stops so abruptly that I slam into his back. "What the...?" I grumble under my breath as I push away from him.

"Shit," I hear him mutter under his breath. I attempt to move around him, thinking there is some issue that needs his attention. It might take a while in this madhouse, but I'm perfectly capable of finding his boss on my own.

I tap his shoulder, attempting to be heard above the noise as I say loudly, "You go ahead and deal with whatever, Jax. I can take it from here."

He whips around, shaking his head and looking uneasy. "Um, no. The boss will be pissed if I take off. Let me get you settled in his office, and then I'll go...er, do, you know, manager stuff."

Is he drunk? I swear, he seemed fine a few minutes ago, but now he's babbling. When I attempt to once again get past him, he moves, blocking my progress and my view. *What?*

Wait a second. Is there something he doesn't want me to see? Tony?

I stiffen my spine, knowing instinctively I'm not going to like whatever I'll find, but I'll be damned if I let him usher me away. So, I feign a step to the right, and when Jax hastens to block me, I dart to his left and quickly slip by. I waste no time plowing forward, having no idea where I'm going, but intent on getting away from the cursing man behind me. The crowd parts almost as if on silent command, and there he is. My future baby daddy standing at the bar with a scantily clad, leggy blonde plastered against his side. He's giving the obviously surgically enhanced bimbo a smile of amusement as she presses her fake tits against his chest and eyes him hungrily. *Back off, whore,* I think cattily. *Hello pot, meet kettle.* I half turn and see Jax waving his arms as he tries to get Tony's attention. But his boss appears riveted by Bimbo Barbie, which is perfect, because I'm suddenly in the mood to do something completely out of character—make a scene. Weirdly enough, my father, murdering monster that he was, never liked to be embarrassed in public. *Well, he's gone, and fuck it all.* Jax groans as I stomp forward and wedge in next to Tony. He's yet to notice me, which seems odd considering he's generally hyper aware of his surroundings and everyone in them. *Another man falling victim to a big pair of plastics.* I grab someone's drink from the bar and toss the dark liquid back. My eyes water as it stings going down my throat. Instead of intervening, Jax simply waits, staring raptly at the scene before him. I dig my elbow into Tony's side and give him a big grin when he turns his head to look at me. "Hey, babe. I'm here to talk about our kids like you wanted."

To my disgust, Tony seems perfectly at ease. Bimbo Barbie, not so much. She scrapes her red nails down the front of his shirt and sticks out her lips in an exaggerated pout. "Who's this?" she asks as she eyes me with thinly veiled hostility.

Before Tony can answer, I extend a hand in her direction. "I'm Lucy, Tony's baby mama. Hey, you're not looking to earn some extra cash, are you?" I look at my flat stomach before adding, "I'd really like to keep my figure, but this one insists that we pop out another Moretti." Then I make a show of studying her body intently. It's difficult to focus on anything other than her braless tits. If it's this hard for me, no wonder Tony was fixated on the cleavage. *Is that what he prefers? Fake and enormous? One wrong move, and we're going to have a nipple sighting, folks.* And I stupidly thought he was attracted to me... Reality check in place, I surge forward. "You have great birthing hips." Giving her an exaggerated wink, I add, "You must be glad that kind of thing is so stylish now." She sputters in indignation. Jax roars with laughter while Tony appears almost bored.

"Are you calling me fat?" she questions shrilly. It probably wasn't her intention, but her voice echoes around the room, causing heads to swivel in our direction. "I'll have you know that I model swimwear *and* lingerie for a living."

Of course, you do. Could Tony be any more cliché? Rich guy with a woman years younger hanging on his every word? God forbid he be interested in someone normal. I'm not jealous. I'm simply possessive of his...sperm. *You keep telling yourself that, girl.* Must the voice in my head constantly point out shit I'd rather not think about? *Why I'm bothering here is beyond me at this point, but I'm too pissed off to stop.* I give BB a look that clearly says I'm humoring her. "I'm sure you do. Now back to my original question. Do you have any interest in being a surrogate? Before you get all excited, I must let you know that there won't any fun stuff involved. We're talking strictly test tube here." I point my thumb in Tony's direction before saying wryly, "He may have a lot of issues, but 'til death do us part and all that stuff. He's my little Pookie."

BB shoots Tony a questioning look. "Pookie? In all the times I've been here, you've never mentioned *her*." *Awesome. Just as I thought.*

"I'm captivated by this beauty," was simply a cleverly worded line to get Edna to back off. *He knew I was coming tonight. Was this what he wanted to show me?* BB is the woman he *wants*—and *has* any which way they both want—and I...*well...*

No need to finish that thought.

Surprisingly—probably for show—Tony moves away from her. He puts his arm around my waist and drops a kiss onto my upturned lips. Even though I know it's all for show, my heart still threatens to jump out of my chest and do a happy dance. *Traitor.* "My business and home life are separate, Amber. I want my woman at home where she belongs." My jaw drops when he slaps my ass for emphasis. *Twice in one day. He really is an ass man.* "You know your way around a kitchen don't you, sugarplum?"

Sugarplum? Even Amber looks faintly repulsed by the endearment. *What am I thinking?* She was all over him moments ago and was very clear that Tony hasn't ever appeared—or acted is my bet—as a *taken* man. *Deep breath, Lacey.* Just keep going for now. I bat my eyes at him, fighting the urge to gag as I simper, "Oh you know it, big daddy." I bat my eyes at Amber before placing my hand on Tony's chest. "He knows exactly how to keep me happy." I lean close to the other woman and say loudly, "And I'm not talking the bedroom moves here. My man makes some serious coin. That's hot. A girl can overlook a lot of *small* issues with a new pair of Louboutins."

Tony pulls me back into his side, making it appear as if we're cuddling. His lips graze my ear as he whispers, "You'll pay for that, Duchess."

Someone is a tad sensitive about his dick size. "You started it, Moretti," I mutter back.

During our little exchange, Amber appears to have taken flight. Sadly, I can't say the same for Jax, who is eyeing us as if we're some rare species he's never encountered before. Tony shakes his head, snapping his fingers in the other man's face. "Don't you have something to do?"

Jax grins, not intimidated by his boss's irritable tone. "Nah, this place is a well-oiled machine as you know. I'm more interested in what's going on here. What's the deal with this whole baby thing? Don't think it works quite that fast."

"None of your damned business," Tony snaps. He loosens his hold on me, then surprises me by taking my hand. "Let's go somewhere private." Jax steps out of the way as Tony leads me past him to the stairs on the back wall. We have just walked into his office when his cell phone rings. He pulls it impatiently from the pocket of his jeans. I see him glance at the display before he hits a button and says, "Marco." His entire body goes tense. His eyes dart around the area as if assessing for some unseen threat, which has me instantly on alert. "Who in the fuck is this and why do you have Marco's phone?" He listens intently for a moment, and then demands a name and address. "Lady, if you're lying to me, it'll be the worst mistake of your life." Goose bumps cover my arms, and I rub them with shaking hands. *So cold.*

"What's going on?" I manage to force out. My throat is tight, and my mouth is dry.

It's as if he doesn't hear me. Instead, fingers fly quickly over his phone before he puts it to his ear again. "Nic, trace Marco's phone and see if it matches the address I have for him." A woman named Nina found Marco in the woods when she was walking her dog. "Don't know the extent of his injuries. She says he's conscious now, but disoriented. He mentioned my name when she asked who to call." He listens for a moment, then sighs, "Yeah, I don't like it either. We need answers." Tony fires off an address I recognize. It's not far from my place in the downtown area. "Call me when you have something." He ends the call and walks across the room until he's behind his desk. He opens the bottom drawer and pulls out several clips of ammunition. Next, his foot goes up into his chair, and I see his ankle holster. He removes the gun inside, checks the clip, then puts it back. He grabs a leather jacket from a nearby chair and puts the ammunition in an inside pocket. He watches me intently as he goes almost methodically through the routine as if he's done it a thousand times before. There's a lump in my throat the size of a basketball at the realization that he could so easily be taken from my life in the blink of an eye. *Or the pull of a trigger.*

"What's going on?" I ask huskily, wondering if he'll bother to answer my question. Marco is Moretti mafia. And I'm not sure exactly what Tony is, but he's certainly no simple club owner.

"I'm not sure at this point. You heard my end of both conversations. Marco's hurt, and I need to go. Jax will take you home. I don't want you out alone at night." *What the hell? No.*

He's almost at the door when I turn to follow him. "I'm coming with you. I'm not letting you go into something like that alone. Marco will probably be of no use to you if something goes down."

For the second time that night, I almost slam into someone's back. Tony spins around. "That's not happening, Jacey. I'm not putting you in that kind of danger. Now stay here, and I'll send Jax up." I don't say a word. I simply wait for him to start down the stairs before I move silently after him. "Are you fucking kidding me?" he growls when he realizes I'm ignoring his command. He's so annoyed when he spins around that I almost lose my nerve.

Almost.

I put my hands on my hips in a show of defiance. "Unless you want to continue wasting valuable time, I suggest you give in now. Need I remind you that Marco is probably waiting on you?" *He's going to kill me.* If he was any other Moretti, he might. Instead, he curses fluently and creatively under his breath before taking my hand and propelling me toward the rear of the club. We move through a fire exit, and I see his Range Rover. The doors unlock when we're within three feet—modern technology for you—but before we get in, I hesitate. "Have you, um...

thought about checking for a bomb? It'll be too late when you press the start button, and we're both blown all over North Carolina."

He blinks at me in confusion. Finally, he opens the passenger door and points impatiently. "Trust me, Duchess, there is a sweep made of everything I own regularly. You'd be more likely to find a bomb at McDonald's than in my car. Now get in. We've already wasted too much time." I feel marginally better at his reassurance. By the time he gets in on the other side, I've secured my seat belt, and he spends a few seconds doing the same. We haven't gone far when his phone rings again, and he clicks a button on the steering wheel to engage the Bluetooth. "What have you got, Nic?"

"You're not going to believe this one. The address you gave me matched the GPS location of Marco's phone. And the woman's name in 1B is Nina. But...if you're driving, you should probably pull over."

"Get to the fucking point," Tony hisses.

But the other man had been right to suggest Tony pull over because the Range Rover swerves a second later when Nic says quietly, "Her name is Nina Gavino. Like you, I don't believe in coincidences. How many Gavinos in Asheville aren't related to Franklin?"

"Fuck me," Tony says. I'm relieved he's managed to steady the car once again, and we're not plowing into the oncoming traffic. "I need some fucking answers, like yesterday." His voice goes deathly soft when he adds, "This could be bad, Nic. Epically fucking bad. No logical explanation puts an injured Marco in the path of Nina Gavino. The Gavinos know what that would mean."

"War. An all-out bloodbath," Nic agrees. "I know that Frankie Jr. is a dumb fuck, but he doesn't have the clout to sanction a hit on a Moretti janitor, much less Marco."

I see indecision play out on Tony's handsome face. Finally, he says, "Listen, Nic. I know this goes against protocol, but I don't want to jump the gun here until I know what we're dealing with. We've worked hard to stay out of the spotlight, and this could put us right back there on a state *and* federal level. We can't afford for that to happen. If it does, we're fucked. People will get spooked and go to ground."

"I hear what you're saying, brother, and I agree. That's why Mike and I are gonna meet you there. You don't go in without us." We slow, and Tony parks on the side of a quiet, tree-lined street. I look around, noting the modern architecture of the apartment complex a few feet away. *Whoever this Nina is, she writes a hefty rent check every month.*

"Absolutely not," Tony argues. "Shit will hit the fan if the family finds out I've gone against the rules on this. Stay out of it and keep your ass clean. I won't drag you and Mike into this. You're in far enough as it is, and I'll take the blame if it comes to that."

"I wasn't asking your permission, Tony." The other man's voice is so icy that a shiver courses up my spine. "I'm a Moretti, but my allegiance is to you, the rightful head of the family as it should be. Draco would expect nothing less of us. I can take care of myself, so I'll pass your suggestion to Mike, but I think his response will be the same as mine is." With that, there is a click as the call disconnects.

Tony stares straight ahead before slapping the wheel in frustration. "Goddammit, does it never end? Can I not just live my life without having to worry that I'm bringing hell down upon the people in it?"

There is anger in his words, but I hear the pain in his voice that he's not attempting to hide. Or maybe I'm just more attuned to suffering than most. Either way, it's genuine concern that has me putting my hand on his arm and squeezing it in understanding. "You can't buy that type of loyalty, Tony. And would you really take away his honor in protecting the man he sees as...um...his boss?" *Okay, so I'm not quite sure how to refer to Tony in the mafia world.* His soft laugh suggests he picked up on my dilemma.

"I'm not his boss, Duchess; I'm a friend. I realize this seems confusing to anyone on the outside. Hell, it's even that way to me, and I've been around it my whole life."

"Yet you can call anyone in your...um, family and give them an order." When he nods, I point out the obvious. "That doesn't sound like the traditional buddy relationship to me. These guys look at you for direction and guidance. You may not sit behind a desk in the Moretti office every day, but they consider you their superior just the same."

He turns in his seat, studying me intently for a few moments. "The last thing either of us needs is for you to be connected to an attempted hit on Marco. Some overeager person might take action first and ask questions later."

"I owe both you and Lee my freedom. I'll never forget that. If not for you, I'd be sitting in prison right now."

His voice is neutral as if he's discussing the weather when he says, "You wouldn't have made it that far. *Every* man in the room saved you. If even one of them told anyone that you and Jade were there, there wouldn't have been enough influence in the world to spare you both. Not to mention the fact that my judgment and loyalty would have been called into question." He gives a bitter laugh before adding, "And that's something I can't afford to have happen. Not when I'm this close to what I've been working toward."

"And what is that?" *Maybe he's planning to take over as head of the family. Wait, do I want a baby daddy who is the big boss?*

Thanks to the well-lit street, I see him shut down. He's said more than he intended to, that much is obvious. As is the fact he won't elaborate further. He ignores my question, instead saying, "You'll stay in the car with Mike. Nic and I will go in and assess the situation."

I narrow my eyes in irritation. *I don't take orders from a man anymore, buddy.* "I have no intention of remaining behind. Plus, I'm pretty sure this Mike person isn't coming here to be my babysitter. You might need our help. You have no idea what you're walking into. This could be an ambush. There might be men up there with guns or even bombs. How do we know that Nina is a woman? Maybe she used one of those voice disguisers to throw you off. Did you think about that, bigshot?"

He appears nonplussed for a moment before he shakes his head. "You watch too much television. Granted this is a bit more suspicious than I originally thought, but it's manageable. As long as I'm not distracted worrying about you." Before I can reply, lights from an oncoming vehicle have us both tensing. Tony checks the rearview mirror when the car parks behind us. "That'll be Nic."

When he puts his hand on the door handle to open the door, I grab his arm, halting his progress. "Shouldn't we like...wait for him to come to us? It's dark outside. How can you be sure it's him? There are probably thousands of cars in Asheville like whatever he drives." *It's left to me to give safety tips to a mobster? What is the world coming to?*

Actually, more to the point, *who the hell am I right now?* I never spoke up like this to my father as it wasn't worth his wrath.

Yet in many respects, Tony is more a man to be feared than Hunter Wrenn. *I went after that bimbo in the nightclub.* Previously, I never would have bothered. *Cared.* I fought to be with Tony now. *Why on earth would I willingly go into something that he armed himself for?* I'm so confused right now.

Who am I?

Despite my valid arguments, he ignores my warning and opens the door. Then he glances at me in amusement. "You've heard of a secret handshake, right?" I nod, thinking this is a strange time for something so random. "Well, Nic and I have a way that we confirm identities in a situation such as this. Therefore, I'm certain it's him."

Intrigued at this tidbit of information, I ask, "So what is it?" Granted I haven't been looking that hard, but I didn't notice anything unusual about the other vehicle.

"If I told you, I'd have to kill you. And with an ass like yours, that would be a damn shame." My mouth drops open in shock. A trail of laughter follows his departing back as he slams the door and goes to meet the other men.

Despite my arguments to the contrary, I don't really want to accompany them into the unknown woman's apartment. If Tony is this uneasy, I certainly have no business being here. But what are my options at this point? Wait with some guy I've never met who may or may not be a bad guy? Or go with Tony and trust that he'll protect me no matter what? There's no decision to be made. Tony has already put his life on the line for me once, and I have no doubt he'll do it again. An unexplainable bond links us together. I have no idea what we're going to walk into, but I do know one thing: Tony Moretti protects what's his, and for some reason, that appears to include me.

TONY

Despite the events of the last hour, I'm still grinning when I approach Nic's Cadillac SUV. The line about the secret identification process was bullshit. But watching Jacey's eyes widen in curiosity and awe was worth it. Plus, it reassured her. Much more so than saying my gut told me it was Nic. Which, of course, was the truth. Nic steps out onto the sidewalk and grins as he pulls me into a hug. Much like Marco, this man is a brother. The passenger door opens, and Mike soon joins us. Instead of a smile, he wears his usual serious expression. Despite that, he returns my embrace solidly. When the greetings are over, Mike says, "I was supposed to meet Marco for dinner, but got called away by Rutger at the last minute. I didn't consider it a great loss because you all know how he loves these dive restaurants. And they never agree with my digestion."

"He certainly does." I shake my head thinking of all the hole-in-the-wall places I've eaten with him before. "I would have accepted any opportunity to avoid it too, brother. This isn't on you."

Mike clears his throat before saying, "I did a bit more digging around on Nina Gavino on the ride here. For one thing, how haven't any of us heard of her, considering she's Franklin's daughter? And she lives right here in the city. She doesn't have much to do with her family and has been on her own for about ten years. It looks like she's fully self-supporting and takes no Gavino money."

"Unlike her idiot brother," Nic mutters under his breath.

"Exactly," Mike agrees.

"You can't convince me that Marco being *found* by a Gavino is a coincidence," Nic states flatly.

"That would be highly unlikely," I agree. Before things can progress further, I hear a door slam nearby and see both Nic and Mike go on alert. The quietness of the approaching footsteps tells me who it is before I even turn to confirm it. "I have an addition to our group," I say wryly. Both Nic and Mike were there that night, and they're not the type of men to forget a face—ever. Especially one like hers.

"You brought a Wrenn with you?" Nic asks incredulously.

I don't bother to apologize or ask for permission. That's not who I am—nor do they expect it. But I do offer an explanation of sorts out of courtesy. "She was with me when I received the call from Nina."

"Hey there, Killer," Nic says by way of greeting as she stands at my side.

Mike nudges him, muttering under his breath, "That's in bad taste, bro." Jacey simply shrugs her slim shoulders as if not overly bothered by my cousin's teasing.

"Was going to leave Jacey with you, Mike, but we stay together. She stays behind me, and you two cover her back. We good?" I take Jacey's arm and turn her away for a moment while Nic and Mike double-check their guns. Another standard rule. No matter how many times you've checked your weapon, you always do it once more before going into an unknown situation. I did the same before Jacey approached us. "Keep your head down and your mouth shut," I warn her. I see defiance in the set of her mouth and the narrowing of her eyes, but she nods in agreement without an argument. *I'll pay for that later, no doubt.* We walk single file down the walkway. Even though I'm looking straight ahead, I scan the perimeter constantly in my peripheral vision, and I know my cousins are doing the same. It's an ability I thought I inherited from my father. Yet a junkie gunned him down. *How in the fuck did he not see that —not feel that coming? The hairs on the back of his neck should have been standing up. And if not him, how did Victor not sense it? So many questions without answers.* I push my obsession with my father's death aside, knowing distractions can be deadly. Another corridor and we're in front of 1B.

"I go in first, Tony. You know that." *Goddamn it to fucking hell.* As the son of Draco Moretti, I am always shielded from danger. The men are to be my human shields in situations such as these, and I fucking hate it. These are my cousins and my best friends. How could I live with their death on my conscience? It's on the tip of my tongue to resist, but that could endanger everyone in our group.

A hand settles on my shoulder as Mike says quietly, "Fall back, Tony. Miss Jacey will go behind you. You're both covered." Without another word, I do what needs to be done. One glance at Jacey's tense face is all the prompting necessary to let go of my pride. It's not the situation making her nervous; it's probably my frustration she can sense. Without thinking, I drop a kiss onto the top of her head by way of reassurance. Nic raises a brow but wisely keeps his mouth shut. When we're all in position, I incline my head for him to ring the bell.

The door opens slowly a few seconds later, and a petite woman with her hair pinned to the top of her head in a messy bun blinks at us. Pencils are sticking out of her hair along with a pair of glasses perched halfway down her nose. *Yeah, she looks like a fucking killer all right.* She glances uncertainly at us before saying, "Can I help you?" I'm impressed she's giving nothing away. Smart.

"Ms. Gavino, I presume?" Nic asks as he scans the area behind her.

"It's Nina," she mutters crossly, not appearing to like being called by her surname. "And you are?"

Are we really having a dick-measuring contest with this waif of a girl? Fuck that. I step forward despite Nic's glare of disapproval. "You called me about a mutual friend. We're here to give him a ride."

Far from being intimidated, the insolent woman, which I outweigh by at least a hundred pounds, puts her hands on her hips and refuses to budge. "I'm going to need to see some ID. I wasn't born yesterday. There's no way I'm letting you in my apartment on your word alone."

"And how exactly would you stop us, Ms. Gavino, if that's what we decide to do?" Nic asks, soundly amused. His smile disappears a moment later when she pulls a gun from her back pocket and aims it at his crotch.

"There may be four of you, and yes, I'll likely only get off one shot, but it'll have you singing soprano forever, asshole. So why don't you and your friends sign the imaginary petition to save your dick by showing me some identification?"

"I like her," Jacey whispers behind me. "She's got potential as a best friend."

Fuck me. I'm almost to the point of lowering myself to provide ID so she'll get the fucking gun off Nic's dick when I see a shadow in the hallway behind her. "Nic," I warn as we all pull our guns as one.

"For God's sake, you need glasses," Jacey huffs out. "That's Marco.

Look at the size of him." A few seconds later, my cousin comes slowly into view. Even in the dim interior, I can see how pale he is.

Heedless of the gun still trained on him, Nic pushes past the spitfire who's been holding us off and rushes toward Marco. Mike and I follow closely. "Dude, you look like shit," Nic says jokingly, but I hear the note of anger in his voice. He's furious. Someone deliberately injured one of our own.

"Smell kind of like shit too," Mike points out dryly. He's not wrong.

"For God's sake," Nina snaps as she nudges her way to Marco's side. Nic stiffens, and his hand twitches. A clear reaction to a threat. I shake my head once. He needs to stand down until we have some answers. On the very slim chance that this is all a coincidence, we can't attack a Gavino who is simply providing aid. *Fucking unlikely.* "Can't you see that he doesn't need to be on his feet? Get him back to the sofa before he passes out again."

"I really like her," Jacey whispers again.

"Then form a fan club later," I grumble as I put one of Marco's arms around my shoulder while Nic does the same on the other side. Nina takes the lead as we follow her into a living area. Marco grunts when we lower him to the black leather sofa.

Nina stands almost protectively over him while I take a seat on the coffee table directly in front of him. There's a trash can a few feet away from where he's obviously been sick recently. *What in the fuck?* He stares at me through disoriented, bloodshot eyes. I see his instincts kick in as he scans his surroundings with barely a tilt of his head. He appears perplexed when he glances at Nina but not alarmed. "Where the fuck am I, and why do I feel like roadkill?"

"Was hoping you could tell us that," I say as I look for injuries. His clothes are dirty, and as Mike so eloquently pointed out, he stinks. But there's no sign of blood other than some thin scratches. He looks hungover—which I know isn't the case.

Marco's forehead furrows, and he appears deep in thought. Before he can say anything else, Nina clears her throat. "Since you appear to be who you're supposed to be, I'll tell you what I know so you'll stop badgering him." Jacey beams her approval at her new hero while Nic clenches his teeth. He's going to hold a grudge on the whole *gun to the dick* thing for a while. *Mind you, so would I.* "I was walking Bixby, my neighbor's dog, in the wooded area behind the complex. I heard a sound, and Bixby was going crazy. Then I saw this big guy lying on his side." She wrinkles her nose as she adds, "That area is mostly used by the dog owners here, so there's a lot of shit around, and I think he fell into some of it."

"I knew it." Mike winces as he looks at Marco in sympathy. We all know how Marco feels about grooming, so this must be rough on him.

Nina pats Marco on the top of the head as if he's the dog she's watching. I bite back a grin, thinking she has no idea who she's treating like a docile animal. "Anyway, I ran over there to see if he was all right, and he started heaving. From the looks of it, that wasn't the first time." She flexes her shoulders and grimaces. "I tried to ask him some questions, but really got nowhere until I mentioned going to get help for him. He went into some kind of bossy he-man mode and tossed me his phone in between barfing. Told me to call Tony and no one else. So that's what I did. Then he mostly crawled back here. I've never been so happy to live on the bottom floor. There's no way he'd have made it any farther. And I certainly wasn't much help to him."

"What the hell happened to you, man?" I ask him in confusion.

He puts a hand to his temple and groans. After another minute, he says weakly, "I have no fucking clue. I had dinner, then did some, er... surveillance work on our case. Next thing I know, I'm sick as a goddamn dog. Head spinning, gut burning, body aching. Felt like I was going to die. My car was too far away, so I headed into the woods. Knew I was going to hurl. That's all I remember until she showed up."

Nic frowns at Marco. "So, you're saying what, that you got a stomach bug or something? You're not injured? No one else was involved?"

Mike appears perplexed too. We all know that a simple stomach bug wouldn't be enough to sideline any of us. We've all worked with stuff like that. It might be a nuisance, but it's not enough to incapacitate any of us. "Something's not right. You're too weak for this to be a regular illness. Did you see anything or anyone suspicious before this happened?"

"Not a damn thing." Marco groans as he shuts his eyes momentarily. It's the strangest thing. It's like I missed a block of time somewhere. I was perfectly fine all day, then I'm on the ground with a dog licking my face and a strange chick hovering over me." When Nina narrows her eyes at him, he adds quickly, "Sorry, didn't mean it in a bad way."

I shift my attention to Nina again. "How about you? See anyone in the area other than Marco who didn't belong? Maybe struck you as unusual?"

Nina purses her lips, then shakes her head. "Nada. But it was dark by that time, and even though there is some lighting, most prefer the sidewalks after dusk. Bixby has a hard time doing his business on cement; otherwise, I wouldn't have been there either."

Nic moves closer to the sofa, then drops onto his haunches next to Marco. "Dude, you realize that you were rescued by a Gavino, right? Apparently little Frankie has a sister."

Marco's eyes fly open as he struggles to sit up. "You're fucking kidding me," he hisses as he flails around weakly. "Franklin doesn't have a daughter."

"Actually, he does, Marco," Mike interjects calmly. "Confirmed it myself." He glances at Nina apologetically before continuing. "She's his stepdaughter, and her mother passed away years ago, so no reason it would have come up. Especially with things being rather peaceful right now."

Nina claps her hands, and the sound is enough to have all of us tensing. *Not very smart in a room full of mobsters.* "When you've finished talking about me like I'm not here, let me know. Then I'd very much like for you to take your sick friend and get the hell out of my apartment. Whether you want to admit it or not, I did you all a favor tonight. I could have left him there or called the police. Instead, I did as he asked and then dragged him back here. I'll be lucky if I don't need a chiropractor after that. And yes, I may not know any of you by name, but I know who the Morettis are and what you're into. I took a chance helping him, much less giving you my address and basically inviting you to do your worst." Her chest is heaving, and her tone is more of a shout now. "You don't know anything about me, because I stay the hell away from people like you and that includes my stepfather. I don't want any part of all of that. My mother may have signed herself over to it, but I didn't. Franklin has never been able to buy my loyalty, nor will he. I take care of myself, period. So, if you're cooking up some convoluted conspiracy theory in your head, let me save you the trouble. I don't do dirty work for the Gavino family. Franklin is all right for the most part, but I fucking hate Frankie Jr. He's an evil turd. I make my living as a writer, and it pays the bills quite nicely, thank you."

"I don't think they were trying to insinuate that you had anything to do with this," Jacey inserts diplomatically. "They're simply concerned about Marco and maybe not wording it in the best possible way."

"Give me a break." Nina snorts. "They know exactly what they're saying. I was around that world long enough to know that everyone on the outside is guilty until proven otherwise. I knew that was a risk when I called Tony."

"How did you know he was a Moretti?" Mike asks.

Nina rolls her eyes, then laughs. "Because the contact said Anthony Moretti." She raises a brow as she looks at Marco. "If you're going covert, you should probably consider the possibility that someone could get their hands on your phone. Don't you people usually have nicknames or something? Hell, I wouldn't have been surprised to find his social security number under his name."

Electricity seems to fill the air as Marco glares at her. *Jesus, he better not even consider it.* "I didn't do that. The numbers were programmed in for me by someone at the...office."

"That's comforting," she mocks. "It's just disappointing that you would be that careless. After all, most everyone in Asheville has heard of Anthony Moretti. He's the crown prince, right? Mafia royalty, and all that jazz?" She tilts her head to the side before asking me, "Do they bow to you, or is it different in your world? Do you have an actual crown? You'd certainly look good with one."

Jacey stiffens at the other woman's compliment, and I feel a smile tugging at my lips. *Don't like her as much now, do you, Duchess?* "I don't think who we are and what we do are any of your business, Nina," I say evenly and pleasantly. To anyone who knows me, it's not a tone you want to hear, but it's lost on her. I'm far from finished with Nina Gavino, but now's not the time to continue. I can find out anything else I need to know without her knowledge or input. Getting Marco out of here and to our doctor is the priority now. So, I get to my feet and motion to Nic and Mike. "You two help him up and to your car. Jacey and I will follow behind you." Nic wants to argue. He can't abide the thoughts of my back not being covered when he's around. Mike hesitates as well. Their loyalty to a man they barely knew is admirable but exhausting. "This isn't the time," I warn as I motion for them to do what I've asked.

Something tugs on my sleeve and I glance back, expecting to see Jacey, but find Nina instead. There is worry as she looks from me to Marco and back again. "Where are you taking him? I know I was a bit bitchy, but he's welcome to stay here. It's probably not a good idea to move him right now."

Despite the irritation I'm feeling at pretty much everything and everyone, I take a moment to mentally compose myself. What she said earlier was right. She could have called the cops—most anyone would have. Regardless of her reasons, she did us a favor, and I owe her at the very least some common courtesy. "He'll be well taken care of; I can promise you that. There's no need to worry." I extend a hand, and after a brief hesitation, she places her own inside it. "I owe you a debt for what you did tonight." I release her hand and pull my wallet from my jacket pocket and extract a white card. My personal cell phone number is printed on it and nothing more. "When you're ready to call in your marker, let me know."

She stares at the card as if it's a snake poised to strike. I'm on the verge of tossing it down on her coffee table when Jacey reaches over and plucks it from my fingertips. She rolls her eyes as she sees it doesn't contain my name. Then she hands it to Nina, who takes it this time. "I know this all looks like a bad gangster movie, but I'll vouch for these guys. If you're in a jam, then they're definitely who you want in your corner." She turns as if to walk away before whirling around once more. "Wait, let me give you my card as well. You know, in case you need to reach Tony and he's not answering, or if you'd just rather talk to someone a little less...intimidating."

Nina takes the second card from Jacey and peers at it. She appears puzzled as she murmurs, "Wrenn. Where do I know that name from?" She makes a quick motion with her hand as her eyes widen. "You're married to Lee Jacks. Victor Falco's right hand." There's something akin to awe in her words as well as trepidation.

Jacey shudders before shaking her head. "God, no. That's my sister."

Something doesn't add up here. I cross my arms and study her body language. "You seem to have a lot of knowledge for someone who claims to have nothing to do with Franklin's lifestyle. Care to explain that?" *And there it is. That telltale shift of the eyes. The tensing of the body. Little signs of distress that most people overlook.*

Nina laughs, but it's forced. "This is Asheville, North Carolina, Mr. Moretti. Not exactly a huge city. People such as Lee, Victor, Draco, and even you are legends around here. Heck, you're probably required reading for some college courses."

"That might be true"—Jacey nods— "but it doesn't explain how you knew Lee Jacks is married to a Wrenn. It was kept out of the papers, and I'm damn sure Lee made certain it wasn't a Google alert. He's rather protective of my sister."

Nina sighs loudly, then throws her hands up in the air. "All right, damn you're both like a couple of drill sergeants. My best friend Minka is—"

"Minka Gavino," Nic hisses in disgust. "Raymond Gavino's hellion daughter."

"We should start keeping a closer eye on the Gavino women. They appear to be coming out of the woodwork," Mike points out quietly.

A headache begins to pound at my temples. This has been a complete mindfuck of an evening, and I'm ready to put it behind me. It's tempting to leave without any further questions, but I ask one more. "So, you have nothing to do with your stepfather and brother, but you're best friends with Minka? Doesn't that defeat the purpose of distancing yourself from the Gavinos? After all, she's the daughter of the second most powerful man in their organization. Not exactly a nobody."

Nina doesn't bother to argue my logic. The tilt of her head says she agrees with my words. "We've watched out for each other since the beginning. It's not a life either of us chose for ourselves. But whereas I've been able to put some distance between the family and me, Minka doesn't have that luxury. She's bound to them by blood—I am not. And before you ask, she's met Lee a few times through the years at various functions. She was surprised when her father mentioned he'd gotten married. I won't betray my friend's confidences any further, but trust me when I say that there is no sinister motive behind it."

Jacey appears to read something in the other woman's words that satisfies her curiosity because she nods, then turns away. I don't exactly feel the same, but I'm done. Nic picks up on my silent command, and as one, we all fall into line to leave. Marco hisses a few times when he stumbles, but we make slow and steady progress. Within a few short moments, he's in the back seat of Nic's SUV. "I'll drop Mike at Marco's car, and he can drive it back. Where shall we go?" Nic asks.

Without hesitation, I state flatly, "To the compound. There are too many people at the club, and we need to get off the fucking streets for now." I take Jacey's arm and lead her to my Range Rover. I open the door for her, and she's securing her seat belt as I get in the other side and do the same.

"Where or what is the compound?" she asks as she turns in her seat to look at me.

My home. No matter where I run, it's always waiting for my return. "It's my old family home. Or rather my father's. I rarely use it. I have a couple who live in the guesthouse and keep an eye on it."

"Why are we going there? Shouldn't we go somewhere more public? Or maybe hang out with others...as in your kind?"

I grin, amused as always by her attempt to put a label on what she can't possibly understand. *She's not exactly an innocent.* I still consider her kill shots self-defense. She did what she needed to do to protect her sister and herself, because it was clearly a "kill or be killed" situation that night. Wrenn would have instructed his goons to take us all out— including his daughters—because he wouldn't have been known if they'd be loyal to him after finding out he'd had their mother killed. "You'll have your answer when you see where we're going."

I fully expect more questions about my childhood home, as she's proven to be relentless in her quest for information. So, the subject change catches me off guard. "Did you find it odd that Nina wanted Marco to stay? I would have been helping you guys carry him out the door, not trying to keep him."

"I didn't notice," I say nonchalantly.

"Please. You're full of it, Moretti. You're like some sort of Mafia FBI agent. There's no way you missed it." She's quiet for so long that I think she's decided to let it go. Then she fans her face before adding, "I guess it's to be expected. Marco is kind of hot. He reminds me of that guy on *Chicago Fire*—Taylor Kinney. Only he's taller and has a better body."

Two thoughts go through my mind. Firstly, this Jacey is worlds apart from the shattered girl who spent night after night in my arms nearly a year ago. She was...*broken*. Understandably. My eyes narrow as something I don't want to acknowledge as jealousy pumps through my veins. *You're just tired. That's all it is. Too many unanswered questions tonight.* "Seems as if you've studied Marco quite a bit. I'm sure he'd be happy to know you're an admirer of his body. Shall I set you two up? Maybe break the ice. You fancy a double date?"

And naturally, she refuses to back down. She really has no self-preservation instincts whatsoever. "Well, he did give me the nifty nickname of Lucy, which is a bit better than Duchess. But I don't know. Who would you bring on the date? I don't think I could stomach an evening with Amber. Plus, I may have ruined that whole thing for you earlier."

"Oh, I don't think so. Trust me when I say that Amber is very... understanding. I feel certain she'd be more than happy to forgive and forget." I'm speaking out of my ass. The girl has offered more than once, but I don't dip in the pool at my clubs. Especially not for someone like Amber who is looking for more than one night with the right man. *And that's not me.* Why I'm not telling Jacey this is what I'm more confused about.

"Don't forget the part about her rolling over on her back with her legs in the air," Jacey adds sarcastically. "After all, I'm sure it's a position she's very familiar with. Probably stays in it most of her waking hours."

She's jealous. Her display of jealousy has my temper cooling. The uncertainty of our places in each other's lives is bound to fuck with both of our heads. *You've agreed to have a baby with her but don't know if you're exclusive. Fucking nuts.* This is far from the perfect time to have a relationship conversation, yet we must define the ground rules very soon. Otherwise, things could quickly spiral out of control. I need some uninterrupted time to decide exactly what I want. *You know what you want. Her. Any way you can have her. Why else would you agree to something like this?* "I never knew you were this catty, Duchess. Amber is a single mother trying to find her place in the world. Shouldn't you have a bit more sympathy for that?"

She exhales on a sigh. "I wish I were a good enough person to wish her nothing but good things, but we both know I'm not. So, before I spout more evil words, we should change the subject."

Luckily, that's not necessary. A few seconds later, Nic turns off the main road and onto a long, winding driveway with us following closely behind. I notice Jacey looking around in curiosity as we travel about two miles before reaching two mammoth iron gates. Nic pulls to the side, and I move around him, rolling my window down to punch in the code to open the gates. The codes are changed so often that neither Nic nor Mike bother to keep up with them. "Welcome to Devil's Cove," I say absently as we pull into the courtyard in front of the huge stone mansion. Well over two hundred years old, the house was designed with a timeless architecture that has kept it from appearing outdated.

"Devil's Cove," she repeats as she strains to see more of the house in the darkness that surrounds us. The grounds are well lit, which makes the house appear almost eerie.

"There's a lake with a cove and waterfall a short distance from the house." Shrugging my shoulders, I add, "I'm certain my father felt the devil part was self-explanatory."

"I'd love to hear more about your father sometime. I've picked up bits and pieces here and there, but not enough to form a clear picture of who he was."

I cut the engine and unbuckle my seat belt before leaning over to tap her chin softly. "He could be your best friend or your worst enemy.

And if you were smart, you wouldn't want to be either. In fact, you'd hope to never be on the radar of a man such as Draco Moretti. He was my father, and I loved him, and he was never hesitant to show his love for me. Yet I, more than perhaps anyone, was privy to the many sides of him. He was a complex person, and I'm not sure even he fully understood who he was. I respected him because he was brilliant at most everything he attempted, but he could also be ruthless and single-minded." I glance at my hands as images of the man I had such a complicated relationship with flash through my head. "Like Lee, he had an extremely high IQ. He was always adamant I attend college, but he never did himself. Said he got his education on the streets. Fuck," I hiss at Nic's tap on the window. So caught up in my trip down memory lane... *What in the fuck is wrong with me tonight?*

"Put your game face on, Tony," Jacey whispers before she straightens and opens her door. "Sorry, I was looking for something," she calls out across the car. *Great, now she's covering for me.*

"Doc is on her way," Mike calls out. "Should be here in less than thirty. Let's get inside."

Lester meets us as we reach the front door. He and his wife are my caretakers, and silent alarms would have alerted him of our arrival. Sensors cover the entire ten acres of the estate. Lester may be retired, but he's far from elderly. He's a retired Navy SEAL who worked for the FBI for over twenty years. He's smart, and better than that, he's well connected. Some would find it ironic that I have a former law enforcement agent working for me, but I call it smart. He's not involved in the Moretti organization. He's an old-school mate of my uncle's, which is how I met him. He knows I'm the son of the founder, and naturally, he's aware that lines not easily explained away are still crossed. But he also believes I'm a good man at heart and understands how hard I've tried to distance myself from the sins of my father. It's something he can relate to since he also has a past that could well have defined his future had he let it. His wife, Cassandra, or Cass as she prefers to be called, is also retired military. Together, they're a force to be reckoned with. They have my back as surely as I have theirs. He pauses a few feet away to ensure that each of us has seen and recognized him before he comes

closer. *Smart man. Never charge into a pit of vipers.* He shoots me a questioning look when he notices Marco's condition. He knows him well as
the three of us regularly have a drink together. "What do you need?" he
asks simply before nodding politely in Jacey's direction. "Ma'am."

"I'll update you when we get inside," I say quietly, then motion for
him to open the door. He turns and enters another code on a panel to
the side, then places his palm on the display that slides out. *My life is
like a fucking* Mission Impossible *movie.*

The house looks as it has for most of my life. A huge chandelier
lights the entryway in front of an ornate, curved staircase. Our footsteps
echo off the marble floor as we cross the foyer and into the study. Nic
and Mike lower Marco to one of the leather sofas, and I'm relieved to
note that although he's still pale, he appears more alert. I go to the bar
in the corner and pour a generous measure of bourbon into a crystal
snifter. I hold it up silently, asking if anyone else wants one. Nic waves
his finger and to my surprise, so does Jacey. "What?" she snaps in exasperation. "It's been a long night, and I, for one, could use a little liquid
courage." When I simply stare at her, she adds, "Don't judge me,
Moretti, just do it." I hear Lester snort in amusement, but he wisely
keeps his comments to himself.

"Ask Cass to come in?" I know it's not necessary, but they need to
know to be extra vigilant right now. It's not just the situation with
Marco; it's also the hornet's nest we're in the process of stirring within
the family.

"She's on her way, son," Lester says as he takes a seat across from
the sofa. "When we saw your car on the monitors, we knew something
was up. You don't normally drop by without letting us know. Especially
with company."

Jacey takes the glass I extend her and tosses it back without hesitation. I must give her credit for controlling her grimace at what I
know to be the fiery feel of bourbon going down. She straightens her
shoulders and takes the chair next to Lester, then extends her hand
to him. "I'm Jacey Wrenn. It seems to be up to me to make the intro-
ductions tonight." Lester freezes as his gaze flies to mine. But he
trusts me. Knows me. He gives her hand a brief shake before

releasing it quickly. A fact she doesn't miss. She frowns before dropping into the chair. "I see you've heard of me or at least my father. I can assure you that I feel the same disdain for the late Hunter Wrenn."

Lester gives her a bored look that I know is anything but. "My loyalty is to the son of Draco Moretti. If he wants you here, then that's the way of it."

Nic snorts in amusement at the older man's words. "Might as well try, Les. Don't think she's going anywhere."

I welcome the interruption as Cass walks in. She's a trim brunette who could never be mistaken for someone's sweet grandma. Thanks to her morning runs on the estate, her formfitting jeans show a body that could pass for a woman twenty years younger. She smiles at me before perching on the arm of Lester's chair. She shoots Marco a concerned look, then nods to Mike and Nic. "It's good to see you, Cass," I say as I take the remaining chair near the fireplace. No doubt Lester will update Cass on *who* Jacey is, but this is her domain, so I ensure they're introduced to each other. "Jacey, Cass. Cass, Jacey," I say to both women. They nod at each other, which makes me respect Jacey even more. She's holding her own in this situation remarkably. "I wanted to update you both on what's been going on. I realize we've discussed some of the things that I've set in motion and not a lot has changed on that front. But I have suspicions about what happened to Marco tonight." I recap the phone call from Nina and the specifics of Marco's condition. "Dr. Atwell is on her way. Hopefully, we'll have some answers after that."

Cass asks Marco to go over what he remembers, specifically the moments after he first felt sick. She studies his face, then gets to her feet and crouches in front of him. "His eyes are dilated. That could be from numerous things, but my gut feeling is he ingested some sort of poison. The things he's described are what I'd expect in that scenario. I can't be certain without some tests being run, but I've seen this type of thing before."

"You mean like food poisoning?" Nic asks, then nudges Marco. "Dude, what'd you eat today? Told you that Chinese food would kill you. The MSG alone is enough to have you riding the porcelain throne for hours."

"Fuck you," Marco grumbles, then rubs his stomach. "Swear to God, I'll never have another hamburger again."

Cass rubs his arm soothingly. "I don't think it was anything like that. Well, the food may have been the carrier, but I'd bet money it was tampered with. Most poisons are fast acting. So, if it wasn't your last meal, it could have been coffee or anything you had a short time before that. No doubt it was tasteless, so you'd never pick up on it."

The buzzer sounds at the gate, and I get to my feet and open one of the hidden panels behind my father's old mahogany desk. Dr. Atwell waves a hand, and I push a button to open the gates. Lester leaves the room to await the doctor. I run a hand through my hair and take a few moments to decompress.

I smell her before a hand touches my back.

Jacey.

What was I thinking bringing her into my world? I turn, and her eyes flicker over my face as if she can see into my soul. I shift, uncomfortable with the scrutiny. "You're not responsible for everyone you know," she murmurs quietly. "They're adults, and they make their own decisions."

I give a laugh devoid of humor. "That's where you're wrong. They were born into the Moretti family, and that makes them mine to protect." A lump forms in my throat as I think of losing Marco. He's always seemed indestructible. I'm more shaken than I care to admit by tonight's events. It's a jarring reminder that regardless of how much we like to believe differently, we're all vulnerable to some degree. I cup her beautiful face in my hand and tilt it until our eyes are locked. "You're mine as well. And you may not like it, but I'll also do whatever is necessary to ensure that no harm comes to you." She surprises me by shrugging off my hold only to move closer and wrap her arms around my waist, laying her head on my chest. My arms encircle her automatically, and we stand in silence, both needing this moment of peace together. I know with every fiber of my being that a storm is brewing on the horizon. Someone is getting braver, and I fear their goal is to put the son to death just as they did the father. But they've made a serious miscalculation because I will destroy anyone who attempts to take my family from me. And that is what the people in this room are. Whereas before I've been cautious as I've looked for clues in my father's death, all bets are off now. If Dr. Atwell confirms Cass's suspicions, then war has been declared, and if I go down, I'll damn well take every traitor in the family with me. Before this is over, the guilty will beg for mercy and the innocent will finally have their answers. Because only then will I truly be free to have the fallen angel in my arms.

5

JACEY

It was after nine in the morning when we left the Moretti compound. I half expected Tony to demand that everyone remain there for a few days, but in the end, it would be too suspicious if all the Moretti men broke from their normal routine. Tony did insist we go by my place and pack a bag so I could stay with him for a few days. He assured me that we'd be safe at his apartment above the club, and I believe him. I know from my previous time there that he has several security guys on payroll, not to mention a state-of-the-art security system installed. I put my hand over my mouth, trying to silence the big yawn that I'm unable to stop. Tony puts his hand on the small of my back and leads me to the stairway to his top-floor apartment. "Let's get a couple of hours' sleep." He enters a code on the panel to release the lock, then guides me through the door.

The open floor plan makes it easy to take in the surroundings with a glance. Probably what Tony had in mind when he designed it. As always, his apartment is spotless. He has a cleaning lady come in a few days a week, but Tony is a neat person. Heck, I didn't even see toothpaste in the bottom of the sink. His apartment has two bedrooms, but he uses one as an office. What are his plans for our sleeping arrangements now? Even though we shared his bed when I stayed with him before, this feels different. With Tony, though, I've learned never to assume. And I'm too damn tired to dance around the issue. "Will you be sleeping on the sofa, or will I?" I figure the blow to my pride will be less if I act as if I don't want to sleep with him.

He lifts a brow at me as if to say *really?* "If you'd like anything from the kitchen, help yourself. I'm going to take a quick shower, then crash." He's a few feet away when he turns back around to face me. "I'll see you in the bedroom."

I childishly stick my tongue out when he's out of sight, and somehow the silly gesture makes me feel better. I decide to get a bottle of water before I join him. The apartment is dimly lit by lights on an automatic timer, so I easily navigate my way to the refrigerator. It's not that I'm that thirsty; I simply need time to process the events of the past twenty-four hours. Not to mention that being in this apartment where I spent a few weeks immediately after killing my father is messing with my head. Tony didn't put it into words, but his eyes probed my face in a way that let me know he's aware of it as well.

I pull a chilled bottle of Evian from the refrigerator and lean against the counter behind me before taking a deep sip. Some water escapes and trickles down my chin, so I raise my arm and wipe it away with my sleeve. Dad would be horrified if he could see me now. Disheveled and unfit to be a Wrenn. *A hopeless disappointment just like your sister. Maybe worse. You have potential yet lack the drive to see it through. Lazy, so fucking lazy. A useless waste of space.* I set the water down hard, and it splashes over the granite countertop, but I barely notice. Instead, I put my hands over my ears as if that will block his voice out. *Thank God your mother didn't live to see how you turned out. I ask you to do one simple thing, and you argue. If you don't care about your sister, then I'll—*

"I shouldn't have brought you here." Tony sighs as he gently pulls my hands away and watches a lone tear slide down my cheek. "I'll get our things, and we'll go somewhere else. It's too much for you."

I shake my head in denial before burying my face against his still-damp chest. His familiar scent surrounds me and offers the comfort I didn't know I needed. "It's not that," I whisper. "Sometimes, I can't stop it. The memories take over at the strangest times. Usually when I'm too tired to fight. If they're really determined, then I'm no match for them." I sniff before adding, "You probably think I'm crazy. Talking about memories as if they're a living, breathing entity."

He pulls me closer and kisses my temple. As always, his touch is tender—almost reverent. "Trust me, baby, I understand all too well. We all have battles being fought within us. There are days that we're victorious and others that we simply must wave the white flag and surrender until we're strong enough to go again. It doesn't make you weak to admit that you're struggling. Only those who are truly strong are able to recognize their vulnerabilities."

The rumble of his voice and the steady beat of his heart lull me into a peaceful contentment. I shift within his arms until I'm staring up at him. For a moment, his face is unguarded, and I see anguish that matches my own. I recall his earlier conversation and ask, "It haunts you, doesn't it? The death of your father. I know there must be so much anger there toward my father." *How could there not be?* He had Draco murdered. "Thanks to me, you weren't even able to avenge him." *I'd give that back to you if I could.* "I acted out of anger and fear that night. I had no idea what I was taking from you until well after the fact."

"We've gone over this several times, Jacey. What makes me more entitled to revenge than you were? He took a parent from each of us. Had you asked me that night before you pulled the trigger, I'd have done it myself for no other reason than to save you from having to live with it."

I ponder his statement for a moment. I'm caught in the intimate moment, and Tony is the only person in my life who probably understands to some degree. "What would you think if I told you that it doesn't bother me that much?" My admission probably makes me sound like a monster. He remains quiet, so I continue. "I mean that in the scope of things I've endured in my life, that isn't the worst. When I lie awake at night, I don't recall the eerie feeling of calm that came over me right before I knew what I had to do. It's not even the second bullet I put in him to ensure he didn't survive."

He rubs a hand soothingly up and down my spine. Several long moments pass, and I think he's not going to reply, but then he does.

"One thing I can promise you, baby. I'll never judge you. If you're concerned about that, then get it out of your head. What you've revealed makes me feel sorrow because I know there are things eating you alive inside and that they're horrific." I tense, afraid he's going to demand answers. "When you're ready, you'll tell me. It'll get to the point that you need to unburden so you can move on. And when that happens, I'll be there for you. But until that time, let's just simply be us. No pressure, no judgments, no drama. We're both surrounded by enough of that. I, for one, could use a safe place to land."

That's exactly what I want.

How does he know? Or are we just so alike?

I move my head until I'm staring at his darkly handsome face and smile. "Is that code for sex?"

He appears startled for a moment by my teasing, then chuckles. "Trust me, Duchess, I don't have to play those kinds of games. I'm far more direct in my approach. When I decide to have you, there'll be no need for clarification. You'll know."

My body, hyperaware as it always is when he's near, literally swoons in delight. But I want to knock his ego down a few pegs. "So, you just assume that you make the rules between us? If the great Tony Moretti wants to have me, then I'm to be available at a moment's notice?" I sniff as if deeply offended. *Thank God I don't make my living as an actress.*

If I hoped to make him feel contrite, his laughter suggests I've failed miserably. But there is an upside because I'm fascinated to see him lowering his head. His mouth is mere inches from mine when he pauses. I fight the urge to say *Are you fucking kidding me right now? Don't you dare stop.* "As cute as that rant was, Duchess, it's totally inaccurate. There are two of us here, and as such, our decisions will be made jointly, especially about sex. Whether you admit it or not, you've been through trauma. And the last thing I want to do is rush you into something you're not ready for."

"Don't you think that's a question I'm more qualified to answer?" I ask quietly. Although I'm touched at the level of concern I hear so clearly in his voice, it still irritates me to have another man calling the shots. *Been there, done that.*

"You're stubborn, Duchess. And you wouldn't want to admit to having a weakness." He touches his lips to mine in a series of short, teasing kisses that set my pulse racing and make me impatient for more. He pulls back without deepening the kiss but doesn't release me. "I know you were frustrated with me when I held back. And believe me, it was one of the hardest things I've ever done. Make no mistake about it, beautiful; I want you. Always have. But I also knew back then that having sex with you so soon after what happened wasn't right. I've done plenty of things in my life I'm not proud of, and I'm far from a saint, but I have never taken advantage of a woman, and I never will." He trails a fingertip down the curve of my face, and I swallow hard at the tenderness in his expression. "I will always do everything I can to save you, even if it's only from yourself." And with that, his mouth fuses to mine, and all hints of teasing are gone. His tongue seeks entry, and my lips part, granting it immediately. He groans low in his throat as he explores and claims. My body goes limp, and he pulls me closer, absorbing my weight into his own. His hands move at some point to my hips, then one settles on the curve of my ass. It's a kiss of both passion and possession. He leaves no doubt that he wants me desperately yet says without words that I belong to him. I wonder if maybe I'm imagining that last part. After all, if he were that possessive of me, would he have waited for me to make a move? To show up in his bar and force his hand? He might have come to me after that, but I got the ball rolling.

I whimper in disappointment when he pulls away. I hope it's to carry me into the bedroom and fuck me senseless—but I know it's not going to end that way, at least tonight. *Why is he the only man I've ever desired?* I'm not surprised when he takes a few steps back and puts some distance between us. If there's any consolation, he appears just as turned on as I am. He takes a couple of deep breaths, and the hand he runs through his dark hair has a noticeable tremor. *I hope you get blue balls.* That evil thought brings a faint smile to my face. His raised brow indicates he noticed. I don't bother to act ignorant. Instead, I say, "I'm glad you're suffering just as much as I am."

My mouth drops open in shock when he reaches down and makes a show of adjusting the bulge that his lounge pants do a poor job of hiding. "You have no idea," he grumbles. "Now, if you're quite ready, Duchess, I need sleep."

Might as well play the part. I stick my nose in the air and assume a haughty manner as I move past him. "I do hope you didn't skimp on your sheets. I don't sleep on anything less than 1000 thread count." *Damn, that was good.*

My victory party is short-lived, though. Because when he clears his throat loudly, I make the mistake of looking back at him. His gaze slides leisurely down my body before he says, "Your performance might be more convincing if your nipples weren't hard enough to cut glass."

Damn you. I curse my treacherous body as he walks off, no doubt thrilled to have gotten in the last word after all. I feel no real anger, though. How could I? He gave me the best kiss of my life—the only one I've ever welcomed—after vowing to always protect me. He's sitting on the side of the bed looking at his phone when I pass through on the way to the master bath. He's laid a towel and a robe out for me on the vanity, and I smile at his thoughtfulness. It's a sad commentary on my life that he's been kinder to me than anyone has since my mother died. I know it can't last because nothing good ever does. If you give someone the chance—if you even consider love in the equation—they'll hurt you and laugh while they're doing it. *I once had hopes and dreams. He could have loved that Jacey, but not this one.*

Who would?

I reach inside the shower and turn the water on. Then I wearily undress and step under the spray. To my horror, I feel them coming— tears. This is the last place I want to have an emotional meltdown, so I'm grateful that the water muffles the sound of my sobs. I half expect to see Tony charge into the bathroom, but he doesn't. I remain in the shower until I'm more in control. Then I get out and dry off before brushing my teeth with the toothbrush Tony supplied. I'm grateful to see my suitcase in the corner, so I bypass the robe in favor of a pair of cotton pajama pants and a tank top. I take a deep breath, then open the door and step back into the bedroom. Tony appears to be sound asleep as he reclines against the wooden headboard. The lamp on his night-stand casts him in a soft glow, and for a moment, I simply stand there and stare. He's such a beautiful man. He'd probably hate that description, but it's true. And his chest: now that's a sight to behold. There's very little hair there, just smooth muscular perfection. In my heart, I believe I could see that face every day for the rest of my life and never grow tired of it. Why can't things be different—why can't I be someone like Jade?

If he knew the truth, he'd never touch me. Never look at me in the same way again. Toss me aside as I rightly deserve. Before my morose thoughts cause tears to return, I block them out—something I've perfected through the years.

Survival.

As I walk to the other side of the bed, I can only hope he follows through with his promise to give me what I've asked for. Because it's the only way he'll ever be a part of my life long-term, and if there's one thing I'm absolutely certain of, it's that I want—*need*—this man in my life forever. I may never completely have him. After all, I saw firsthand what he's offered night after night, and I could never compete with that. But to have his child would keep me in his radar, which is exactly where I want to be. *It would be enough. Would have to be enough.*

6

TONY

I wake with a hard-on. That is no surprise. You learn early on that it's a common occurrence and don't think much about after a while. Don't get me wrong, it's fucking great when there's someone around to take care of it, but if there's not, you either do it yourself, or it gives up and goes away—for a while at least. The warm body pressed against me certainly means there's a good chance I won't be jerking off today. Still half asleep, I run my hand under the cover and give an approving grunt at what I feel. My mind, still hazy, moves sluggishly. It takes me another moment to register that I'm in my apartment. *I don't bring women here.* It's too much of a shit-where-you-eat thing. This place is my sanctuary, and no one has ever been in this bed with me—*except her.* Then it hits me. My hand freezes on her ass.

Jacey's. The hard-on was simply uncomfortable before, but now that it knows she's near, it has a mind of its own. I wouldn't be surprised if it jumped out of my fucking pants and into her. *Don't think she'd believe that story.* She picks that moment to yawn before stretching. Her tits push into my chest, and one of her legs comes to rest between mine. *It's going to happen. I'm going to come in my pants for the first time ever.* I hear the strain in my voice when I say, "Jacey, for fuck's sake, stop moving."

She moves again, and I groan in frustration. I can feel her eyes upon me now, but I can only make out her outline in the dimness of the room. "Tony?" she asks uncertainly.

Does she have to sound as if she doesn't know who she's in bed with? I attempt to turn my hips away since she's too close for comfort. But my hand on her ass makes that difficult. So, I yawn loudly, then lift both arms to stretch. *There, problem solved.* Well, one part of it at least. Now I need her to move to the other side of the bed—hell, across the room would be even better. *Sleeping together without sleeping together might not have been the best idea.* I interject a relaxed tone into my voice that I'm far from feeling. "Yeah, it's me, Duchess. You good?" My cock throbs insistently, and my noble intentions are beginning to fray rapidly. *For the love of all that's holy, stop wiggling!* She has stretched three times in less than a minute, which has plastered her entire body against my side. *Is she doing this shit on purpose?* I'm in seven kinds of hell when my phone rings. The sound is like a bomb being dropped, and I nearly jump out of my skin. Then I shift and grab it from the nightstand like a lifeline. *If it's a telemarketer, I'll buy every fucking thing they're selling just for this timely interruption.* But it's my uncle Marcel— even better. My dick is waving the white flag since talking to my father's brother feels like the equivalent of being caught making out by your parents. "Uncle," I say, then hear him chuckle. *I might have sounded a bit more enthusiastic than usual.*

"I didn't wake you, did I?" he asks, knowing I sleep odd hours thanks to owning a nightclub.

"No, I'm up," I answer wryly. *Well, part of me was.* Luckily, he takes that statement at face value. Jacey moves away from me and sits on the other side of the bed for a few moments. I flip on my lamp so she can see. Blackout curtains are a must with my hours, but Jacey's probably a little disoriented. She gets to her feet and goes into the bathroom, shutting the door behind her. *Thank God.* "I'm glad you called," I say truthfully. Even without the need for a rescue, I'd have felt the same. I've always had a close relationship with my father's brother. He's the exact opposite of my father in most every way other than looks. They weren't twins, but there is an uncanny resemblance. Had my father still been alive, I have little doubt that would still be the case.

"I've missed you, kid," he teases as he always does. I might be a man of thirty-eight, but he continues to call me *kid*. And truthfully, I don't mind. It's always reminded me of something a normal father would do. My own called me either Tony or a shortened version of my full name, Ant. When he was pissed, it was little asshole or fucker. Not exactly a Norman Rockwell-type moment, but it was normal to me since it was all I ever knew.

"Yeah, me too," I agree without hesitation. It's been at least a month since I've seen him, which is unusual. Normally, we see each other every other week.

"I'm going to be in the area this afternoon. I wondered if you'd be interested in taking your old uncle to lunch?"

Jacey wanders out of the bathroom and mumbles something about coffee before leaving the room. I hear my uncle ask if I've fallen asleep, and I shake off my Jacey-trance and answer his question. "Absolutely. The club's closed tonight, so I've nowhere to be. Mind if I bring someone?"

He's quiet for a moment, and I can only imagine the look of surprise on his face. I've never brought a woman to meet him before.

"I didn't know you were seeing someone."

Fuck, this is awkward. I feel like a teenager. "It's, um, kind of a recent development. We've known each other for a while, though, so it's not as if we just met. I mean, obviously, in that case, I wouldn't be bringing her around to meet the family." *Shut the fuck up. You're rambling.* Yet I continue to drive the train straight off the cliff. "I'm not bringing her to meet you at all. It's more of her being here, and you know, she needs to eat. Although, I do have plenty of food in the apartment, and there are restaurants nearby that deliver." A movement in the doorway has me looking in that direction to see Jacey standing there with a bemused expression on her face. My uncle is laughing on the other end of the line. Yeah, I sounded just as bad as I thought. I drop my head forward, wishing everyone would just go the fuck away. "Where do you want to meet?"

"How about Leo's on Main?" The Italian restaurant is a favorite of ours, and we've been there many times. My finger is over the button to end the call when he adds, "Oh and, kid, bring your girl. I think I should meet her." *Fuck my life.* Jade is still standing there when I toss my phone back on the nightstand. "Don't even ask," I grumble, sounding for the world like a sulky child.

She holds her hands up in a sign of surrender. "I wasn't going to. Something tells me I'd rather not know. Plus, there's the fact that eavesdroppers never hear anything good about themselves."

I don't comment on her observation. At this point, I'll probably say something else insane, and I'd rather not. "I'd like for you to have lunch with my uncle and me. We're going to Leo's. You seemed to enjoy it at the last family dinner that Lee and Jade had there."

"I love it," she agrees. Then adds, "But I should really think of going home. There's no need for me to stay here, Tony." She lowers her eyes and shuffles her feet. "I know we have this...er, thing we're going to do, but that doesn't mean we need to be joined at the hip. Although parts of us will have to connect at some point." My lips twitch as she begins stuttering. Apparently, I'm not the only one talking out of their ass today. We seem to have that effect on each other. "You know. That came out wrong, like really wrong. I shouldn't have put it that way. Even if it is kind of true." She looks fucking adorable as she flails around, resembling a fish out of water. It's a side of the normally polished and composed Jacey I haven't seen before, and I like it. She is nothing like the Duchess right now. "God, why did I have to even mention that part? I might as well draw you a picture, right? I practically am with my words."

"It's rather appalling." I nod in agreement, then bite my tongue to keep from laughing. "Your whole dirty side is unexpected. I think you'd fit in well with some of the men who unload the liquor shipments."

She blinks rapidly as if struggling for a response. I wait with bated breath, hoping the awkward Jacey will come back out to play. But sadly, the Duchess makes the next appearance. I can almost see her straighten her crown and stiffen her shoulders. "As I was saying, I need to go home today. I have some work to do, and then I'd like to prepare for the week ahead. That's what I generally do on Sunday, and I don't like to deviate from my routine."

I take my time getting out of bed. I know without looking that she's getting impatient at my lack of response. I'm tempted to make the bed, but figure that might be pushing my luck. Never turn your back for long on an angry woman. *Especially not one who killed her father.* Her eyes are narrowed in annoyance as I approach her. "Is there coffee left?"

"Yes," she snaps. "Did you hear anything I just said?"

"I did. Now, why don't you go ahead and get ready while I'm having my coffee? We're meeting my uncle in a few hours."

She sounds panicked when she grabs my arm. "I can't do that, Tony. Just drop me off on your way." Her eyes are pleading as they meet mine. "It's better this way. You won't have to pretend I'm someone special to you."

The bottom drops out of my heart. It simply falls somewhere around my feet and shatters. *So much pain.* It's there whether she knows it or not. This beautiful woman before me feels as if she's not good enough to share a meal with the son and the brother of a fucking mafia king. A man who had more blood on his hands than she could possibly fathom. I'm certainly not an angel and have done necessary things that would cause her to see me in a very different light. For all her references to the mob and whatever fucking movies and television shows she's watched, she really has no clue what it's like to be a part of my world. To have grown up that way. I cross the room to her in a few long strides, still shaken by the naked emotion she's showing. The Duchess is back when I reach her side, and for once, I'm grateful. If being someone else is what it takes to get her through the day, then I have no complaints. We all adopt certain protective shields to deal with the ugly side of life. Those who aren't capable of what I think of as self-soothing will slowly lose their mind. *How do I deal with this?* I was prepared to pull her into my arms and offer comfort along with reassurances, but I'm not convinced that's what she *needs.* My gut says to go the annoying guy route. Her eyes are flicking around the room as if waiting for my move. I smirk at her before saying, "Just wear those yoga pants of yours. I can't imagine a man alive who wouldn't find you special in those."

"Wh-what did you say?" she sputters as I move past her.

"You heard me, Duchess," I toss over my shoulder. "I'm going to take my coffee to the office for a bit. I need to check in with Nic. You can either use this time to do whatever it is you women do, or you can go the way you are. But make no mistake, you are going. Even if I have to carry you. Actually, I'd enjoy that." I hear her say something that sounds like "asshole", which makes me smile. I'll hold off on congratulating myself for handling this one correctly until she's seated at Leo's. She's a stubborn woman, and if she decides to be difficult, it will be an interesting few hours. *Bring it on, Duchess. Bring it on.*

JACEY

"I still don't understand what was wrong with my black suit. I wear it to the office, not to funerals as you so rudely suggested." I smooth my hands down my jean-clad thighs, feeling underdressed to meet his uncle. When I walked out of the bedroom in my black suit, he took one look and shook his head. I tried to argue, but he was adamant that lunch was a casual meal and his uncle wasn't a snooty person.

"If you don't want to be called Duchess, then you shouldn't dress the part. In that outfit, you're simply Jacey. Still wound a bit tightly, but so hot that I could give a fuck. Don't get me wrong. You're beautiful no matter what you wear, but you don't need the armor with me, sweetheart."

How in the hell does he know? I attempt to look confused, but what I feel is closer to shock. No one has ever figured out what my clothing is all about. "I have no idea what you mean. I pick out the things that I like. I'm the president of a company, Tony, and it requires me to look the part." *Even I want to roll my eyes at the uppity tone of my voice.*

"You're not going to work today. So why the need for the power suit? My uncle sells insurance, so it's unlikely that he'll be a future client."

Tony is far too insightful. Arguing with him is pointless because it'll just make him think he's right. *He is.* I decide a subject change is in order. "So, you and your uncle are close? Is he...in the family business?" Strange how these types of questions seem almost normal now.

Tony chuckles, then shakes his head. "Hell, no. Never has been, and never will be. And yes, I think the world of him. I don't see him nearly as much as I should, but I know he's always there for me."

I turn in my seat, wanting to know more about Tony and the famous Moretti family. So much of what I do know is based on rumors. "How about your father...did he get along well with his brother? Are there any other siblings or just those two? Wait, you're an only child, right? Does your uncle have children? A wife?"

I smile sheepishly when Tony says, "Whoa, sweetheart. Let me answer those before you throw any more at me." He tosses an amused smile my way when we stop at a traffic light. "You're certainly a nosy little thing, aren't you? If I didn't know better, I'd say you're trying to get to know me better."

"You wish," I say disdainfully. "It's called idle chitchat, Moretti."

I swear he's enjoying this far too much. "Oh of course, Duchess. I apologize for forgetting my manners. I'll endeavor to answer your questions to the best of my abilities, Ms. Wrenn." If he wasn't driving, I'd throw something at him. But since he is, I'm forced to endure his sarcasm to appease my curiosity. "As for the relationship between my uncle and my father...it was mostly cordial but strained. My uncle didn't approve of my father's lifestyle, and he especially didn't want me involved in it. But he was also a personal confidant to my father and probably knows more about Draco Moretti—the man—than anyone else, including me. They had no other siblings, but their father had eight—all boys, if you can believe it. So, there are plenty of Moretti relatives out there. I am indeed an only child to the best of my knowledge, and before you ask, I do not know who my mother was. Draco was never forthcoming with that information. He only said that she had no desire to be a mother and had asked to be left alone. It's one of the few questions I asked him over the years that he adamantly refused to answer. And no, my uncle is not married, nor does he have children."

Tony slows the Range Rover, and I bite back a curse as I realized we've reached the restaurant. There's so much more I want to know while he's talking so freely, but it's going to have to wait. Maybe his uncle will have some stories to tell. Isn't that what families are for, to embarrass you? *Or hurt you.*

Don't. Not today. Push it away.

I force a bright smile that probably doesn't fool him for a moment. "Great, we're here. I'm starving." *God, that sounded fake.*

When Tony pulls to the curb, a valet walks to his door and opens it. Tony hands over the keys and some money. He comes around to my side and takes my hand to help me onto the sidewalk. Whatever his faults, Draco certainly raised a gentleman. A few feet away, a man sitting on an iron bench gets to his feet, and I know immediately it's Tony's uncle. The resemblance is so strong that I'm momentarily taken aback. Somehow, I hadn't expected them to look so similar. It's almost like a glimpse at the future Tony. "Uncle Marcel," Tony says enthusiastically. They embrace for a moment, and strangely enough, it's one of the most touching things I've ever seen. The affection between them is so obvious, and neither shies away from showing it. Tony takes a step back and puts a hand on my waist to pull me forward. "Uncle Marcel, this is—"

"A Wrenn," Marcel whispers. He gawks at me in disbelief. "Your woman friend is a Wrenn? I...had no idea." *I fight the urge to hang my head in shame. I hate the ripple effect of my father's legacy.*

Tony appears nonplussed as he stares at his uncle. "How do you know she's a Wrenn?"

This is beyond awkward. Of all the questions I asked Tony, why hadn't the first been if his uncle knew what had happened that night. But right now, I'm also curious why he knows who I am. He could have easily seen me in the society pages of the paper, but I was a blonde then. Plus, I haven't attended any high-profile events since my father's death, so he should not have identified me so easily. I extend a hand to the still rattled man, saying uneasily, "I'm Jacey Wrenn. It's nice to meet you, Mr. Moretti."

For a split second, I wonder if he'll return the greeting, but his manners kick in, and he clasps my hand between both of his own. I detect nothing but sincerity when he says, "It's a pleasure, my dear. I apologize for that little bit of drama. It's just that you look so much like your mother that it startled me."

I forget all about the fact that he's still clutching my hand as I whisper, "You knew my mother?"

I can literally see the walls going up around him. For some reason, he's not happy he revealed that. He squeezes my hand once and then releases it. "Not really. But I met her a few times when she was...visiting Draco." He darts a questioning look at Tony as if to ask if it's okay to say what he has. Tony shrugs his shoulders indifferently, but I know he's as curious as I am. It's there in the slight tensing of his shoulders. "On one occasion, she was a blonde, and then a few months later, she was a brunette. Said she felt like being someone different for a while. My brother had complained because he preferred the lighter color."

I open my mouth to respond, but Tony clears his throat. "We should continue this inside. We're going to be late for our reservation."

"Oh yes, absolutely," Marcel agrees jovially. His odd behavior of a few moments ago seems to be over, and he appears completely relaxed. *Why do my parents still control so much of how I'm identified? Will that noose ever loosen?*

I bite my tongue as we approach the hostess station. Jade told me on one of our previous visits that the woman standing there, Zola, is Leo's daughter. And that she had the hots for Lee. So much so that Jade has feared a few times that she was in the kitchen spitting in her food. She's not an attractive woman in any way. *That nose...so big.* "Mr. Moretti," she beams when she spots Tony. "It's great to see you again. I have your table all ready for you. One of your friends, Mr. Jacks, and his wife are here, so I seated you near them. I hope that's acceptable."

No, not Jade. I don't want to see them. Tony appears to pick up on the tension in my body because he raises a brow questioningly. I shake my head, telling him without words that it's nothing although that's not the way I feel. I see Jade a split second before she spots me. She's sitting in a booth next to Lee, and he's staring at her indulgently. He looks at her as if she's his world. *So happy.*

I'll never have that.

The pain hits me again. The searing knowledge that any chance *I* have for a normal life is gone and has been for a while. *I gave up my dreams to save yours, Jade.* I hate myself for the spurt of resentment and jealousy that always threatens to consume me when she's near. *She doesn't know; it's not her fault. Can't blame her.* And I don't. If given the choice of knowing now what would happen, I'd still take the same path.

Promise me you'll always protect your sister.

And I had. To Jade, I've been the biggest monster in her world. She only managed a taste of our father's other side once, and it scared the hell out of both of us. Even in the end when he gloated about our mother's death, she didn't fully realize what he was capable of. Only I knew—I'd lived it every day. I survived, but at what cost? Lee is getting to his feet now, having spotted our group. My sister's gaze follows, and I see surprise and pleasure as her eyes meet mine. "Tony." Lee gives the standard bro hug before turning to Tony's uncle. "Marcel, I can't believe it. Damn, you look so much like Draco." Another hug is exchanged, and then he reaches me. I must give him credit; he's one cool customer. He doesn't appear to find it unusual that I'm here with Tony and Marcel. My relationship with my brother-in-law isn't exactly warm and fuzzy. He is always courteous, but he blames me for putting Jade in danger that night. For basically abducting her and delivering her to our father. *I did what I had to do. If I hadn't, he would have sent one of his goons— alone.* "Jacey," he acknowledges me by a tilt of his head, then steps aside so Jade can get up.

My sister doesn't hesitate to walk right up to me and pull me into a hug. I return the embrace automatically but with much less gusto than her. I see by the slight narrowing of Lee's eyes that he notices my luke-warm response to his wife, and he doesn't like it. *Another strike against me.* "This looks promising," she whispers before pulling back. I know Lee is watching, but I can't pretend with her. We're not confidants. We'll never be best friends, which, if I'm honest, breaks my already fragile heart. But it's her comment suggesting something is real between Tony and me that scrapes at the walls of the useless organ within my chest. *No, sister. It doesn't look promising. Tony will never look at me the way your husband looks at you.*

I ignore her comment and instead ask, "Where's little Victor?"

"He's having a play date with Lia and Lara." She grins. "Lara pretends that she's the big sister and bosses him around. He just loves her, though." The men are discussing a recent business deal that Lee closed when Jade peers around before leaning in and whispering, "Zola still despises me. She gushes all over Lee, but as soon as he turns his head, she narrows those beady eyes of hers at me. I wouldn't be surprised if she runs her bony finger across her throat one day."

The other woman walked off at some point while we were greeting each other. I grin despite the usual unease I feel around my sister. "She wasn't thrilled to see me either, but she lit up like the Fourth of July for Tony." I wince as I add, "What's the deal with her makeup? She's got enough strikes against her without making herself look like a vampire clown. Her eyebrows are double the size they should be."

Jade snickers. "I'm not a fashion icon by any stretch of the imagination, but even I know that. She'd be better off not to use any." Jade appears pensive for a moment. "I know it's wrong to talk about someone this way, and I wouldn't want to hurt her, but it's just that she's so flipping evil. Lee thinks I exaggerate since he rarely catches her being anything but nice."

"You should stop eating here so often," I point out. "You realize she's probably done things to your food that would make you swear off eating."

Jade runs her hands down her hips as she says, "That wouldn't be such a bad thing. I could stand to lose some of this." There's no real distress in her tone, though. She's come a long way in the past year. My sister is very much a woman who knows that her husband is insanely in love with her. And she's blossomed because of it. *Since you stopped tearing her down as well.* I push that thought aside and study her when she turns her head to answer a question from Lee. *She's beautiful.* Regardless of what I told her to the contrary, Jade has always been attractive. Whereas I am tall and bordering on too thin, she is shorter and full of curves. She's a pinup girl from the days when women weren't so obsessed with being thin. Men always gave her a second look, but she never knew. *Thanks to you.*

When Jade turns back to me, I'm tempted to change the subject, but I say, "You're fine the way you are. If you're comfortable and happy with yourself, then screw anyone who says differently. There are those who are so unhappy with themselves that they have to insult others to feel good." *I never enjoyed it. I hated myself with every single hateful word I said to you, and I wish I could tell that.*

Jade smiles brilliantly, and I see Lee pause as if spellbound by his wife.

Oh, how I want that.

She is oblivious to it, though. She's so thrilled over the compliment that she's focused only on me. "Thank you for that. I like who I am now, and you know I haven't always." She glances at her hands as she says wistfully, "You and Mom were always so tiny. I felt like a giant in comparison."

"I'm sorry," I murmur softly, and she has no idea how many things those words encompass.

"It's no big deal." She waves away the apology airily. "It's not like we have a say in those things. I mean, the build we're born with. Although I could have certainly done more to improve it," she says ruefully. She nods her head in Tony's direction before asking, "I'd ask if you're here on a date, but his uncle is with you." Her eyes widen, "Wait, is this a meeting-the-parents moment?"

"Not really. I was at Tony's place when his uncle called to invite him to lunch, so he asked me to come along."

When a hand grasps my elbow, I look over my shoulder to find Tony there. "If you're ready, we'll take our seats now. I just heard my uncle's stomach growl." Marcel laughs ruefully and moves to a table a few feet away. Before we join him, Tony says Lee's name to stop him from returning to Jade's side. "We had a problem last night. Come by the club around one tomorrow?"

Lee's eyes are assessing as he processes Tony's vague request. But he asks no questions. "Of course." I get his standard greeting and parting for me, "Jacey."

"Thanks, brother." Tony claps him on the shoulder, and we both bid farewell to Jade. Tony pulls out my chair before taking his own. Both he and Marcel order the chicken piccata with a side of pasta, while I settle on the cavatappi in a light cream sauce with fresh vegetables.

"I swear that man is ageless." Marcel grins as he inclines his head in Lee's direction. "He looks very different than he did when he was a boy of less than half his age now. Even then, he was a force to be reckoned with." He takes a drink from his wine glass and points it in Tony's direction. "Your father was somewhat in awe of him. Said he was a child prodigy and that had he been born into a different life, he'd have been somewhere like Harvard by the time he was ten. I think both Victor and Draco were conflicted about it. They had the means to do something like that for him, yet they wanted him with them."

We all glance toward Lee and Jade's table for a moment before turning away. "Lee would have never been happy at an Ivy League school. He would have turned them down if they'd made the offer. Even as young as I was back then, I could see that."

"He's like you in a lot of ways, kid. You both walk just outside the family. Close enough to keep your ear to the ground but far enough away to protect your own interests."

"That's basically the gist of it," Tony concurs. "It's the best I can do. You know that. It's nothing short of a miracle that I've managed to disassociate myself to the degree I have." He's looking at me now, and his next words sound like a mixture of warning and apology. "I'll never be completely free, though." *Nor will I.* Being held captive to who we are is the invisible tie that binds us together. I have more of a relationship with Edna and Mel than I do with the man I asked to father my child. Yet the link is there between us. It has been since I opened my eyes that night after passing out in his arms. With everything that happened, I should have been freaking out, but his presence had soothed me. I'd always scoffed at the idea of soul mates and love at first sight, yet the feeling of having known him forever was there. What was left of my soul had recognized him that night and with that had come a type of peace.

I'm pulled from my thoughts by Marcel's question. "Anything new with your side project? Or have you decided to leave it alone as I suggested?"

The waiter arrives with our food, and I've already forgotten the unanswered question, but apparently Tony has not. After a few bites, he picks up where the conversation had halted. "Actually, we had an issue last night with Marco." Tony lowers his voice and briefly summarizes what had happened.

Marcel's face is a picture of concern as he asks, "And Dr. Atwell believes it to be something other than food poison?"

"She couldn't say for sure, but she's going to run some bloodwork, and that should tell us more. I expect to hear from her soon."

Marcel lays his fork down and puts a hand on Tony's arm. "Son, you need to back off this. I also want answers, as he was my brother, and for the past twenty years, I've been haunted by what happened to him. It never really felt right to me. But I also realize he was from a different world. His normal and mine varied wildly." Marcel picks up his glass, but instead of taking a drink from it, he simply stares at the liquid as if seeing something we're not privy too. Finally, he says, "He'd grown overconfident those last years, whereas before he'd always been almost paranoid. In the end, I believe it was his downfall. No man in his position could afford to feel invincible. He and Victor were on top. They were both feared and revered, but they made the mistake of thinking they were untouchable, and it cost them their lives." He lifts his head to study his nephew intently. "Don't go down that same path. You are your father's son and, as such, have been off limits. Yet greed and jealousy are powerful motivators. They will make a smart man do stupid things. In the end, just as the family couldn't protect your father, they can't shield you."

Tony doesn't appear to be shaken by his uncle's dire warning, but I have a lump in my throat the size of a small car. I'm not naïve; I know being a Moretti is dangerous. Yet Tony seems larger than life to me. I see him in a similar light to Marcel's perception of his brother. *Invincible.* This reminder that he is anything but scares the hell out of me. I've survived so many things, yet losing Tony would break me. Other than my mother and sister, he's the first person I've allowed myself to care about. *The only man.* As uneasy as it makes me, he sees the Jacey beneath the armor, and no one has ever cared enough to notice that I'm not who everyone perceives me to be. *He has no idea.* "I can't stop," Tony says quietly, but there is a note of finality in his tone. "But rest assured, I won't let my guard down. Maybe my father was simply careless, and everything is as we've always been told. If that's the case, then I'll move on. He always told me never to accept anything at face value. To check it twice, then do it again until that weird feeling you get in your gut is gone."

We finish our meal in silence, each of us lost in our thoughts. Tony's uncle shoots a look full of concern in his nephew's direction several times but doesn't broach the subject again. Lee and Jade left about fifteen minutes earlier, and we exchanged a brief goodbye, but it had done nothing to break the tension filling the air. Marcel pushes his chair back and pats his flat stomach. "I'm stuffed. This place never disappoints, does it?"

Tony finishes off his wine and sets the glass down. "No, it doesn't. I'm glad you called today. I've been meaning to contact you. I won't let it go so long the next time."

Marcel smiles at his nephew before looking at me with a raised brow. "So how did you two meet? It seems an odd coincidence." *He doesn't know? How could he not?*

Tony puts a hand on the back of my chair, and even though I know it's probably for his uncle's benefit, I still feel pleasure as his fingers graze the nape of my neck. "Through Lee. I'm sure I've mentioned attending some of his family events. So, with Jade and Jacey being sisters, she was there of course."

Marcel nods, then his expression sobers. "I didn't know your father, and what I do know doesn't make me think much of him. But I am sorry that you lost your last parent. That couldn't have been easy."

I have no idea how to respond. Why hadn't Tony prepared me for this? I assumed that as close as he was to his uncle he would have told him some version of the truth. Yet I don't want to blurt out something and contradict Tony's story. "No. No, it wasn't." *Well, that much is true.* I have no intention of going into the reasons, though. Let him assume it's simply grief.

I want to drop to my knees in gratitude when Tony pulls his wallet from his pocket and tosses some bills on the table. "I hate to, but I need to deal with a few things before it gets any later." He turns to me, asking, "Are you ready?" I nod with probably a bit more enthusiasm than necessary, and we get to our feet.

We are waiting for the car to be brought around when Tony's uncle gives him a hug goodbye, before doing the same to me. Having received so few hugs from a father figure in my life, I want to cling a little longer than is appropriate. *I never realized how much human touch comforts.* "I look forward to seeing you again, Jacey." He elbows Tony in the side playfully. "Don't screw this up, kid." We both wave goodbye when Marcel gets into his non-descript sedan and drives off.

When Tony's Range Rover arrives, we both get settled inside, and Tony pulls away from the curb. "You don't have to say it," he says dryly. "I know you were put in an awkward spot several times, but if it's any consolation, you handled it like an ace."

I roll my eyes. "Gee, thanks. I felt like I was swimming in the ocean with weights tied around my ankles when your uncle brought up my parents at the end. What *does* he know? We should have had this conversation ahead of time, don't you think? Or were you going to leave off my last name if he hadn't recognized me?"

"Truthfully, I didn't think that far ahead," he says. "And that's on me. I don't normally overlook details, but then again, this is not a situation I've ever been in before."

"What do you mean? I gather you see your uncle on a regular basis."

"I do, but I was referring to having a woman with me and specifically you. I've never brought anyone other than one of the guys to a meal with my uncle. So, this was very much an unprecedented event." *A commitment phobe like most men—shocker.* I keep that thought to myself, because I really have no room to talk. Although my reasons probably differ wildly from his. "My uncle assumed that one of the Moretti men *handled* your father, and I never corrected that assumption. It's safer for everyone involved that he keeps his distance from the family. He is my uncle, so it's impossible to disassociate him completely, but he is not privy to most things concerning the daily operations of the Morettis."

"But he knows about whatever it is that you and Marco are doing? And he's warning you against it."

"It's unfortunate that I had to tell him a bit about it because he is one of the few people with inside information about my father. Most of the family knew him only in a generic sort of way. They might have been related, but he was basically their boss. He only let them see what he wanted them to."

"The whole thing sounds dangerous," I say softly as we drive through the downtown district and back to Tony's club.

He shrugs. "Just existing comes with certain risks for me, Jacey. It is a part of my life, and it's not likely to get any better. If there is a coverup pertaining to my father's death, I want to expose the guilty party, which might allow me to rest easier. After all, if someone didn't like him in power, then they likely don't like me moving around semi-freely with little oversight. I'm a liability if what I believe is true." He runs a hand through his hair and snorts. "I shouldn't be telling you any of this. It's safer for you to be oblivious. Yet with the link between your father and mine, you're connected regardless of how little you know. I don't want to worry you, yet you need to understand why I'm concerned for your safety. If I'm a loose end, then you may very well be. And before you ask, Lee has taken precautions for his family. It would be a very stupid person who laid a hand on a Jacks. The family has always been wary of him. My father and Victor built him up as Satan himself, and that's why he's been allowed to live free of them. They want no part of him."

"Then as a part of his family now by marriage, would that also offer me some protection? I mean, I know I'm not his wife, but I am his sister-in-law."

Tony pulls up in front of the club and cuts the engine before turning in his seat to face me. "It's possible," he answers slowly. "It depends largely on the people involved and how good their information is."

I glance out the window, not wanting him to see the pain. I consider not responding to his statement at all but think that may be more telling than a reply. So I pull the Duchess from within as I say emotionlessly, "You mean if it's common knowledge that Lee detests me. If it is, then they might not fear retaliation."

"That's correct. You could easily be a warning kill. Someone close to Lee, yet not a direct hit on a Moretti. They might do it to rattle cages. To see what, if anything, happens." As if he'd sugarcoat his words. He's straightforward as always.

"You're saying I could be bait. An attempt to lure you out or scare you into backing off without taking the risk of actually harming the Moretti prince."

Tony inclines his head in agreement, and we sit quietly for a moment. The sound of an approaching vehicle has us both looking behind us. "That'll be Marco."

"Is he feeling well enough to be driving this soon after his...illness?" *What else do I call it? I need to learn more mobster lingo.*

A grin pulls at the corners of Tony's mouth as he murmurs, "I won't go into any details, but apparently, he's gotten most of everything out of his system."

I step to the side and watch as Tony and Marco share the usual hug, then laugh at some shared joke. Probably more of Marco's tales of woe from the past twenty-four hours. As I study Tony's handsome profile while he speaks to the man he considers a brother, it hits me that even though Tony was an only child, he has more family than I'll ever have. Sure, there's Jade and Victor, but that is nothing like what Tony and Marco share. I don't know how to have close relationships like others do. I've been in an isolation of my own making for so long that it's physically painful for me to witness the camaraderie of others. It's not simply that I'm jealous; it's also that I don't understand it. Jade wants that with me—it's there in her eyes every time we're together—but I can't. Even as I yearn to experience it, I know in my heart that it's too late for me. It would never be natural, and it would be yet another role I'm forced to play. *You have that with him.* There is the link with Tony, but it's a different kind. And as much as I want to let down my walls and open myself fully to him, am I capable? I've been Hunter Wrenn's daughter too long because I have no idea who Jacey Wrenn is anymore... *maybe I never did.* Tony motions for me to go inside with him and Marco, and I follow behind them on leaden legs. Maybe it would be a blessing to be the warning kill for some madman. Of all of us, I'm the only truly expendable one.

No one would grieve.

No one would notice the loss.

No one's life would be altered.

Except mine.

And that would no longer matter.

7

TONY

Marco and I take a seat at the bar in my kitchen area. Normally, we opt for a beer at the very least, but his appetite hasn't returned to normal, and after the few glasses of wine with my meal earlier, we're both fine with water. Jacey went to the bedroom earlier and closed the door behind her. Probably to give us privacy as well as to have some of her own. Even though it's temporary, she's not used to this type of living arrangement, and neither am I. The two weeks she was here before were the closest I've ever come to living with a woman. "You still look kind of rough, brother," I point out. "You should have let me come to you."

He grimaces before saying, "I'll live. I'm sure I look worse than I feel. I'm mainly just sore from all the puking." He shudders. "I swear to Christ, I hope I never have anything even close to that happen again. I don't know how people survive those stomach bugs that go around." He shifts on his stool, then pulls a sheet of paper from his pocket and pushes it in front of me. "I talked to Dr. Atwell. Speaking of bugs, I had an herbicide in my system. Luckily not the worst kind. And thanks to a constant barrage of calls during my meal, I'd only eaten maybe half before it had gotten cold and I'd left it. Doc says that kept the symptoms mild. She said I'd probably have been all right without that damn char-coal stuff she forced down me since I had thrown up so much. Although it saved me from having my stomach pumped."

I rub the side of my face as the realization that Marco was poisoned sinks in. Even though we all suspected it, I hadn't wanted it to be true. Yeah, he got off lightly, but someone had been beyond brave to attempt a hit on a Moretti. "Fuck," I hiss. "Does whoever the fuck is behind this not realize that they just made themselves look guilty?"

"This could be unrelated to our digging around," Marco points out. "The family has plenty of enemies, and it could have been any of them. We don't need to automatically assume that this is connected to Draco's death. Plus, Doc said it was possible that the restaurant had been using the herbicide, and it had accidentally gotten into their water or food. Although, she did check and no other complaints have been made relating to illnesses at that restaurant."

"I get what you're saying, but my gut tells me this is linked. It feels like too big of a coincidence that someone outside the family would suddenly decide to take out a key Moretti. That is fucking suicide, and you know it."

"I do," he agrees quietly. "My next question is, how do we play this? Do I inform my father as I normally would in a situation like this? Or do we keep our mouths shut knowing it's going to make us look like we are up to something to whoever is behind it? Hell, I've even wondered if that was the goal. Not to kill me, but to see if I'd break protocol afterward."

"That's a good point." I sigh as I ponder our dilemma. "I could easily make an argument for either side. If we wanted to buy a little more time, then we probably need to report it. Make whoever it is keep guessing. Or we keep this on the down-low and smoke them out of hiding? It was pretty damn brazen, so they're already spooked."

"And when you're scared, you get emotional, which means you get sloppy," Marco says, spelling out what I'm thinking perfectly.

"Exactly. But that approach is by far the riskier of the two. We'll have to be careful and watch our backs. I figure we back off nosing around for a few weeks to further confuse whoever is behind this, but we don't report it to anyone in the family. They'll either watch and wait for us to make a move, or they'll attempt to push the issue again."

"I'm firmly behind plan B, but we'll need to run it by Nic and Mike and make sure they're on board since they're involved." He nods his head toward the bedroom. "What about her? You brought her here, so she's a direct link to you now. They could try to hurt you through her." He gives me a look that clearly says he doesn't understand my reason for having her here. *Given how everyone is reacting to her, should I have left her alone?* Surely, she doesn't want this additional stress in her life.

"If you'll recall the whole baby-daddy audition in my club, you'll realize that she came to me. Yeah, I could have shown her the door that night and continued to watch her from afar. But if whoever is behind this shit got wind of that little show, then finding out she's a Wrenn will put her firmly on their radar. I need her close until we know what we're dealing with. And with you being poisoned, I'm more convinced than ever that I made the right decision. She's too vulnerable."

"There's no way she's going to hole up in your apartment until this shit is solved. She has a company to run. If you want to maintain some semblance of normalcy, then she needs to be at her office tomorrow just like she always is."

"I've already thought about that. You know I've had someone watching her since that night. I figure I'll give her the option of them accompanying her to work each day and staying inside Wrenn, or she works from here."

Marco laughs, shaking his head. "You gonna tell her you've had her followed for a year? If I were you, I'd leave that little piece off. That's enough to freak a woman out."

I lift my bottle of water and tap it against his. "I'm no fool. They'll be warned ahead of time to keep their mouth shut. That's all I need is her getting pissed and taking off."

Marco begins peeling the label from his bottle of water. He still looks pale but much better than the last time I saw him. Still looking down, he asks, "So, kind of a big surprise how I ended up near Nina's place, right? Considering none of us knew she existed. She's...feisty. She might be little, but she's strong. She damn near carried me back to her apartment. Fuck, I think she even rubbed my back while I was puking. Who does that shit? What did you think of her?"

"It was pretty damn shocking," I agree. "She was angry when we voiced our suspicions. Said she had nothing to do with the Gavinos now."

He's still acting almost sheepish, which is not like Marco at all.

Ah fuck, he likes her. Goddammit.

"What was your take on her? You're good at reading people, Tony. Did you sense she was lying about the Gavinos? I had no idea who she was until you all started talking about it before we left. And I was so out of it that it only sunk in later when we were at the compound."

"I don't know, bro," I answer truthfully. "There was nothing I could put my finger on, but I keep going back to the odds of her finding you. Fuck, you know how many people live in Asheville? About ninety thousand. So, how is it even possible that you were poisoned for the first time and then passed out near the home of Franklin Gavino's step-daughter? Fuck if I know what to think about it. My father always said there is no such thing as a coincidence. Especially one of that magnitude."

His already pale skin appears almost translucent now, and I know he's had enough for tonight. And he sure as hell isn't driving himself home. Without asking him, I shoot a text to Nic and ask him to pick Marco up. When he gets here, I'll also tell him that either he stays with Marco or Marco stays with him. *What-the fuck-ever.* Why does it suddenly feel as if I'm babysitting everyone? There's Jacey, who wants to go home, and then Marco, who is mooning over a Gavino. Then there's Nic and Mike, who I should have never involved in this shitshow. The dull ache in my temples is now a full-blown throb. I want nothing more than to go take a fucking nap and forget it all for a while. But Jacey will be waiting to pounce when Marco leaves. As much as I loved my father, this is one of the many times I wish I were born into a normal family. One where violence against myself and those I care about isn't a strong possibility. Tomorrow I'll push the mental weariness that threatens to consume me aside, and I'll put a plan of action together. But tonight, I simply need to shut down and regroup. Jacey, of all people, will understand that.

JACEY

Tony has been so quiet since Marco left that it's beginning to make me nervous. Like most women, I've read countless magazine articles about how men disconnect in times of stress. *And this is certainly one of those times.* But considering I've never been in a long-term relationship, I haven't witnessed it firsthand. My father certainly had plenty of mood swings, but I don't recall him going through this weird quiet one. That would have been a blessing. But even as irritated as I am with him over my house arrest, I'm still worried. He calmly walked into the bedroom about an hour ago and advised that one of his men would be with me at the office for my protection until he felt it no longer necessary. And that if I insisted on going home, someone would be there as well. I opened my mouth to let him have it, but he simply turned on his heel and went into the bathroom. The shower started a few moments later. I paced the bedroom the entire time, livid at his high-handedness. Then he was back with a towel wrapped around his waist. *Okay, I lost my train of thought for a moment. So hot.* That mind freeze allowed him time to go into the closet and come out wearing a pair of low-slung basketball shorts. *He's killing me here.* "I...um, Tony," I croak out, before stopping to clear my throat.

He turns to stare in my direction, then lifts a hand when I open my mouth. "I'm done for the day, Jacey. You're angry with me; believe me, I get it. Take a place in line behind everyone else who'd like a piece of me. I'm no good to any of you unless I have some space to process. To plot out the next moves because, believe me, a misstep at this juncture could be fatal to any or all of us." I stare at him in surprise, not knowing what to say to this insight into his head. I have a feeling that few people have ever been privy to the inner workings of Tony Moretti. "I'm sorry that you're unhappy with the arrangements I've put into place. I wish I could give you some alternatives, but I have none. Please believe that I wouldn't be putting you through this unless I thought it absolutely necessary."

From out of nowhere, a horrible thought occurs to me, and I cannot stop myself from giving voice to my suspicions even though I should wait. "You never intended to father my child, did you? Your capitulation was all an act. You needed a way to keep me close while you worked through this game of yours." I put my hands on my hips, my voice reaching a near shout as I snap, "Did it ever occur to you that you were thrusting me into the spotlight with this farce? It's been a year since my father died. If anyone wanted me, they'd probably have done it by now. Like you've already pointed out, Lee isn't likely to get his boxers in a wad over my death. Hell, he might be offering a reward for all I know. It would certainly save him from having to humor his wife by looking at me across the dinner table at Christmas."

I'm in a self-righteous rage when he pulls the rug out from under me. "Your baby-daddy audition in my club made this necessary. If you're looking for somewhere to heap the blame, then start by dumping it at your own feet. If anyone *had* forgotten your existence, you made sure they got the reminder loud and clear. I realize you had no idea that your timing was extremely bad, but regardless, the damage is done." I'm speechless when he finishes delivering my verbal slap down. He didn't raise his voice, nor had there been any anger in it. He simply stated the facts as if he were discussing the weather. *Cloudy with a chance of you fucked yourself over.* I remain where I am, uncertain how to respond. An apology doesn't seem quite right, nor do I think he expects one. "I'm going to sleep," he says before moving away. He has already turned the covers back and is sitting on the side of the bed when he adds quietly, "And I wasn't lying about the baby thing. When this is over, if you still want to have a child, then I'll be the father. I asked Dr. Atwell to schedule full physicals for both of us along with STD tests, although I've had both recently as a part of my annual physical. I thought we could get the details out of the way now, then proceed when it's safe to do so." He turns off the lamp on his nightstand and lies down.

I decide to go about my own nightly routine while I mull over Tony's revelations. When I came up with the insane scheme of taking applications for someone to father my child, I hadn't stopped to consider the repercussions. Oh, I knew Tony would be pissed—in fact, I counted on it. But what I hadn't considered was what the very public venue could mean. I put not only myself but him in danger as well. Granted, I hadn't known what he was involved in, but still, I had inadvertently made myself a possible target to a murderer. And I took Tony along for the ride with me. By rights, he should have left me to fend for myself. Yet here I am at his apartment under his protection. *And acting like a spoiled bitch.* Even with all that, he's still willing to give me what I asked him for. What I attempted to push him into.

I make a mess of everything I touch.

I lean my head against the cool tile in the shower and let the water cascade over me. I stay there so long that I resemble a prune when I finally get out. I dress in the same pajamas from the previous night and quickly brush my teeth. I have no idea how long I've been in the bathroom, but when I come out, I expect him to be asleep. But the light from my side of the bed shows his eyes still open as he stares at the ceiling. He doesn't react at all to my presence, and I once again feel uncertain. I square my shoulders, and murmur, "I...I'm sorry. I didn't think things through before I acted. If I had known—"

"Jacey, it's fine. Please let it go. We'll talk later." Then with a note in his voice that clearly ends the discussion, he adds, "Good night."

What now? I have no idea if I should get in the bed with him like last night or go elsewhere, and he gives me absolutely no indication of his preference. I'm pretty sure at that moment if my hair caught on fire, he'd point at the bathroom and tell me to handle it. To me, there is really no decision here. He has asked for time and me tossing and turning next to him is not going to give him that. Nor does he need for me to ask his approval for everything. So, I take the pillow from the other side of the bed and rummage in the closet until I find an extra blanket. He voices no objections when I walk out the bedroom door and shut it behind me. To say his behavior unsettles me is an understatement. In the short time I've spent in his company, I've witnessed many facets of the man. Playful, caring, serious, angry, and thoughtful are some that come to mind. But this somber mood isn't one I expected. It's not that he is scared or anxious. Rather, he's off somewhere in his head where no one can reach him. I have little doubt that he's making, then discarding plan after plan. Tony isn't a man to leave very much to chance. And with Marco, Nic, Mike, and now my life possibly on the line, he's going to be very careful in every move he makes.

I made this so much worse for him without realizing it.

Instead of taking the sofa, I curl up in a large, overstuffed chair and lay my head back against the cushion. With a sinking sensation in my stomach, I know that regardless of what happens in the days and weeks ahead, I'll release him from his promise when this is over. If I want a child, then I can do as Jade suggested and go to a clinic. What good did I believe could come from basically blackmailing a man to be the father? Eventually, he'll resent me for it, which is completely under-standable. He's under enough pressure trying to navigate the minefield that is the Moretti family. If my presence makes him more vulnerable, a child will make him that much more so.

Your selfishness clearly knows no bounds.

I cannot or will not stand in the way of someone else's happiness. For Tony to be linked to me because having a child is selfish and wrong.

And really, what have I been thinking? Why do I believe I could be anyone's *mother*? I've lived thirty-seven years of woeful and loveless ugliness. *What do I know about love?* About the true selflessness of being a mother? So desperate for love that I'd *willingly* subject a child to having a fucked-up woman like me as its parent?

God, I'm repulsive.

I'm not Jade. There's no Lee Jacks to love me unconditionally. No incredible man who wants a family *with* me. Any man, including Tony, will run if they're aware of the things I did for my father. No, when this is over, I'll return to my life and only see Tony at family events as before. He never has to know the true Jacey, and I never have to endure the look of revulsion in his eyes if he did. I'll go back to being the cold-hearted bitch everyone hates and expects nothing of. There's safety in the familiar, and I've played that role for long enough that it's almost effortless. No one knows that beneath the façade, I just want to belong —to be normal. But I can't go back, nor can I move forward. Instead, I'll remain in a state of suspended animation.

Alone, so alone.

As deserved.

8

TONY

Clint will accompany a very subdued Jacey to her office, so we both sit quietly at the bar sipping coffee as we await his arrival. Shutting down the previous night had been inconvenient but necessary. Jacey has no idea of course, but it is how I process things. Some might call it an adult time-out, but it's what I've done for as long as I can remember. It was effective and a hell of a lot cheaper than therapy. Oddly enough, my father had been the same way. Many times, I found him in his study lying on the leather sofa or simply sitting behind his desk with his feet propped on it. And he'd be staring off into space as if his body was there, but his mind was millions of miles away. He'd remain in that position for hours, and I learned from an early age that interacting with him when he was in that state of mind was useless. It wasn't that he became angry; he simply ignored me.

I have no idea what time I finally drifted off to sleep, but I woke in the early hours by the dream again. The same one I've had on and off for years. Sometimes, months pass between occurrences, then other times, it happens several times a week. I have noticed a pattern, though. They occur more when I'm overly tired or stressed. Both of which I'm experiencing right now. I've had this dream for many years now. When Jacey passed out in my arms, I wasn't so much shocked by what happened, but by the fact that I *intimately* knew her face. Before that moment, I never actually believed my dream girl existed in the flesh. I was much younger in the dream, and so was she. I fell in love with her as a boy, and as I got older, the feelings were still there, but it was more of a fondness as we were both frozen in time in my head. There was nothing unusual about the dream. We were swimming in the big pool at the compound. We joked and splashed each other before getting out and having some ice cream. I think we were about ten. The sunlight had glistened off her blond hair, almost creating a halo effect. Even then, she was a beauty. So carefree and full of life. But last night, the dream was different. The setting had been the same, but we were the age we are now. I swallow hard as I recall the next part. Jacey walked out of the pool, and when she turned to face me, her stomach was round with my child. I fought it, but the dream ended abruptly, and I woke with a longing in my soul I've never experienced before.

I wanted it to be real.

I want it to be real.

I wanted her to be happy, for us to live a normal life where we have a family without the constant threat of someone trying to take it all away. I long to give her everything she wants. But first, I have to find and eliminate those who wish to destroy it. The sound of Jacey's barstool scraping across the floor as she gets to her feet brings me back to the present. She's in one of her power suits and looks very much the Duchess this morning. *She's always been a blonde in my dreams.* She thought changing her hair color could help her become someone else, but there is no magic pill. That can only happen from within.

"You're very quiet this morning," she murmurs as she pours out her remaining coffee and rinses the cup.

"Sorry." I smile, attempting to put her at ease. It's obvious that the distant Tony from last night has thrown her off. She's unsure how to act around me now. She watches me warily as I stand and approach her. I place one hand on her hip and the other cups the side of her face. "I miss the blond hair," I say truthfully.

She lets out a short laugh. "I hate to admit it, but I do as well. It has nothing to do with the whole blondes have more fun thing because believe me, that's a myth." She appears pensive for a moment, then admits, "I don't know this person sometimes looking back at me in the mirror. I thought my hair would help...you know, give me a fresh start. But it's a constant reminder of why I did it in the first place." Shrugging her slim shoulders, she adds ruefully, "Leave it to me to simply make things worse instead of better."

"I understand." I pull the neckline of my shirt aside and point at the cross there amid the other tattoos that dot my chest. "I had that added after my father was killed. At the time, I sought comfort in what so many do when they suffer a sudden loss. You either turn to God or turn away from him when you lose someone you love in such a brutal fashion. I've never walked through the door of a church before, but regardless of the life my father lived, he still believed in a higher power. I think the idea that there was a hell gave him pause at times, but he believed he was living his destiny, and that it was the inevitable price he'd pay at some point. It was as if I thought having the cross so close to my heart would save him from purgatory or even make it more bearable to never see him walk through the door again. To never hear him laugh at his own jokes or to lose his shit when I blew off school for a few days and he got a call from the principal. Yes, I had an unconventional upbringing, but I didn't really realize that fully until later. He wasn't ever a Boy Scout leader, but he loved me. Yeah, he cursed, he smoked, and he drank. Hell, he did just about everything in front of me that the books tell you not to do around your kids." I pause, running a fingertip along her bottom lip. "Maybe the hair helped you at the time more than you realize, just as the cross may have given me some comfort. If it's doing the opposite now, then you change it. There are plenty of things we have no control over. But in this instance, you do. So, try it, beautiful, and see if it helps."

She turns her face into my hand much like a kitten needing to be stroked. "I love hearing stories about your father. I know it's weird, considering he had a thing with my mother, but I'm kind of fascinated by the man who built such an empire. His life sounds like a movie."

"Much of it was," I agree. "But like most people, he had his good days and his bad ones." I lean closer and inhale the fragrance that is so

Jacey. It's delicate, floral, and utterly feminine. I could happily drown myself in it without complaint. I allow my lips to graze hers lightly, and her slight gasp has me instantly hard. I want her so much my fucking body hurts. *Can't hold out much longer.* Now more than ever I need my house in order. She's here where I've wanted her for so long and more than willing. Yet everything is such a fucking mess that I'm afraid to bring anything else into the fray that could cloud our judgment. If my head isn't in the game, people could die—*she* could die. I keep the kiss light and unhurried. A leisurely sampling of her plump lips. I also keep a few inches between our lower bodies. The last thing I need is the head downstairs losing his mind and taking advantage of her proximity. Jacey was timid the first time I kissed her, and I put it down to nerves, but it hasn't changed. Not that we've shared that many kisses, but I have the distinct feeling that no matter how confident she is in the business world, she prefers to follow instead of lead in the bedroom. We've never discussed our past relationships, so I have no idea about her sexual history nor do I really want to. No good ever comes from bringing up stuff like that. It could cause problems where there have been none. She's a beautiful woman, and I assume she's had her fair share of sexual partners, but that doesn't necessarily mean she'll be immediately comfortable with me. Everyone is different, and I certainly have no problem taking the lead. In fact, I prefer it. When I deepen the kiss, things begin to spiral. Her tongue in my mouth has me ready to disregard every reason why this is a bad idea. I've bridged the gap between us, and we're grinding against each other like a couple of horny teenagers. "Fuck, I want you," I groan against the curve of her neck.

Her hands are in my hair and never has that turned me on as much as it does now. Swear to Christ, if she touches my dick, I'll probably blow my load immediately. "Yes, please." Her voice is breathy and low as she moves even closer.

The sound of the intercom has us both jumping as if we heard a gunshot. The next beep is accompanied by Clint's voice. "Hey boss, I'm here. I'll wait in the car for Ms. Wrenn."

As painful as the throb of my dick is, I still chuckle when Jacey grumbles, "You have to be kidding me."

My hands ended up on her ass at some point, so I give it another squeeze and then shift them to her hips. I risk giving her one last kiss on her now-pouting lips before releasing her completely. She wobbles for a moment, and I reach out to steady her until she gives me a nod. "I more than share your sentiments, Duchess. But we've waited this long, and a quickie isn't what comes to mind when I think of having you for the first time." I don't bother to hide my painful grimace as I adjust myself to keep my zipper from cutting my dick off.

She's giggling as she turns away, and I can't resist slapping her ass. Her gasp of outrage is purely reflex because the expression on her face says otherwise. *My girl likes it a bit rough.* She collects her purse and briefcase, and we take the stairs to the bottom floor. I'm so accustomed to the layout of the club that I have no problem moving around in the dim lighting, but after Jacey bumps into a barstool, I take her hand and lead her through the maze until we reach the back door. A black BMW sedan idles in the alley. The driver's door opens, and Clint gets out to greet us. He's former military and was hired by Lester, as were all the security personnel on my payroll. He's tall and built like a fucking tank. He's wearing his usual black suit, and I wonder idly where he has them custom made. We shake hands as he says, "Good morning, boss." Then he turns to Jacey and inclines his head. "Ms. Wrenn, I'm Clint, and I'll be accompanying you today. If you need anything at all, please let me know."

"Thank you, Clint, and please call me Jacey. I'm not used to having a shadow, so it will take some adjustment."

Clint darts a look in my direction, no doubt amused by her statement since he's been watching her for some time now. It's a credit to his skills that she doesn't recognize him. I clap him on the shoulder and then put a hand on Jacey's lower back, leading her to the car. I open the back door and set her briefcase and purse on the seat for her. Then I kiss her as if we've done it every morning for years. *And it feels just like the dream. Right.* "Have a good day, beautiful. Call me if you need me... or even if you don't."

Her eyes are soft and her lips still rosy from our earlier kiss. "I will," she says before folding her long legs into the car. I shut the door behind her and rap on the top of the BMW to signal to Clint to go. As the tail-lights disappear, my chest feels unusually tight. I fight the urge to call Clint and demand he bring her back. I feel almost panicked that she'll be on her own for hours today without me there to watch over her, which is irrational since Clint is more skilled than I am in every kind of combat. He'll protect her with his life; I have no doubt.

I'm in trouble.

It's what I've known since the moment she passed out in my arms. There will be no in-between. Heaven or hell awaits, and it's too late to stop the momentum. She will either be the center of my life or the predominant reason I lose it.

TONY

I spend the morning working out some of Jax's issues. Then he leaves to fly to Florida. He'll visit the club there first before stopping at the other locations in Georgia and South Carolina. Normally, I would make the rounds myself, but this is not the time for me to be away from North Carolina. Jax is single and has no obligations here, so he can easily handle the traveling for now. I glance at my watch. Lee should be here any time, so I walk out the front door of the club and await his arrival. *Fuck, I need a smoke.* I have once again given up smoking, and it's been rough. Stress makes me want nothing more than to feel the calm that inhaling and exhaling brings. But it's a nasty habit I'm determined to break. Plus, there's Jacey to consider. She made it plain when she stayed before that she can't stand cigarette smoke, and I don't want to subject her to something that could harm her. When I throw open the door, Lee is climbing out of his Porsche. *Bet there's no car seat in that.* It's still hard for me to reconcile the Lee I've always known with the family man he is now. Oh, I know with a certainty that he could and would still kill a man with a toothpick if necessary, but still, I never expected him to marry much less have a kid. For anyone wanting a little payback, Lee now has several weaknesses to choose from. His wife, his son, a daugh-ter, and a granddaughter. Each one of them with a target on their forehead for the right person. *I'm no better.* "Tony," he says as we give each other a brief hug. "Out taking a smoke?"

"I wish." I sigh in irritation. "Trying to quit again, but couldn't have picked a worse time. I'll probably need to drink more now to offset it."

I lead the way inside, and we go directly to my office. I've been too lax with sensitive conversations as of late. Now more than ever, as many as possible need to be held in a safe environment. I bypass my desk and take a chair in the seating area, and Lee does the same. I quickly bring him up to date on Marco along with Nina Gavino. His expression changes very little, which is what I've come to expect from him. A sign of panic on his part would probably freak me the fuck out. The most emotion I've ever seen from him was the night Jade was abducted, and we were following her cell phone signal. He kept his cool for the most part, but I knew he was deathly afraid for her. "A few days have passed, and things appear to be the same here. So I know you haven't informed the family of the attempted hit on Marco. Otherwise, the club would be crawling with Moretti men."

I lean forward and clasp my hands between my knees. "I decided against it. A shake-up of that magnitude would put everyone on high alert. If the person responsible is one of ours, they'll go to ground for a while. No one would be foolish enough to make another move until the heat dies down."

Lee studies me for a moment before inclining his head in agreement. "Very true. Apparently, Marco wasn't meant to die, but the act was merely to get your attention. Otherwise, they would have dosed him with something more lethal. It wouldn't matter to Rutger, though. Marco is his son, and there would be hell to pay. He will view this as an act of war, which is quite possibly the goal of whoever the hell is involved. Get the Morettis gunning for another family—more than likely the Gavinos since Nina was involved—and there is mayhem. Easier for things to slip through the cracks. Plus, a fatal hit on you would be blamed on them. Ties things up nice and easy."

"My thoughts exactly. I'd like to avoid that. I refuse to give this bastard an easy road to taking me out. If he wants it, he'll have to fucking outsmart me to get it." I snort in disbelief as I say wryly, "I can't believe all that just came out of my mouth. Fuck, we don't even know if anyone in the family murdered my father, much less tried to take Marco out. It could be a Gavino, for all we know, or Hunter Wrenn's claims that he engineered and executed the whole thing is a possibility as well."

"All valid points," Lee says. "But you don't buy that any more than I do. We've both always had a gut feeling that nothing was as it appeared to be even before Wrenn and the Gavinos came into play. Don't get me wrong. I believe Hunter did everything he fucking boasted about including taking down Draco and Victor. Yet there are things that simply do not add up. As we've both said many times, Draco and Victor were not careless men. Overconfident at times but not sloppy. Letting a junkie get the jump on not one but both is an anomaly that cannot be explained rationally."

"Same. The uneasiness has only increased. Even if I wanted to let this go now, I don't think the party or parties involved would. I'm a marked man, and my only choice is to eliminate them before they get to me or someone I love. I know this goes without saying, but for the foreseeable future, be very diligent about your family's security. I have no reason to believe they'll go after you, but don't relax your guard."

"Jade and Victor are more than covered, and in addition to the men I have on Lia and Lara, Lucian also has some as well. No one is getting close enough to touch a hair on their heads."

I notice he makes no mention of Jacey. I know there are a lot of unanswered questions about her role in Jade's abduction, but I've always believed there was something more there than we knew. "I assume you have men on Jacey as well? She's as much of or more of a target than anyone right now."

I see the look of distaste on his face for a split second before it once again becomes expressionless. "Of course. They stay on the sideline, but if she's in distress, they'll step up. You also have her covered, so I don't see any need for concern there. She's staying with you?"

Anyone who believes that women are the only ones who gossip amongst themselves is deluded. Men may be more covert about it, but word still gets around. And considering we have the same ties, it would be strange if he wasn't aware. On the outside chance Jade hasn't told him about the baby thing, which, again, is unlikely, I decide to keep my response brief. "For now, yes. I'm not comfortable leaving her on her own until I have more information."

Lee is quiet for a moment, but he has something more to add. Finally, he says, "I never thought what happened that night would create this type of bond between you and her. Granted, I have spent very little time around her, but that's largely by choice. My wife might be able to forgive and forget, but I cannot. She probably didn't have an easy time as Hunter's right hand, but she chose to remain in that role, siding with him in every instance against Jade. My wife would grieve if harm came to her, and that's why I'll always protect her if possible. Otherwise, I'd leave her to fend for herself."

His words are emotionless and flat. I want to defend Jacey, yet I don't have a leg to stand on. Anything I offer would be based on feelings, not facts. To a man like Lee, I might as well save my breath. Considering I would normally be the same, I can't play the hypocrite and rip into him over it. When this is over, Jacey and I are having a long talk. She's given me enough to know that she had her reasons for what she did, and I doubt they have anything to do with hating her sister. On the contrary, if my hunch is right, it's the opposite. The only question is why? Even if it's necessary I find out, with a monster like Hunter as a father, I really don't want to know the answer. Lee is waiting to see how I respond. He's always been a man who enjoys baiting people for a reaction, and it's served him extremely well in the past. "That's not exactly news to me, brother," I acknowledge. "We all play the part we're given. I believe Jacey is no exception. But I have no proof to back that up, so we'll leave it at that. I appreciate the added protection you have on her. Regardless of our differing personal feelings, any kind of loss within our circle is unacceptable."

"Agreed. Keep me informed."

I relax as we move past the subject of Jacey. I don't want to be at odds with Lee, but I won't side with him against her without a helluva lot more proof. Although if our positions were reversed and Jade was my wife, I'd undoubtedly feel the same way. "By the way, I appreciate that information on Caulder Construction. They're starting next week. The fucking fire marshal is making us jump through hoops. Don't get me wrong, I want my clubs to be safe, but it's like they're constantly adding to or amending their requirements. Anyway, if Caulder does a good job here, I'll use them at the compound next. Lester has a list of things that need to be taken care of. Fuck, it's always something."

"You should try being married," Lee quips before getting to his feet. "I need to get back to the office." I accompany him downstairs, and we embrace once more. Fucking thankful for the man. *Wonder if my world will ever come full circle like his has? Lucky bastard.*

I remain in the doorway for a long time. The hair on the back of my neck prickles, and I know it's coming. A reckoning over twenty years in the making. Outside of my small circle, who is friend or foe? A wise man would run, but the son of Draco Moretti is no coward. Never has the weight of responsibility that I carry been heavier. To be victorious, my friends and brothers in arms will have to let me fight beside them. For a war such as this cannot be won without each of us playing our parts. *And I will not allow them to shield me.* A fleeting image of Jacey comes into my head. I've never had as much to lose as I do now. And even though it fucking infuriates me to think her life is in danger because of me, my heart feels some unexplained peace.

I found my dream girl.

And I won't lose her again.

9

JACEY

Is Tony avoiding me? Granted, our schedules are very different with me now back at work from early morning until the evening and Tony's nocturnal hours in his club. He goes to bed a couple of hours before I get up in the mornings and is either already in the club or preparing to go when I get home. I spend my evenings working or watching television. He hasn't mentioned me going to the club, so I can only assume he doesn't want me there. At best, I'd be a distraction, and I don't think he needs the added stress.

Clint and his partner, Bishop, cover me at the office, yet thankfully, I don't feel smothered. Other than transportation, they stay out of sight. There is some comfort knowing they're there if I need them. In fact, for the first time in a very long time, I don't feel so alone. *Isolated.* When I'm at Tony's, his security takes over. If a window or the door is opened in the apartment, someone will know about it.

I'm packing my briefcase in preparation for leaving the office when there is a knock on my door before Clint steps inside. "Ms. Jacey, the boss asked me to take you to the compound this evening instead of the club. Dinner will be there as well."

Well, well, maybe he's not avoiding me after all. *Or he feels guilty.*

Whatever the reason, I'm excited, which is crazy since I've seen Tony at some point every day. He's even continued to kiss me good morning on the days he's been late getting to bed. So, the fact that I feel as if I've been invited out on a date is silly. If he wants me at the compound, then this probably pertains to the family. Marco, Nic, and Mike will probably be there if there is news. I've been so out of the loop lately that it's easy to forget there might be a threat out there waiting to take one or all of us out when we least expect it. *God, that sounds so dramatic.* I wonder if Lee will be there and if he is, then Jade and little Victor might be as well. I feel the same complex array of emotions when there's the possibility of seeing my sister. Longing, bitterness, and anxiety are the prevalent ones. For a moment, I consider having Clint tell Tony I'm not feeling well, which isn't exactly a lie. Being around Jade and Victor cause something akin to sickness every time. *Gotta get past this. Be the Duchess.* A small smile pulls at the corners of my mouth as I realize how easily I've come to think of myself as Jax's nickname. Of course, Tony calling me that so frequently has caused it to stick in my head. And in a way, it is fitting. I do act like someone else to protect the person inside me.

It's my reality, and now I no longer hope for that to change.

The drive to the compound takes longer in rush hour, and it's after six when we pull up at the tall gates and wait to be admitted. I know there are cameras along the miles-long driveway, and I look for them as we pass through the wooded landscape but see absolutely nothing. I'm surprised when we approach the house and half a dozen vans and work trucks sit off to the side of the drive. I recall Tony mentioning something about some. The car comes to a stop, and I wait as I always do for Clint to walk around and open my door. I've learned from experience that he isn't happy when I pop out on my own. "Thanks, Clint," I murmur as he takes my arm to help me.

"I'll leave you in the foyer for Tony while he finishes up with the tradesmen. I need to debrief with Lester." *Debrief. Who are these guys?* I forget all about the covert lingo as my skin tingles knowing Tony is near. I self-consciously smooth my hands down my pencil skirt and brush an imaginary piece of lint from my silk blouse. *This isn't the prom. Get it together.* Then it hits me that someone is probably watching me on a security monitor. My hands drop to my sides instantly, not wanting to look like some club groupie all giddy for Tony's attention. Clint keys in a code and does the handprint thing to open one of the massive entryway doors. I hear power equipment in the distance and see Tony deep in discussion with two men. "Looks like he's busy," I say to Clint as we walk across the foyer. We pause a few feet away, waiting for Tony to acknowledge our presence. Tony comes here for privacy, and it's something I respect. My eyes drift around the area, noting all the intricate details I missed last time I was here. It really is a beautiful home. When I feel eyes on me, thinking it's Tony, I look up, only to gasp.

Can't be.

No. God, no.

I begin to shake; I can't control it. My vision blurs as I stumble backward. "No, no, no."

Sick.

Feel so sick.

Clint must notice my sudden movements because I hear him calling my name faintly over the roar in my ears.

All I see is *him,* the face of my nightmares. And then he takes a couple of steps toward me. That arrogant, evil grin leering at me.

I'm falling into space.

There are hands on me, but I fight them with everything I have.

But, once again, I'm no match for them.

Then there is nothing. Only darkness. Blessed oblivion.

TONY

I turn as the commotion behind me grabs my attention. Jacey is white as a ghost and trembling violently. I start toward her at a run. *What the fuck is happening?* Clint is trying to calm her, but she's fighting. She lunges away and teeters in the heels she's wearing. Time seems to stand still.

I'm not going to make it.

I can literally see the strands of her hair sliding through his hands as she tumbles backward. Her head strikes the heavy door sharply before she crumbles to the marble floor. "Fuck," I hiss as I reach her a few seconds behind Clint. I drop to my knees next to her prone form, scanning her for injuries. "What in the hell happened?" I ask as my hand comes to rest on her pale cheek. Her eyes are closed, and I have no idea if she passed out or was knocked out by the fall.

Beside me, Clint gently lifts her hand and presses his finger against a point on the lower side. "I have no idea, boss. We were waiting for you to finish. One minute, she was fine, and the next, she was freaking out. Saying no over and over. I...I've never seen anything like it. She's always so calm and controlled." Looking up, he adds, "Her pulse is steady. But she hit her head hard. We should call 911."

Then I remember that Dr. Atwell is upstairs checking Marco one last time to make sure he has a clean bill of health. "Clint, Marco and Doc are upstairs. Go find her."

Jeremy Caulder and a few of his men are standing to the side uncertainly. "Get your men and get out," I snap without looking up. They're smart enough not to question my command. They scurry toward the back of the house to round up their crew without saying a word. "Duchess," I murmur as my hands move over her gently. When I saw her go down, I thought she'd been shot. There's no sign of that from what I can see, and I'm afraid to move her until Dr. Atwell gives me the all clear. "Come on, sweetheart, open those beautiful eyes. You're scaring the shit out of me right now."

What happened?

The look of terror on her face had been unmistakable. *What were you afraid of?* I rack my brain but can't come up with anything out of the norm.

Rapid footsteps sound on the stairway, and a few seconds later both Dr. Atwell and Marco are next to me. "What the fuck, Tony?" Marco asks as he literally stands guard over her against some unseen threat.

"I don't have a clue. She got spooked by something. Lost it. Clint tried to calm her, but she pulled away and lost her balance. Fell backward and hit her head hard on the door."

"Is she—" Marco's question trails off as Jacey shifts slightly before releasing a pained groan.

I caress her arm soothingly. "Duchess, try not to move. Let the doc check you out first."

Not surprisingly, the stubborn woman ignores my command. Her eyes open, and she blinks rapidly as if trying to process what's happened. Dr. Atwell speaks slowly and clearly, "Jacey, can you tell me where you're feeling pain?"

"Head," Jacey croaks out, still seeming disoriented.

Dr. Atwell brings a penlight from her pocket and begins inspecting Jacey's pupils. "Any nausea or dizziness?" When Jacey says no, she runs through another series of questions and appears satisfied by the answers she receives. Even though she's still dazed, she is noticeably more alert. Thank fuck. "She doesn't appear to have a concussion. Let's move her from the floor so I can see the back of her head."

I put my arms under her as gently as I can and scoop her up against my chest. She's so thin that I have no problem balancing her weight as I get to my feet. "Tony." She sighs and lays her head against me.

I attempt to comfort her around the lump in my throat as I say, "Yeah, baby. I've got you. Don't worry; you're going to be fine."

I've just placed her on a sofa in the study when she asks, "How? What happened?"

I take a seat next to her, holding her hand between both of mine as she stares at me in bewilderment. "I'm not sure what happened, sweetheart. You panicked over something and jerked away from Clint. I couldn't reach you before you fell and hit your head."

In a split second, I see the confusion clear before she freezes. She scrambles backward, her eyes darting around the room. The trembling returns, and her face goes even more ashen. Her fingers dig painfully into my arm as she gasps out, "Keep him away from me. Tony, please. Please." *Who the fuck is she talking about?* She moves toward me, and to my shock, she climbs in my lap and wraps her arms around me. She's crying now, and it's a horrible keening sound. As if each sob is wrenched from her very soul.

Dr. Atwell rushes from the room and returns with her bag. In moments, she is holding a syringe to Jacey's arm. "It's a sedative," she explains as I shoot her a questioning look. "Just to calm her. Yes?"

"Do it." I can't bear to hear Jacey so distressed.

Once she's done, she asks, "Do you have any idea what this is about?" Dr. Atwell isn't one to ask questions of a Moretti. She'd rather not know. She wouldn't work for me if not for being a friend of Lester and of course needing money to put her son through college. I answer truthfully. "No fucking clue. Listen, I'd appreciate it if you'd stay here overnight. I was planning to go back to the city, but that's obviously not happening."

"Of course, Tony. While she's sedated, I want to get a closer look at the back of her head, so if you'll tilt her forward a bit." Jacey appears to be sleeping, and I marvel at how quickly the injection worked. Dr. Atwell finally appears satisfied with her examination. She peels off her rubber gloves and drops them in a nearby trash can. "She has a pretty good-sized knot, but there is no blood. Normally, I wouldn't advocate giving a sedative to someone with a head injury, but in the case where the risks outweigh it, I saw no choice. She would have caused herself more damage if left unchecked."

"I appreciate it, Doc. Is it all right to take her upstairs now?" When she nods, I add, "And you know your way around. Why don't you find Cass and have some dinner? Then make yourself comfortable. I'll send for you if I need you." She promises to check in soon, and then with one last curious look at Jacey, she leaves the room.

Marco remains silent, but I know he's following along behind me as I carry Jacey to my room at the top of the stairs. She murmurs in her sleep, but nothing I can make out. I sit heavily in a chair beside the bed once she's settled and run a trembling hand through my hair. Marco clears his voice as he paces the room. "Bro, that scared the ever-loving shit out of me. I didn't see it the first time, but her reaction in the study was pure terror. What's she afraid of, because I'm ready to tear someone apart?"

"You and me both." I sigh. "I'm fucking lost here. No idea what happened." Hell, she's been with me for a couple of weeks, and everything has been fine. Granted, we pretty much just pass each other due to our different schedules, but she's seemed perfectly relaxed when we've seen each other. Things have been quiet at the office according to Clint, and she hasn't been overly stressed. Fuck, she's looked great the past few days. She's been the Duchess less and Jacey more. At least the Jacey I've seen glimpses of. "I haven't seen her that horrified or frightened since she shot her father." I pause, rubbing my hands over my face before adding, "What you saw in the study was nothing. I...fuck, I thought someone had hurt her...shot or stabbed..."

"Fuck, man." Marco looks just as worried about her, which doesn't surprise me.

"Clint said she kept saying no over and over. I just don't—"

"He's not supposed to be here." Marco and I both freeze before our heads swing in unison to the woman on the bed. Her eyes are open but heavily lidded. She's staring straight ahead as if she's talking in her sleep. "Why was he here? How could he be?" She shakes her head, then groans. My heart almost shatters when she turns and tells me in a childlike voice, "He hurt me."

"What the fuck?" I hear Marco whisper, but my focus is her. Only her. *Who hurt you, baby?*

They'll die.

"Duchess," I say softly. "Who scared you tonight? Who hurt you? Tell me and I'll make it go away." *For-fucking-ever.*

Her small frame shivers, and for a moment, I think she won't answer, but then she talks. "Jeremy. He hurt me...too much." She drifts off while I sit there in confusion. *Jeremy?*

My blood runs cold and rage flows through my veins like molten lava.

"Is that an old boyfriend or what?" Marco asks.

A man dared to raise a hand to her? I will find him, and when I do, he'll rue the day he was born.

"Fuck if I know, but I'm damn sure going to find out." I pull my phone from my pocket to call Lester with the intention of having him start digging when it hits me with the force of an atomic bomb. "Holy fucking hell," I roar, then lower my voice when Jacey moves restlessly in the bed before settling. I get to my feet and turn to Marco, saying incredulously, "It's Caulder. It must be. The guy who owns the construction company I've been using. I was in the foyer talking to him and a couple of his men when Jacey came in."

Marco's eyes narrow, and I recognize the look of calculation there. "His name is Jeremy, isn't it?" I don't bother to reply, but instead, I start for the door. I'm almost to the stairs when a hand on my shoulder stops me. I attempt to shake him off, but he holds firm. "Tony." His voice comes out as a near shout as he tries to get my attention. "Listen to me for a goddamn minute before you go off halfcocked."

"What?" I snarl, ready to bodily shove him aside if necessary.

"Think for a minute. I know you want to go yank this piece of shit out of his house in front of God, man, and everyone else who happens to be around, but you know better. We need more information from Jacey. It's too big a coincidence not to be him, but we need to know what we're dealing with and then put a plan together. How are you going to be any help to any of us—including her—if you're sitting in prison somewhere? And despite your influence with the local police, they'll have no choice but to toss your ass behind bars if you do something so blatant they can't ignore."

I almost despise the rational side of my brain that kicks in. I want nothing more than to get my answers from the source—and hope to fuck I have to beat them out of him—but Marco is right. This can't happen how I so desperately want it to. It would be suicide, and I'm not a stupid man. "I fucking hate you sometimes," I mutter as I push by him and retrace my steps to my room. I'm in the doorway when I stop and look back at him. "If this is anything like I think it is, then he dies."

It's a testament to our lives and the way we grew up that Marco doesn't look surprised. "Doesn't matter much to me." He shrugs. "Any man who elicits *that* reaction from a woman as strong and courageous as our Jacey deserves to die. Consider it done."

Oh hell, no. I stalk back to him and do something few would dare: I invade his personal space, going almost chest to chest with him. "There will be none of this protecting me shit. When and if I need you to step in, I'll ask, but I won't be denied the right for retribution again. We clear?"

If I expect anger, it's not there. Instead, there's humor along with respect as he stares at me. "Perfectly. I hear her moving around in there. If you're finished with your tantrum, maybe we should go in and see what's what. You're such a little bitch sometimes."

10

JACEY

The room is awash in light when I awake. I yawn and automatically turn my head to look at the clock on the nightstand. Only—it's not there. Then I become aware of two things: the unfamiliar surroundings, and the fact that my head feels like there's a marching band inside it. *What the?* I struggle to push away the last vestiges of sleep and make sense of what is going on. Then on my second sweep of the area, my eyes fall on him. *Tony*—asleep in a chair a few feet away. *This just gets weirder.* My thoughts are so cloudy I'm beginning to wonder if we got drunk last night. Maybe we passed out at someone's home. *Marco's?* My head is throbbing so badly that I don't want to move, so I reach out with my foot and tap Tony on the arm. "Tony, wake up," I whisper. I have no idea why, but I feel the need to keep my voice down until I know where we are.

His eyes open, and he sits up, looking instantly alert—and impossibly hot. *So unfair.* Does he ever have a bad hair day? "You're awake. How do you feel?" His eyes run the length of my body as if inspecting me for damage.

I wrinkle my nose before saying, "Other than a monster headache and not knowing where we are, I'm just peachy. Did we get high or something?" When he simply stares at me, I quickly add, "Not that I make a habit of that, but since I feel like shit, we're both sleeping in our clothes, and apparently, we had a sleepover with someone I hope is a friend of yours."

He gets to his feet and stretches before approaching the bed and sitting on the side of it. He extends a hand and gently pushes a tendril of my hair off my face. His look of concern is beginning to unnerve me. *Why isn't he saying anything?* "Jacey." *God, it's worse than I thought. He's calling me by my name instead of Duchess.*

I'm beyond frustrated at this point. "Either get to the point or find me some coffee, Moretti. And maybe some Advil. I'm too exhausted for this guessing game you have going on."

To my surprise, he does as I ask. He returns a few minutes later with a bottle of water and a couple of small pills. I don't see any coffee, but I decide to let that slide for now. I wince as I sit up in bed and toss the pills in my mouth before downing half the water. He hovers for a moment, then sits on the edge of the chair he's recently vacated. *What is wrong with him?* Tony never stays in one spot for very long, so this is completely out of character for him. I set the bottle on the nightstand and run my hand through my hair, attempting to smooth it down. When I make contact with a tender spot in the back, I'm shocked to find a lump there the size of an egg. *That explains the headache.* I'm still examining it when Tony finally speaks again. "Do you remember Clint bringing you to the compound after work last night?"

"Not really." I shrug. But there's something. An elusive memory just out of reach. I shut my eyes as I attempt to concentrate. Yes, it's there. Clint coming into my office to tell me that Tony wanted me to meet him at the compound. Excitement because it felt like a date. Driving through the gates and waiting while Clint entered the code for the door. Tony talking to some men.

And then it hits.

A bolt of pure agony sears through my head as the rest comes back to me.

Fear, panic, run, need to run.

I'm gasping for breath when the bed shifts and Tony comes down over me. His hands are on my arms, and he's scared, so very scared.

"Duchess, look at me." He repeats this slowly but firmly until my eyes lock with his. "That's good, baby. Slow your breathing." When that doesn't work, he says, "Hold your breath until I tell you to let it out." It sounds insane, but he's my lifeline right now, and I do as he's instructed. He has me blow it out, then we repeat this several more times until my breathing begins to slow. "Keep looking at me, Duchess. You trust me?" The question is so strange it gets my attention. When I nod, he gives me an approving smile. "Then you know I'd never let anyone or anything hurt you. You are safe here with me. You'll always be safe. Whatever happened to you in the past is a memory to deal with, but it can no longer hurt you. I won't allow it."

He knows. How? My eyes blur, and tears drip down the side of my face as I process his words. I'm filled with shame and self-loathing. I never wanted him to know. But he does. Jeremy was here, and he must have told him. But why? *He probably lied to make himself the victim.* Tony gently brushes the tears with his thumbs, but they keep coming. *I don't cry. This isn't me.* "I'm sorry," I croak out as I try to turn my head away. I don't want him to see me. *So ugly.* "Never wanted you to find out. You won't want me anymore. Nothing will ever be the same."

"Jacey." He sounds helpless as he once again calls me by my given name.

Things are already different.

I'm so caught up in my misery, so despondent that it takes a moment for me to realize that he's lifting me from the bed and into his arms. Then he rests against the headboard and arranges me on his chest. He rubs my back in soothing patterns. Instead of calming me, I begin to sob. I had never cried like this in my life, even when my mother died. But it's as if a dam has burst, and I cannot stop. He rocks me like a small child and murmurs words I don't understand against the top of my head. I'm faintly aware that someone has come into the room at some point, but I don't look to see who. I don't care. I have no idea how long I cry, but Tony's shirt is soaking wet when the sobs quiet to hiccups, then finally silence. He shifts me in his arms so he can remove his shirt. He uses it to wipe my face before tossing it on the floor. My head is now against his warm muscular chest. *How I wish I could stay here forever. It feels like home.* "Are you all right, sweetheart?" he asks tenderly. *Why does he sound like that?* I must be imagining things. Making them the way I want them to be. There is no way he could know and still sound as if he cares about me. *No one loves a whore.* Then he pulls the rug out from under me again when he says, "I need you to tell me exactly what Jeremy Caulder did to you. I know it was him that you were afraid of yesterday, and I need to know why. I promise I will deal with it, and you'll never have to fear him again."

I'm already shaking my head before he finishes speaking. *There's no way.* "I...don't know that name." I attempt to pull away, but he won't allow it.

"Jacey." There's a hint of exasperation in his voice now, which I'm oddly grateful for. It's easier to handle than the pity.

"Stop calling me that," I snap, then ruin the tough act by wiping my face with the back of my hand.

"It is your name." He sounds confused now, which isn't surprising. I could probably make a strong case for being bipolar. I don't care, though, if it distracts him from his questions. But my relief is short-lived because it sounds as if he exhales heavily before saying, "You told me last night that Jeremy was the one. You gave me his name."

Lie, must lie. "Maybe I recognized him from somewhere." I'm getting defensive now, which also sparks my anger. I want him to leave it alone. "My past is none of your business, Tony. Have I asked you about all the women in yours? Stop. Let me go." I sound like such an ungrateful bitch, and I hate it. He's never been anything but good to me, but he's backing me into a corner. If I tell him the truth, he'll be disgusted by me. If I don't, he'll be angry, but there is at least a chance he'll get over it.

He catches me off guard when he shifts me off his lap and moves to the edge before getting to his feet. I'm wary at his apparent capitulation. *Too easy.* "Normally, I'd agree with everything you said. No good ever comes from oversharing with a romantic partner. *But* this isn't a typical past relationship. I have a man working for me who you're terrified of. Even if I felt nothing for you, I'd still want to know why. When anyone, especially a woman, has such a strong reaction to a man, it needs to be investigated."

"Then just fire him," I huff out. "I'm sure you've done it before. You don't need a written report for that. Tell him you don't require his services any longer."

"Sure, I'll do that right now, and while I'm there, I'll get *the truth* out of *him*. In any way necessary." He turns and heads for the door. "Remember, this is what you wanted," he tosses over his shoulder.

Wait—what?

Oh my God.

My stomach lurches. He's not going to let it go. And part of me can't blame him. I don't remember everything that happened after I recognized Jeremy, but I recall enough to know that it can't be explained away easily. My reaction was too extreme. "Tony, stop!" He pauses as if waiting for me to say more. "You win," I whisper.

He puts his hands in his pockets, then spins around to face me. There is no triumphant smile or smirk there. His expression is solemn. "This was never about winning, and you know that." He returns to the chair instead of the bed as if needing to keep some distance between us. I could give him some version of the truth that he might find more acceptable, but I'm so tired. I've played one game after another for most of my adult life, and I'm spent. A part of me is afraid of what I'll see on his face when he knows, yet another part doesn't care anymore. This is the real me. And it's ugly. He may never want to see me again when I'm finished, but there is an odd sense of peace in letting go. And that's what I'm doing. One year after I killed my father, I'm finally putting his ghost to bed where it belongs.

TONY

I feel like the world's biggest prick. I'm not that much better than Jeremy Caulder at this point. After all, I've bullied a defenseless woman into telling me her secrets. She's given in. I see the exact moment it happens. There is a sad resignation in her eyes as she pulls her knees to her chest and wraps her arms around them. I want to let it go—I wish more than anything I could—but what transpired the previous night stops me. She might believe this is business to me, but I could give a fuck about that. I'll fire him without a moment's hesitation. No, this is all about her. What *he* did to elicit such a strong reaction from *her*. And I know it's bad—I can feel it in my gut. But I cannot allow her to live in fear of Jeremy Caulder when it's within my power to do something about it. The only other option would be to deal with him without fully knowing the truth, but I'm too much like my father to accept that. No, the level of his sins will determine the way retribution is delivered. In this, I am very much a Moretti to my core. "Whenever you're ready." An apology is on the tip of my tongue, but it would be meaningless to her at this point. *I only hope that in telling me what happened, her heart will be less burdened. God, how I hope for that.*

"To tell you about Jeremy, I'll need to explain my role in my father's life." Her voice is neutral when she speaks. There is no emotion there; she is simply blank. "Don't interrupt me to ask questions or make comments because if I stop, I will not start again." She appears to take my silence for agreement as she continues after only a slight pause. "My mother was big on family traditions, which is kind of a joke now, considering how fucked up the Wrenns turned out to be. She impressed upon me many times that I was the big sister, and that I was always to take care of Jade as if she were my own. I realize now that it was probably because she wanted to leave us to be with your father. I can only hope she had no idea the type of man our father truly was when she considered abandoning her children to be with him. This didn't amount to much while she was still alive. I looked out for my sister, but we had a nanny, a cook, and a housekeeper, so it didn't require much of me. I was a teenager when she died. When he killed her. I stepped in, attempting to comfort Jade and give her what I could as a substitute mother. I came to think of her as mine even though I'm only a few years older. That proved to be a costly mistake because *he* noticed and found a way to use it against me." Her voice has gone raspy, and I pick up the bottle of water and hand it to her.

"Jacey," I begin, noticing how pale she's become.

She waves my concern away with a flick of her wrist and picks up where she left off.

Where does she get this strength from? How is she so unbelievably resilient?

"When I graduated from college, everything changed. The man I knew as my father was a stranger to me. Oh, he looked the same, but he was not a good man. He called me into his study one evening and told me I would be working for him at Wrenn, and that I would do whatever he asked of me without question or Jade would suffer the consequences. I didn't believe him. But in the next few weeks, he drove his point home to me. There was a freak accident where Jade supposedly tripped on the stairs and fell. Then one night as I was going into my bedroom, one of Daddy's flunkies was coming out of Jade's bedroom. I ran in after him only to find her still asleep and obviously undisturbed. My father was waiting for me in the hallway when I came out of her room. He told me that had been a warning. Next time, it would be real. Another three incidents occurred over the next week, and that's when I knew I couldn't protect her. If he really wanted to hurt her, there was little I could do to stop him. When I threatened to go to the police, he let me know in no uncertain terms that they were for sale to the highest bidder. I knew he wasn't bluffing because the chief of police had been to our home for dinner on more than one occasion. So, I had no choice. The bitch was born. I pushed Jade away from me to protect her. I wanted her to have no reason to hang around the house any more than necessary, which wasn't easy since my father wouldn't let her move out until she went to work for Lee. He needed her close to keep me under his thumb."

A knock on the bedroom door startles us both. I smother a curse before getting to my feet and opening it. Dr. Atwell is standing there giving me a questioning look. "I wanted to check on Jacey before I left."

I feel like an asshole, but I know if we stop now, this is all I'll ever know. So, I lower my voice as I say, "Could you possibly stay a bit longer? We're in the middle of something. I wouldn't ask if it wasn't important."

Dr. Atwell nods once in agreement. "Of course. Let me know when you're ready. I have an appointment after lunch, but I'm free until then."

I thank her, then go back inside, closing the door behind me. "Are you good to continue?"

Again, she doesn't reply to me directly; she simply starts talking again. "At first, it was fairly simple work, but then as I became more knowledgeable about the business, he started having me play hostess for some of his gatherings. Some that were all right, but he had several associates who were completely unsavory. A few even assumed I was a perk of doing favors for my father. I thought that was insane...until it...."

Fuck. Please let me have misunderstood. Her voice is now so hollow that I wonder if she's even aware of what she's revealing. "I was forced to be the whore for my father's business associates. He said if I didn't, then it would be Jade."

"Fucking hell," I hiss before I can stop myself. *That son of a bitch.*

"None of them hurt me until that last night. None had any idea I wasn't with them of my own free will. I had to play the part. They all treated me *well* until Jeremy... He was different. There was something wrong with him, and I knew that the first time I met him. He had a cruel streak, and unfortunately for me, he was more than happy to join my father in one deal after another, which made him a valuable ally to the old man. He also didn't buy into my act. He knew I wasn't with him of my own free will, and it...excited him. He got off on feeling as if he was raping me. He liked it rough. The first couple of times, it was spanking, so hard I couldn't sit the next day. Then he moved up to choking me. Each time I went to my father, telling him I feared for my life, he waved away my concerns. Told me he would get Jade to take my place."

I don't think she's even aware of the lone tear that trails down her cheek. I'm sick to my stomach. *The things he made her do. That monster.* I'm not even sure I can handle hearing anymore. There is already enough for me to know that Jeremy Caulder will die. And it will be slow and fucking painful. "Baby, let's stop now. You don't have to go on."

Fuck. She's not listening to me. I wonder if she's even aware I'm still in the room. It's as if now she's started, there's no turning back. "The last time, it was bad. He brought friends. And all three of them took turns. Viciously. I...I thought I would die. That they would kill me. The blood seemed to scare Jeremy. He called my father in a panic, and when he arrived, he had a doctor with him. One of his men took me out through a service elevator, and I don't know what was said, but that was the last time I ever saw him. Until...yesterday. My father stopped doing business with him, mainly because he now had enough of Jeremy's contacts to cut him out of the deals they'd been involved in together. I didn't delude myself into thinking it was out of concern for me. I was simply a convenient excuse. No doubt he blackmailed him as well." Then she absolutely slays me when she adds with forced cheer, "Oh, but don't worry. Jeremy was paranoid and always used condoms. I've been tested yearly, and I have no sexually transmitted diseases. And the doctor assured me that I would have no permanent damage from that...encounter. I had a small hemorrhage and needed some stitches, but I'm perfectly healthy."

I get up and begin pacing the room like a caged animal. *Keep it together just a little longer.* "Christ, Jacey, do you think I give a fuck about possible STDs? That's the furthest thing from my mind, believe me."

She shrugs in a matter-of-fact way that makes me want to shatter her control. *Why am I the only one losing my shit here?* "Just thought you should know since we've discussed having a child together. I realize after finding out about all this, you're probably no longer willing. And I understand. There are no hard feelings. Anyone would feel the same way."

"Damn it, Duchess, stop with the fucking assumptions. I don't need you to make my decisions or to do my thinking for me. I'm quite capable of both. And how about canning the ice-princess routine long enough for us actually to talk."

She appears bewildered when she asks, "Isn't that what we've been doing?"

Putting my hands on my hips, I snort, then feel like a dick. *What do I want from her?* Would it make me feel better if she were a sobbing mess? I draw in a deep breath and release it. Then I lower my voice so I'm not shouting at her. "You've been talking, and I've been listening."

"But it's my story to tell," she points out. "Why would I need input from you since you weren't there and have no idea what happened?"

Fuck, I'm making a mess of this. I run a hand through my hair and release a ragged laugh. "Hell, I don't know. I guess it kinda freaks me out the way you talk of everything like it happened to someone else. So coldly clinical when I know you're anything but. Maybe I could buy it if I hadn't seen your reaction to Caulder last night."

She stares at me for a long moment. "I'm scared of him. Yes, he fucking terrifies me. I've looked over my shoulder ever since that happened. I had slowly begun to relax, thinking I'd never see him again. So, seeing him standing in this very house talking to you... It was as if I were back there, living that night over again. It was playing on a loop in my head...I needed to run."

I drop my head forward, hating that I've forced her from her safe place. I have questions—up to and including the night she shot her father—but she's been through more than enough today. And really, I don't think I can deal with anything else right now. I need time to sort this out in my head. He will pay but only when I've planned how. I want —*need*—to hold her, to comfort her. But she's so detached from her nightmare—for now—that any softness would shatter her. So, I go with facts. "Dr. Atwell wants to check you before she leaves," I say, thinking she'll be grateful for a subject change. But if her frown is any indication, that's not the case.

She smooths her hands over the wrinkled sheets as if it's of the utmost importance that they be returned to order. "So that's it then?" she asks in a small voice. "After I've confessed to you that I was my father's whore, you have no comment?" I'm frozen in place at her words. Whether she realizes it or not, there's so much self-loathing in her tone. But more than that, there's also a sick kind of acceptance that what she believes of herself is true. "You're what...going to avoid any more awkward conversation until you can get away from me? Bet you wish you hadn't insisted I stay with you now. Certainly makes things harder, doesn't it?"

"Jacey, shut the fuck up," I bellow. Her mouth drops open, and her eyes go wide. Yes, it feels all kinds of wrong to yell at someone who just shared something so abominable, yet I know instinctively that tenderness would be scoffed at. Her brain works differently than other women. There have been some tender moments between us, but I know those made her uncomfortable. She's spent so many years walling herself off from others that she has a hard time accepting and processing kindness. And knowing now how her father blackmailed and used her, I understand her suspicion of others. She doesn't trust that anyone could genuinely care about her. *She doesn't believe she's worth it.*

Her eyes narrow, then she almost has me smiling when she shoots me a bird before saying, "Up yours, Moretti. A rabid dog has better manners than you do." She's pissed, but there is color in her cheeks again. And she no longer sounds like a robot. Although, maybe it would have been better to leave her in that state for a while longer if it made it easier to deal with what she's been through. *Too late now.*

I twist my lips into a smirk. "You're probably right. But you must admit, I'm much more attractive." I extend my arm and deliberately flex my muscles. "Impressive, right?" My action and comment literally have me gagging, so I can only imagine what her reaction will be.

"Are you serious?" she chokes out, then actually begins laughing. *Ouch, a direct hit to the pride.* "My God, your vanity is out of control. Of course, with nitwits like Amber hanging on your every word, I guess it was bound to happen."

My father once told me that sometimes even the best of us must "take one for the team." And that's what I do now. If making fun of me keeps her from falling into an abyss of painful memories, then I'm more than happy to do it. After all, I've spent years around Marco and Nic—who constantly argued with each other over who was better looking. It appears I've picked up a few things along the way. I lean against the wall, feeling the weight on my shoulders lighten as our verbal banter distracts us both from the conversation we've just had. "Don't be so hard on Amber. I'll have you know she has a college degree."

Jacey lifts a brow in inquiry. "Oh, really? I wasn't aware they offered a degree in stripping. But good for her for making the most of her profession. I'm sure there's plenty of room for advancement."

The barbs continue to fly between us, and when Marco barges in without knocking a few minutes later, I am flaunting my rock-hard abs while she has a finger in her mouth making a gagging sound. It's one of the few times in my life I can remember rendering him speechless. He moves across the room, picks up Jacey's empty water bottle, and sniffs it. Obviously disappointed, he sets it down again. "That would have explained so much. What? Wait, never mind, I don't even want to know." He gives me a shit-eating grin before he adds, "But rest assured, the guys are going to hear about this weird exhibition. Have some pride and put your shirt on, man. No wonder the poor girl is about to upchuck all over herself."

"Thank you, Marco. You're my hero," Jacey declares fervently. There is a decided spring in her step when she slides off the bed and crosses the room to the bathroom. "When you're finished admiring yourself, maybe you could find me some clothes to wear home." I hear a giggle as she closes the door behind her.

Marco is still grinning, but he also looks confused. *Join the club, pal.* I find Jacey one of my old T-shirts and a pair of sweatpants—they will be too big, but they'll have to do for now. Then I get a shirt for myself and put it on. I knock on the door and tell her I'm leaving them for her. Then I motion for Marco to follow me out into the hallway. "Don't even fucking say it," I growl as he opens his mouth, then shuts it again. "It wasn't what you think."

"Hmm, well it looked as if you were doing your best gigolo imper-sonation, but possibly I misunderstood. I gotta admit, it wasn't exactly what I was expecting to find. Far from it." I pull my phone from my pocket and quickly fire off a text to Dr. Atwell letting her know that Jacey is in the shower, but that she can check on her shortly. Then I start down the stairs and hear Marco fall into place behind me. I go directly to the study and pour myself a double bourbon and toss it back. Then repeat it. "Hard liquor before noon. Must be pretty serious," he says with no hint of amusement in his voice now.

I cross to my father's desk and take a seat behind it. There's something almost comforting about sitting in the same chair he spent so much time in. It makes me feel close to him again. I put my feet up and lean back, closing my eyes. "It's worse than I imagined, brother. God, for what I now know, I fucking wish I killed Wrenn. But I understand now why she needed it. Hell, pulling the trigger that night was the only way she had any hope of getting her life back. I'd have emptied the entire cylinder into him if I were her...then reloaded and done it again."

Marco lowers his frame into a nearby chair and runs a hand over his neck as if bracing himself for what is to come. "How bad are we talking here? She dated Caulder at some point?"

I lay my head back and shake it as I stare at the ceiling. "Fuck, no. I shouldn't share her story without her consent, but if anything happens to me, promise you'll go to Lee and tell him. I want him to understand why she treated Jade the way she has. I want her to have a chance for a normal relationship with her sister. She desperately needs to mend that fence, even if she thinks it's too late."

"Lee's only a phone call or short drive away."

I straighten in my seat as I prepare to repeat Jacey's story. When I'm done, he'll understand why I can't go to Lee right now. Because when I walk out that door, it will be to exact revenge on Caulder. I will not rest until he has drawn his last breath. Violence is not something I enjoy, nor is it my first choice, but the sins are grave enough, so this time, there is no other choice. Evil cannot be allowed to roam unchecked. There is a balance in the world that must be maintained, and it is up to those who have the courage and the abilities to do it.

Jacey will live a life free of Caulder, even if I must give my own to ensure that.

11

JACEY

Tony has been called away on business—some issue in his South Carolina club—so Marco drove me back to his apartment. The club only opens on Thursday, Friday, and Saturday unless it's a special event, so all is quiet when we arrive at *Nyx*. "I've never asked Tony how he came up with the name for the club. It's a bit unusual."

We made the trip mostly in silence as Marco seemed to have something on his mind and wasn't his usual outgoing self. He parks the SUV near the back door before turning to look at me. He gives me a distracted smile. "It means goddess of the night. Tony has always been a fan of Greek mythology."

"He certainly has many different sides," I acknowledge, thinking of his crazy antics from earlier. It didn't occur to me until I was in the shower that he was doing it for my benefit. Pretending to be horribly vain to distract me from my thoughts of Jeremy. Oh, I'm sure he's aware of how handsome he is, but he's not the type of man to flex for attention. *Just breathing gains enough.*

"You have no idea," Marco tosses over his shoulder as he unlocks the door and turns to wave me in ahead of him.

When we walk into the apartment, Marco immediately checks each of the rooms. I assume to make sure someone isn't hiding under the bed, but I don't ask. In fact, I'm not that thrilled about being here alone with the club closed, so I'm grateful for his thoughtfulness. When he walks back into the kitchen where I'm getting a bottle of water, I'm surprised to see him pull out a barstool and sit. "How about a pizza and beer? I'll call Leo's for delivery. And if there's no beer in the refrigerator, I'll grab some from the club."

"You're staying?" I ask in surprise. It had never even occurred to me that he wasn't simply dropping me off. I know Tony has security lurking around somewhere, so I figure he considers that enough.

"Of course." Now he's the one who appears startled that I'd think otherwise. "This is no place for a woman to be alone at night. I've always told Tony he was nuts for living here. If someone breaks in the club, then it's not a big stretch that they'll stumble upon this place."

"Gee, thanks for pointing that out. And I'm sure Tony is prepared for most anything—including that." I pull up the baggy sweatpants I'm wearing and turn toward the bedroom. "Pizza is fine with me. I'm going to go change out of these clothes. I'm tired of tripping over the pants."

I take my time, in no hurry to rejoin Marco. He's a likable guy and easy to get along with, but still—I barely know him, and I'd rather not have to carry on a conversation for hours if I can avoid it. I figure I'll delay until the food arrives, go eat, and then shortly after fake a few yawns. I could use an early night anyway since Clint will be here around seven in the morning. I need to be at the office early to make up for missing the day today. I sit on the edge of the bed as I wait and glance around the room. There are no pictures here or many personal effects. It's almost as sterile as a hotel room. The whole apartment is that way. *My clutter is probably driving him crazy.* I mentioned it to him once, and he said simply, "This is where I sleep most nights, but it's not my home." It was a sentiment I could relate to. I've felt that way most of my life. Only, there was no home somewhere waiting for me. I felt like a prisoner when I lived at my father's house, even when I moved out to the guesthouse. When I sold it after his death and bought the condo, I went from feeling like a prisoner to a guest in someone else's home. Strangely enough, I've felt more at home here than anywhere else.

My mind again goes to my conversation with Tony earlier. The ability to remain detached in times of extreme stress served me well as I recounted what I had done in the past to protect my sister. Even with the mask firmly in place, I noticed his reaction. I didn't detect any revulsion in his expression, only rage. He was so angry. No. He was deadly furious. I never want to be on the receiving end of that look. I'm under no delusions that he'll storm my castle, and we'll ride off into the sunset together. When he has time to actually consider what I've done, he'll want no part of me. And he certainly won't be willing to have a child with a...whore. Because no matter the reason, I still slept with men for financial gain...*even if it wasn't my own.* I can attempt to rationalize it fifty different ways, but it will always come back to that simple point. How many hookers love their job? Sure, some might, but most probably do it for the money or some type of gain. *I'm no better.* I'm far from over my past, and I seriously doubt I ever will be. But maybe—just maybe—at some point I'll make peace with it and move forward without the cloak of self-hatred attached to my skin. That's the very best I can hope for. Even with that, it will always haunt me, and I'll always hate myself for it—but I can't go back in time. Finally telling someone the truth has made me feel lighter. I know that will change when Tony ends whatever this is between us. But for now, the demons in my head are quiet, and I'm going to enjoy it for as long as I can. Marco yells from the other room that our dinner has arrived, and I get to my feet. I have no idea where it comes from, but I freeze as something Tony said earlier fills me with dread.

You'll never have to fear him again.

Oh, dear God, why didn't this occur to me before now?

Tony isn't like other men. He's a Moretti. *You'll never have to fear him again.* It's on a loop in my head as I take off at a run to find Marco. He's startled when I skid to where he's standing in the kitchen. "He's not in South Carolina, is he?"

He takes my arm, looking at me as if I've lost my mind. "What are you talking about, Jacey? Are you okay?"

My voice comes out in a near shout as my fear grows. "Dammit, Marco, answer me. Tony isn't at his club in South Carolina, is he?"

I see it then. The shift of his eyes. Most wouldn't notice, but I've spent so many years reading my father's moods, and I'm somewhat of an expert at picking up on those types of tics. I put my hands on my head as the ramification of what I've caused sinks in. "He's going to kill Jeremy, isn't he? I can't believe I didn't think of it sooner. I-I just thought he'd fire him and, hell, maybe even knock him around a little if he tried to argue. But Tony would never be satisfied with that. He's going to ruin his life for me...because of me."

Marco is staring at me. Nothing in his expression says I'm being ridiculous. He opens his mouth, then closes it again and turns away. "I got the pepperoni with extra cheese. Hope you're okay with that." He calmly opens the pizza box and picks up a nearby plate.

Are you kidding me? "Ignoring me isn't going to work, Marco. I'm not a child."

"Then stop acting like one," he says calmly. *I want to hit him with something.*

Tears of anger and frustration fill my eyes and threaten to spill over as I cry out, "Why won't you answer me? Don't you care anything about Tony?"

He whirls around so quickly that I take a step back in alarm. His calm demeanor of a moment ago is gone, and in its place is one filled with anger. *Shit.* "Don't I care about my brother? You have no fucking idea, lady, but you've just insulted me in the worst way possible." He's shouting now, and my bravado is rapidly disappearing. "I'd die for Tony Moretti without a second thought. I've had his back for as long as I can remember. My father has had to live with Draco's murder on his conscience for twenty years, and that will not happen to me. If I believed for one second that Tony was in danger, I wouldn't be here babysitting you. The greatest risk Tony has ever taken is falling for you. Granted, we were all pretty gone on you the night you gunned your old man down. Any one of us would have married you on the spot. Hottest thing I've ever seen. But you see, Tony has always been different. As similar as we are in so many things, we look at the world a little differently. *He* had to get to know you. Figure out who you are...what's going on inside your head. Hell, the fact that you shot to kill should have told him most of that, but it wasn't enough. He sat back, waiting for you to come to him. I told him he was nuts. That he should just make the first move because obviously you were never going to do it. But then you showed up at the club pulling that asinine stunt. Again, impressed by your balls. I guess it was easier than just putting it out there and telling him how you feel." He's calmer now, which is almost worse than his anger. He moves toward me, and I force myself to stand my ground. Only a few inches separate us when he stops. "The biggest risk Tony has ever faced is you, Jacey. You're a weakness to a man who had none. You came along at the absolute worst time possible for him, and he hasn't been the same since. Everything he's done in the last year has been because of you."

I'm stunned by his words. "A-are you talking about his father's death? He said he's been looking into that for years. It has nothing to do with me." *Does it?*

Marco shrugs before leaning back against the bar. "Sure, we've tossed around some theories, but after he finally met you in person, saw that you weren't just a figment of his dreams, he was determined to put things in order. He's tried for most of his life to keep some distance between the family and himself. He doesn't want that lifestyle. Never has. And I respect his choice. But there are those who resent that he's allowed that choice while still having the protection and resources of the Morettis at his disposal. They forget that without Draco, there would be none of it. Everything we have is because of him. Tony makes his own living and doesn't depend on anyone for anything. He's a lot like his old man in that regard, so he deserves more than he ever takes. But then there was you, and suddenly, he wanted answers. Yesterday. Wanted to be able to sleep at night without the threat of someone taking him or someone close to him out."

One thing he said sticks out to me, and I ask, "What did you mean by a figment of his dreams?" *Surely not the white picket fence kind of dreams. That's not us.*

He shakes his head before turning away once again to get a slice of pizza. "You'll have to ask Tony about that. I won't betray his confidences any further. Pizza?" he asks as he holds his piece up.

I twist my hands nervously in front of me, making one last-ditch attempt to reason with the man before me. "Bu-but what about Jeremy? We need to stop him before it's too late."

He takes a bite of his food and chews it slowly. Then washes it down with some beer from a nearby bottle. "*That* was too late the moment he met you. I'd never stop him from doing what I would most certainly do if our positions were reversed. He'll handle his business as he sees fit. And if he decides to take out the trash, then I'll be there to dispose of it. You cannot and will not interfere. If you care about the man who's put himself at risk for you, then you'll sit down, shut up, and eat your fucking dinner. Are we clear?"

His tone brooks no arguments. I do as I'm told. I fix a plate, grab a bottle of water from the refrigerator, and take it to the sofa. There is an old western on television, and I stare at it as if fascinated but see nothing. Because all I can think of is the man, who, at this very moment, may be killing someone to avenge me. And no matter what Marco thinks, I have no concern for Jeremy. If I had the courage, I would have killed him myself ages ago. No, I fear that Jeremy will take Tony by surprise and hurt him first. I don't care what Tony has done or can do. I've faced monsters without a soul or an ounce of remorse. Tony is neither. But I can't let go of Marco's words. *You're a weakness to a man who had none.* If I didn't feel guilty before, I certainly do now. I'll never deserve the type of retribution Tony is exacting tonight. Never. I'll never deserve to be any man's weakness, especially not one as incredible as Tony Moretti. *If you care about the man who's put himself at risk for you, then you'll sit down, shut up, and eat your fucking dinner.* I do care about Tony. So much. And I will not allow him to sacrifice his life for me. I set my untouched pizza aside and approach Marco again. He lifts a brow in inquiry, and I notice his appetite is fine if the pizza crusts littering his plate are any indication. "Just promise me one thing. This doesn't touch him. If for some reason you can't...do whatever it is you do to fix stuff like this—"

"Excuse me?" He sounds offended that I have the audacity to question his...skills.

"Just listen," I snap, tired of his heavy-handedness. *Men and their egos.* "If for some really strange reason this goes badly, I will turn myself in, and I want you to back me up." He's the one who looks stunned now. He was *not* expecting that. "I will not let him take the fall for avenging me. Believe me, prison would be a picnic compared to the hell I've lived through. I'm tough. I can survive it. So, if it comes to that, you will back whatever story I come up with. A Moretti in prison would be dead before a week passed, and you know it. How many would love to kill someone of his stature?"

I've got his attention now. He's no longer scowling, but something akin to respect reflects in his eyes. "I knew you were something that night I met you. I'm not gonna lie. I've questioned it a few times since then, but you just redeemed yourself. Tony will probably kill me, but you are right about his survival odds in prison. Me, or one of the guys, would be bad enough, but the Moretti prince would have a price on his head immediately. There would be no saving him somewhere like that. But it will not come to that. I will protect him, and I will protect you. You've earned that much."

"So what now?" I ask, feeling nerves return as the adrenaline recedes.

"We wait. That's all you can do sometimes, Lucy. Wait."

"We wait. Okay." I can't eat any food now, as my heart is in my throat. Instead, I go to the bedroom and lie across the bed.

So this is what it's like? Feeling something so strong for someone who isn't my blood? I only know that if I lose Tony, I won't survive it.

I won't survive it.

TONY

Finding Jeremy Caulder didn't take long. As luck has it, he's working late in his home office tonight. He has no wife or children and lives on at least ten acres of land with the closest neighbor several miles away. I'm sitting in the passenger seat of Nic's Cadillac Escalade while he and Mike scout our surroundings. I was adamantly opposed to dragging anyone else into my personal vendetta against Caulder, but Marco left me little choice. He fully intended to accompany me himself and had been fucking pissed when I pointed out that he was the most likely to be noticed should he go off grid. After all, he is Rutger's son. Nic and Mike, however, are off duty tonight, and Marco insisted either they go with me or he would. We argued as always about him protecting me, but he held firm. I have just checked the clip of my 9mm when I see shadows approaching. They pull the ski masks off, and I lower my gun. Nic's usual smirk is nowhere in sight when he gets in the vehicle and shuts the door. "What?" A sense of foreboding runs down my spine. From the moment we entered the property, I haven't been able to shake the feeling that something is off.

Nic turns to me, more serious than I've seen him in a long time. "Apparently, you're not Caulder's only enemy. Someone had quite a party here, and we weren't invited."

"What the fuck does that mean?" I ask, irritated that everyone around me seems to speak in some ghetto code now.

Ever the serious one, Mike leans forward between the seats and puts a hand on my shoulder. "He's dead, Tony. And we're not talking just a shot to the head here. Whoever killed him made it slow and painful. I've seen some fucked-up shit, but this is right up there."

I sit in stunned silence for several long moments. *Who else did you piss off?* "When you say 'fucked-up shit,' exactly what are we talking here?"

Nic whistles low before shaking his head. "His hands were removed. Fucking gone. He was naked. So, there was no missing the knife wounds all over his body. Ears were severed, and his eyes were held shut with metal hooks. He had a bullet hole in his forehead, but my guess is that was done last. You don't do shit like that unless you want the person to suffer. You're not going to gift them with a mercy killing first, then carve them up like a jack-o'-lantern."

"You have got to be fucking kidding me," I say incredulously. *I'm denied retribution yet again?* "You sure it's him?"

Nic snorts as if to say *really?* "When have you ever known us not to do our homework first, Tony? I can assure you that the mess on the floor in that house is Jeremy Caulder." He leans over and pulls his gun out of his ankle holster. "But I know you're not going to take my word for it. So, let's get this shit over with." He opens his door, then stops before getting out to say, "I'm not kidding. It's fucked-up shit. If you think there is any chance at all you'll puke, then you better take something with you to catch it. We leave nothing behind that the cops can use."

I open my mouth, ready to chew his ass out for that insulting remark, but then I think better of it. As always, he's simply trying to cover me. Neither he nor Mike is under any obligation to be here with me tonight. In fact, they'll be in a fuckload of trouble if anyone in the family finds out. We have enough to deal with without me taking my frustration out on him. "I'm good," I say as we each put on masks and gloves. We crouch low and steadily make our way through the wooded area surrounding Caulder's house. Nic insisted on taking the lead with Mike following behind me. The killer could still be in the area, and Nic's trained to scan the perimeter with skill beyond me. After all, he's trained extensively with retired Navy SEALs. When we reach the back of the old farmhouse, Mike hands us each booties to slip over our shoes. It doesn't occur to me to question why he has them. Mike is a person always prepared for anything.

"His office is the second door on the right," Nic whispers before easing the door open. We move slowly, careful not to alert anyone who might be in the house to our presence. Nic and Mike checked it earlier, but that's not a guarantee someone didn't escape detection. *Or come back.* When we reach the office and I get my first look at Caulder, I understand Nic's warning. It's grisly—and the smell is enough to make my stomach roil.

"Fuck," I hiss. Deep breaths are not an option. I do my best to block out the stench and study the scene. Nic's description was gruesomely accurate. This isn't your run-of-the-mill killing. No, this shit was personal. Someone took a lot of time and effort to inflict this type of carnage. The knife wounds show rage. Caulder might have made it worse by saying something to piss off his assailant. That's not my gut feeling, though. Even though this was most certainly premeditated, there's also an element of carelessness that I bet the killer hadn't planned on. Torture? No doubt about that. But the sheer brutality of the killing suggests this person lost control—at least for a few moments. And when that happens, you make mistakes. Maybe the police will find something but maybe they won't. Something must have been left behind, but we don't have time to confirm that. Nor do we need to risk leaving behind something ourselves.

Now the shock has lessened slightly, I study the body intently. If not for the fact that I've had several meetings with Caulder in recent days, I'd be hard pressed to identify him. The blood covering much of his face makes it challenging, but it's him. I thought the diamond earring in his ear odd the first time I met him because it seemed out of place in his otherwise clean-cut persona, but now it helps confirm his identity. Mike comes to stand beside me. "I hope he deserved to go out that way," he says as he stares at what's left of the man.

I haven't shared the full story with them out of respect for Jacey—I didn't have to. They trusted my judgment without question. Nic was astute enough to read between the lines. But Mike deals in facts. He's not comfortable with guessing games. "I don't necessarily agree with this type of flashy brutality. I think there's a strong possibility he had a history of violence toward women. For that reason, he had to be stopped. Obviously, someone agrees with my sentiment. His sins caught up with him as they do everyone."

"We need to go," Nic murmurs when he finishes a quick inspection of the room. "Someone may miss him sooner than later, and I don't think the police will be too understanding of our presence here."

We're careful not to disturb anything as we make our way back out. No one speaks until we're in the vehicle and heading toward the city. "That was fucked up." Nic sighs. I'm startled from my inner musings when he asks, "Do you think this is connected to you?"

"Wait, what? What the fuck?"

Nic stares straight ahead as he navigates the busy road. "Just feels like an awfully big coincidence to me. We're racking up weird occurrences each week it seems. Thinking we can't afford to assume that anything out of the norm isn't connected to you."

"He's right," Mike says quietly from the back seat. "Granted, there is no logic to base this theory on, but it's probably safer to question every-thing, even if it sounds absurd."

I mull his words over and grudgingly agree. We need to be careful that we don't cross the line from being thorough to paranoid. If Caulder hadn't been working for me recently, I would have discounted this vague link. But Nic's raised a valid point, and I nod despite how farfetched this whole thing sounds. "Agreed. We add it to the list and see if we can find any way to tie it what we've been doing."

"I'm getting a bad feeling about this," Nic mumbles as if speaking to himself.

"I've had one for a while," Mike chimes in. "Not that we're all involved. We wouldn't let you do this without us. It feels as if nothing is as it seems."

"I second that," Nic says. "Almost like I could pick up a can of Coke and find it's Pepsi even though nothing indicates I should question it. If it says Coke, then it should be."

"That argument is completely without merit," Mike deadpans.

I shake my head as they argue back and forth. Their bickering is comforting to me in a way. I've always been amused by the way Mike's levity clashes with Nic's *unusual* thought process. By rights, they shouldn't be able to stand spending so much time together, but I think they secretly enjoy the arguments. This continues until we reach the club. I hope Jacey is asleep so we can tell Marco what happened without her overhearing us. It's not something I want to share on the phone. We walk through the darkened club and up the stairs. I've just opened the door and taken a step inside when I see a blur of move-ment. I'm in the process of reaching for my gun when Marco shouts, "For God's sake, don't shoot her crazy ass. Well, maybe just wound her enough to shut her up. Oh, and by the way, she knows. Sorry."

She knows? What the fuck? Her arms and legs are wrapped around me so tightly that I can't move forward without face planting. I'm nudged to the side as Nic and Mike move into the apartment. "Duchess—"

Hearing her nickname appears to bring her to her senses because her legs loosen before dropping from around my waist. She hangs by her arms awkwardly, and I grunt in exasperation before putting my hands on her hips and lowering her feet to the floor. If I think this bizarre display is over, I'm wrong, because her hands begin patting at my chest and stomach. I hear laughter from the kitchen area when she walks around behind me and inspects my back before returning to stand in front of me once again. When she moves lower, I put a stop to this. I grab her wrists, stilling her movements. I gather that's the wrong thing to do when she snaps, "What in the hell were you thinking, Moretti? You repay my trust in you by going off to play mafia vigilante? And you leave Marco here to babysit me? By the way, he sucks at it."

"Hey!" Marco says indigently. "I think I handled your PMS-Barbie mood swings pretty damn well."

I don't need this shit tonight. I motion for her to step aside so I can close the door behind us. Then I cross to the kitchen cabinet that holds the hard stuff. I grab the first glass I can find and fill the fucking thing with bourbon. I down half of it in one swig. *Can't put it off forever.* I take a couple of deep breaths, then turn to face the others. I glare at Marco who's still glaring at Jacey. *I'm surrounded by fucking children.* Nic looks vastly amused while Mike appears oblivious as he flips through my *Wall Street Journal. Wonder if he has room for one more in his happy place?* I set my glass on the bar with a little more force than necessary, but the thud gets everyone's attention. My voice is unnaturally calm. "Let's start with how and why there was an exchange of sensitive information here?"

Whereas she was practically growling at him moments before, Jacey comes to his defense. "I'll have you know, Anthony, that he didn't tell me shit. If you want to point your finger at someone, then turn it right back on yourself because you told me earlier." Before I even attempt to figure out the fucking riddle she's tossing out, I down the rest of my drink and strongly consider fixing another. But now probably isn't a good time to pass out even though it's damn tempting.

I put a hand to my throbbing temple and rub it wearily. I know I'll regret it, but I ask anyway. "And how exactly did I tell on myself, Duchess?" *God, women fuck with your head.*

"You said, '*You'll never have to fear him again,*' meaning Jeremy." She crosses her arms over her chest, giving me a look that clearly says, *ah-ha, gotcha.*

Before I can respond, Nic looks at her in confusion. "You realize that makes no sense. He could have been talking about a mouse. That's a totally generic sentence."

"I second that assessment." Mike nods without looking up.

Jacey's eyes are narrowed into slits now as she scowls at my friends. "Oh, I see. This is the boys' club." She points at each of them before scoffing. "All for one and one for all. Well, I'm impressed by this show of camaraderie, but what you're all ignoring is that I was *right*." Her scowl is more of a smirk now as she motions to Nic. "Care to explain that away, Einstein?"

I think I've finally discovered what makes a grown man cry. I'm tired, frustrated, and still dealing with the shock of Caulder's murder. The last thing I need is this sideshow playing out in my fucking living room. As a result, my voice comes out as a growl when I say, "E-fucking-nough already. Obviously, she knows. At this point, I don't care if she read tea leaves, flipped a fucking coin, or dialed the goddamn *Psychic Network*." I pinch the bridge of my nose, then continue. "Let's move past that and go over what happened tonight." Jacey's face pales, and she appears to brace herself. "I didn't touch him," I say directly to her.

When I pause, Nic steps in. "Someone else already had their *fun*. In quite an impressive way."

"The fucker was dead?" Marco asks in disbelief.

"That would be correct." Mike nods, finally appearing to actively join the conversation. "I will spare Ms. Jacey from the graphic details, but suffice to say, he had at least one more very angry enemy."

Marco appears stunned as I give him a nod, letting him know without words that it was bad. "I can't fucking believe it. That's way too much of a coincidence. Someone knew you were after him and took him out before you could."

"Agreed," Nic chimes in. "But why? What could they have to gain? Hell, if anything, they did Tony a favor. Caulder was sent to his maker, and none of us got our hands dirty. If you look at it that way, we have a fucked-up fairy god-murderer on our hands. Bastard clicks his heels together and says, 'There's no asshole like a dead asshole,' or something catchy like that."

Did he just say that? Instead of refilling it, I push my empty glass aside. *Maybe I've had enough.* "That's...yeah, thanks for that analogy, Nic. I would have possibly put it a little differently, but I think everyone gets the gist of it."

"We do?" Jacey wrinkles her nose in bewilderment.

I almost laugh despite my irritation with pretty much everything and everyone right now when Mike attempts to explain Nic's rambling musings to her. "Ms. Jacey, I believe what Nic is so inarticulately attempting to say is that he wonders what the person in question had to gain by removing Mr. Caulder from the picture. Because it saved us from having to deal with it. In fact, it was quite the good deed where we're concerned. So if this is connected to the Morettis as we suspect, then we're unsure what they're hoping to accomplish with their elimination of the now deceased."

Jacey is momentarily speechless. Finally, she murmurs, "I'm not sure which explanation I prefer now. Er...thanks for your insight, Mike. It was very...detailed."

Enough. I've reached my limit for the night. Shutting down is inevitable because I can't process any more. Clearing my throat, I say in a quiet voice that everyone in the room except for Jacey understands. "We'll break for the night and pick this up tomorrow. Speculation is all that we have. Go home and get some sleep, then meet here for lunch. I'll contact Lee as well. Now more than ever, we need to hold our meetings where it's most secure." They know my office and apartment are regularly swept for bugs and fully soundproof, so I don't need to spell that out. "If our suspicions are correct, we're in dangerous and uncertain waters. We cannot afford to lower our guard."

There are nods of agreement as they move toward the door. Nic and Mike are already in the hallway when Marco pauses beside me. He inclines his head in Jacey's direction before saying under his breath, "I'm sorry about that. Shocked the hell out of me. Wasn't much point in denying anything since she wouldn't have believed a word of it."

I clap him on the shoulder, giving him a weary smile. "It's fine, brother. Thanks for being here. Watch your back."

"Always do," he says, before frowning. "Well, except for that whole poisoning thing." He joins the others, still muttering under his breath.

I shut the door and lean wearily against it for a moment. *She's watching me. Can't deal with anything else right now.* I know it's childish, but instead of approaching her, I veer toward the bedroom and directly into the bathroom. I turn on the shower, letting the water heat while I remove my clothing. *So much blood.* I've never been more grateful to have a roomy shower with a bench seat built into the wall. I adjust the showerhead and let the water cascade over me as I lean my head back and attempt to make sense of this latest mindfuck. As close as I am to Nic, Mike, and Marco, we don't talk about the fucked side of what they do for the family. They're not your garden-variety thugs, so they don't spend their days and nights killing. Taken a life? Undoubtedly. An innocent one? No. My father didn't operate that way, and I have no reason to believe that Rutger does either. The Morettis primarily run a diverse and varied operation. There are legitimate businesses, but there are also some lucrative ones that are not. It is those that pay off the most but provide the biggest risks. And along with that comes the type of people who are necessary to deal with. The ones who will kill to protect their turf and those looking to attain money and power by stealing it from another. Nic, Mike, and Marco primarily provide protection when engaging with them. I have little doubt they've seen far more in their line of work than I have in my limited capacity with the family.

There was very little chance I would have left Caulder alive tonight. Taking a life is not my first inclination. Ever. I could have ruined him financially or made him suffer by stripping away everything he owned, but a man like that wouldn't have left town with his tail tucked between his legs. No, as a general rule, the more evil the man, the more reckless. He made the connection between Jacey and me when he saw her at the compound. Even with her dark hair, with Clint calling her name loudly when she panicked, he recognized her. I probably said her name as well. He left knowing, and there was no way around it. Jacey would have been back on his radar. Hell, a woman such as her probably never left it. He might not have gone after her immediately, but he most certainly would have started digging around. Hunter Wrenn basically gave Caulder his daughter, jerked her away, and then took a chunk of his business as well. Getting revenge would have appealed to the piece of shit.

Leaving him alive hadn't been an option. Quite simply, it had come down to him or Jacey. There was no way I'd let him hurt her again. And he would have. I never want to see that look of terror on her face again. If ridding the world of one sadistic fucker is what it takes, then I'll do it every time. Any man who gets his kicks out of hurting women doesn't deserve to draw a breath. *No choice.* And that's what it came down to. Yes, I was beyond furious, but once Marco stopped me, I took time to think. I have the right *and* the obligation to protect those I love.

Love?

What the...

Do I even know the true meaning of love? The purest love I've ever felt is in that damn dream. Was she so intertwined with the girl in the dream that I can no longer separate fantasy from reality?

No. I've always seen her.

I relax as I acknowledge the truth of it. My response each time Jacey's near can't be denied. I have feelings for her—strong ones. I'm not sure if either of us really knows how to love in the way that *romantic* love is portrayed. But who-the-fuck-ever said that everyone is supposed to be the same?

I turn off the water and get out of the shower, feeling more at peace with that part of my life. As for whoever beat me to Caulder, that's on the back burner until tomorrow. There's nothing I can add that hasn't been said or suggested. Considering conspiracy theories will add nothing but a sleepless night, and I need to recharge for the game ahead. Because I'm done. I want this over with, and I'm ready to do whatever it takes to accomplish that. But for now, fuck it all. I'll sleep, and it will be with Jacey in my arms. I need her softness. The comfort I feel when her body is tight against mine.

I just need her.

Tonight, that's as close to heaven as I can get.

12

JACEY

I use the other bathroom to shower since Tony isn't coming out of the one in the bedroom anytime soon. No doubt he needs some time alone. Not that I can blame him, considering the night he's had. Neither of us is used to living with someone else in such close quarters, so I take my time as well to give him some privacy. Half an hour has passed when I walk softly into the now darkened bedroom. I tug the short T-shirt I'm wearing down farther, wishing I'd put on my pajama pants. I'll need to go to my apartment for clothing tomorrow. I have one clean suit left to wear to the office, but that's pretty much it. The lamp on my side of the bed is still on, but his is off. He's lying on his back with one arm over his head and the other resting at his waist. I creep across the room and do my best not to disturb him as I ease my way under the cover before flipping off the light. I don't know why, but the darkness seems oppressive tonight. Despite my good intentions, I shift around as I attempt to push away my unease. I almost jump out of my skin when a hand touches my arm. "What's wrong? You seem nervous." *How can he possibly know that?*

Even to my own ears, my voice sounds unnaturally high when I say, "Oh, no. I'm fine. Just trying to get comfortable. You know how that is."

His sigh says he doesn't believe a word. The bed shakes as he moves. Then his body bumps against my side. "Come here, Duchess. If there was ever a need for a fucking cuddle, it's now." He doesn't have to tell me twice. I make a few awkward maneuvers before ending up with my head on his chest and one arm around his waist. His arm comes around me, and I'm snuggled in a warm cocoon that smells amazing. "Better?" he asks, sounding faintly amused.

"Mmm, much." I love feeling his skin beneath me. Without thinking, my fingertips begin drawing lazy circles across his stomach— marveling at his hard abs. *Not an ounce of fat there.* I circle his belly button, completely lost in the moment.

I'm not a virgin...*far* from it. I had a few short relationships in college. I intentionally block out the men I slept with at my father's directive. But this is the first time I've ever really felt the desire to explore a man's body. And unlike past experiences, I don't want to stop. In fact, I feel as if it will cause me physical pain if I do.

Tony's voice is strained when he asks shakily, "Duchess, what are you doing?" My hand is on his lower stomach now, just inches away—

"I don't know," I murmur truthfully. *What am I doing? Must stop.*

But I can't.

Something inside me needs this heady feeling of control. I know Tony isn't the type of man I should have some kind of sexual therapy session with, but I want this. I need it in a way I don't fully understand. Then my fingers close around him, and instead of fear, there's only wonder.

I want him. The throbbing between my legs tells me I'm not imagining it.

"Jacey," he hisses but doesn't attempt to pull away. Instead, his hips lift as a ragged groan escapes him.

As much as I want to make him come in this unguarded way, my body is humming with desire. I remove my hand, wiggle out of my panties, and scramble onto my knees until I'm straddling him. His cock rests against the curve of my ass. "I want you, Tony," I breathe.

His hands come to my hips, holding me in place. "Need condom," he mutters in frustration.

I laugh. I can't help it. Something about that is funny. I glance down, able to make out the outline of his face in the dark. "Really? Of all the things that might kill us, you're worried about an STD?"

"Fuck, no," he growls. "I've been tested and so have you. But you could get pregnant."

"I'm still on the pill. Damn, Moretti, this whole safe-sex discussion isn't very mobster-like of you. You're kind of ruining the whole spontaneous moment we were having." Before I can even process what is happening, he picks me up by my waist, positions me just so, and impales me on his hard length. I cry out in surprise, and he freezes.

"Duchess, are you all right? Fuck, you make me so crazy. I didn't think."

Oh, my God. I am *perfectly fine. And amazed.* I stretch to accommodate his size. I'm not experiencing discomfort, but rather an adjustment to the unfamiliar fullness. Tingles of pleasure are shooting through me, and I smile at the gorgeous man beneath me. *This feels right.* "I'm good," I assure him.

He lifts his hand and strokes the side of my cheek, and I can honestly say the look in his eyes is awe.

When looking at me.

After the day we've had...

Only this man.

I can tell he's still concerned, so I go with something ridiculous. "You know we could avoid this next time if you give me a little warning before you shove your dick inside me. Something like, 'Hey, Duchess, batten down the hatches, I'm coming inside.'"

He's shaking. I'm certain he's not crying, so I figure he's found my humor funny. "And *I'm* ruining the moment, Duchess? You sound like you work on a loading dock somewhere. I'll admit, though, it's kind of hot."

I pull my T-shirt over my head and toss it on the floor. Then I lift my hips just enough to get his attention and lower once again. His indrawn breath tells me I've more than got it. I force out a loud yawn and stretch my arms over my head. "I'm pretty tired now. Could we pick this up later? Maybe next week? I have to work tomorrow, and it's getting late."

I smirk at when he grunts, "No fucking way," before tightening his grip on my hips and raising me several inches, then bringing me back down again. I moan at the exquisite feeling coursing through me. He sets an easy rhythm, and we move perfectly in sync. After a few moments, I grow impatient, needing more. *Harder. I doubt this man has ever held back like this, and for the first time, I want him to take charge. I want my body to be his.* I kick upward with my legs, and his hands drop away, letting me take the lead, which turns out to be better than imagined. Because now that he's not guiding my movements, his hands are free to roam. He cups my breasts, then rolls the nipples between his thumb and forefinger. I've never known how sensitive they were. His fingers dance over my nipples, and I'm struggling to keep focused. I feel him everywhere. I throw my head back and lean into his hands more, loving the way he's touching me. Caressing me. The soft touches against the hard pulls. Pleasure. Pain. I'm tingling everywhere. *It's never been like this.* The grunts he's making and his ragged breaths.

"God, you're so fucking sexy, Duchess. Want you so bad." Then he drops one hand between my legs to where we join and begins rubbing my clit.

"Ride me, beautiful. Ride me hard. However you want me."

His words. His touch. His body flexing beneath mine. The warmth of his skin beneath my hands. I've never come during intercourse before, so I'm in shock as my orgasm approaches. I'm coated in a fine sheen of sweat. The sound of our slick bodies coming together is intoxicating. I look at his face, and what I see nearly tips me over. This strong, amazing man is looking at me in...wonder. Me... Then his thumb, coated in my essence, presses firmly on my clit. "Tony...I'm, God, yes," I shriek as my body spasms around him. His hands are back on my hips as he pulls me down harder while thrusting upward. The added stimulation is enough to send me over once again. A few moments later, his harsh exclamation tells me that he's found his own release. It's probably not what you're supposed to do in the afterglow, but I collapse on his chest in a limp heap. I'm too tired to even separate myself from him, so I'm grateful when he gently lifts me off. *Holy shit. Is that what sex is meant to be like?*

"Wore you out, didn't I, Duchess?" he asks, then laughs before smacking my ass lightly. I don't have the energy to protest, so he can do whatever he wants to it. *Wait, not that.* To my surprise, he keeps me in his arms and maneuvers to the edge of the bed before getting to his feet. "We'll take a quick shower before we crash," he explains as he moves toward the bathroom.

"I don't have the energy," I protest sleepily.

"Unless you want to sleep in the wet spot all night, I think you'll appreciate it. Don't worry, I'll do most of the work." And he does. He puts me in the shower, keeps an arm around me, and washes first me, then himself. It occurs to me that I should feel awkward about him seeing me naked. The bedroom was dark, but that isn't the case now. I probably look like a homeless person, but I don't have it in me to care. When you practically maul a guy in bed, it's a little late to have an attack of nerves after the fact. Besides, I might be on the thin side, but the girls are still perky and where they're supposed to be. Plus, I've had a recent wax job, so I don't look like a yeti down there. Wait, when did I last shave my legs? *Shit.* Okay, so maybe there was a little extra hair in places, but he didn't seem to mind. And if the way he constantly had a hand on my ass was any indication, he approved of that area. I've often wondered how things would be between us when and if we ever had sex. A part of me has feared it would be as disappointing as all my experiences have been. *That night, when Caulder...*

I block it.

I *will not* let him ruin this for me.

He took too much of my fucking life. I refuse to give him another second of it.

Even though it was fast and furious at the end, tonight was perfect. I was comfortable enough to joke around. I had no idea I could ever be that way with a man—especially during sex. But with Tony, everything was easy. So natural and effortless.

Tony Moretti is the right man for me at this point in my life. *I want more, but I won't presume he'll want me when this is all over.* He's shown me something I didn't believe exists. Sex isn't simply an act of going through the motions. Or trying to go somewhere else in your head until it was over. No, it can be fun, exciting, fulfilling, and everything else written about in books that I've never believed existed. As Tony dries me and leads me back to bed, I have only one thought left in my head: *maybe there is someone out there other than a child who could love me unconditionally.*

And I allow myself to feel something I gave up on long ago.

Hope.

13

TONY

"You two finally did the deed, didn't you?" Marco smirks in a way that makes me want to punch him. *Bastard.* "You forget I read people for a living. Not necessarily to see if they'd had sex with their crush."

"Who had sex?" Nic asks as he walks in the door of the club with Mike trailing a few steps behind. "I can tell you who hasn't lately." He grimaces.

"Are you referring to me?" Mike asks, looking up from his phone. "Not that it's any of your business, Nicoli, but I had relations with a nice lady a few nights back. And before you ask, no, I will not tell you her name. I had no clue that you were not as fortunate. I'll be happy to give you some advice if you'd like."

"What the fuck?" Nic groans. "You've been out getting lucky, dude, while I've been sitting at home watching reruns of *Jeopardy*?" He looks at us incredulously. "What is wrong with this picture, gentlemen? Who would you have said was the least likely to have gotten laid?"

Marco glances at me and grins before looking at Nic once more. "Well, apparently that would be you, buddy."

Nic narrows his eyes at Marco before saying, "Well, at least I'm home relaxing instead of riding by Nina Gavino's place a dozen times a night in hopes of seeing her out walking the neighbor's dog." He leans a hip against the bar and lifts a brow, "So tell us, oh ladies' man, what's the grand plan? You see her, park your car, and start strolling down the sidewalk? Pretend you were in the area?" Shaking his head, he adds, "Dude, you were as sick as a dog at her place. You can't come back from that—ever. In her mind, you'll always be the guy who nearly shit his pants in front of her. Wait...that didn't actually happen, did it?"

The humor has long since fled from Marco's face as he glares at the other man. "Mind your own fucking business, *Nicoli*. Your time at home would be better spent brushing up on your barbecue skills. I mean, after that embarrassing loss to Tommy, it's obvious there's work to do."

Despite my irritation over Marco's weirdly intuitive guess that Jacey and I slept together, I can't help smiling. He's hit Nic where it hurts— his cooking skills. Over a year later and he hasn't gotten over losing to Tommy. "Guys," I interrupt, attempting to break this up before they draw their fucking guns on each other. From the look on Nic's face, that's a possibility.

I've never been more grateful to hear the door open and see Lee walking in. "This isn't over, asshole," Nic snaps at Marco...but wisely decides to let it go for now. Apparently even he doesn't want to look like a whiny little bitch in front of Lee.

Handshakes and hugs are exchanged, and we head to my office. I had one of my guys pick up some sandwiches and drop them off, so by unspoken agreement, we eat first, making small talk until everyone finishes. I get to my feet and lean against a nearby wall so I can see everyone easier. It's much the way I handle staff meetings in the club when I attend them. I'm in no way the authority figure here—we're all equals in my mind. But it's simply the way I'm most comfortable. When I open my mouth to tell him about Jeremy Caulder, I realize that Lee needs to know why I was after Caulder. *Fuck.* This is going to require an explanation I'm not comfortable with. Lee needs to know what Jacey has been through and why, but it doesn't make me feel any better about it, though. She's already shared things with me that were technically none of my business. And in turn, I've told Marco, Nic, and Mike deeply personal and humiliating things about her. There simply is no choice, though. Lee must know—not only because of the possibility of a link between Caulder's murder and our current investigation but also because of his hostility toward her. He thinks she's a cold-hearted bitch who turned her back on her sister long ago. *The woman he loves wouldn't exist right now without her.* Lee appears relaxed as he always does, but I know it's an illusion. His mind is usually firing off in a dozen different directions. He is the most intelligent man I've ever known, and that's saying a lot, considering my father and Victor were brilliant in my eyes. "There have been some new developments since we spoke last." Then knowing no way to sugarcoat it, I get right to the point. "Jeremy Caulder was murdered."

His eyes widen slightly, the only indication I've caught him off guard. But he simply says, "I see. This information hasn't been made public."

This next part is trickier, and I'm struggling with where to begin. *Fuck it.* "Two nights ago, Clint brought Jacey to the compound. When they walked in, I was meeting with Caulder and a couple of his guys in the foyer. She recognized him, lost it, fell, and hit her head. She was terrified. Thankfully, Dr. Atwell was there checking Marco again, and she sedated Jacey because of her distress. When she woke and cried out again in fear, *very* long story short, I made her tell me who and why she was so afraid of."

When I pause, Lee motions with his hand. "And?" *He really doesn't give a fuck.*

It's hard, but I manage to push back my irritation. I keep reminding myself that I'd feel the same way if our positions were reversed. But he's not heartless. "Your father-in-law forced Jacey to *entertain* men beneficial to the company. One of them was Jeremy Caulder." Again, there's a flicker of surprise, but it's quickly gone. "Jeremy was a sadistic bastard who hurt her, then brought over some friends to join the party one night. I don't want to go into all the details, but she was injured badly, and has since felt terrified of seeing him again."

Lee shrugs his shoulders before saying, "Why did she agree to be Wrenn's and therefore Caulder's entertainment to begin with?"

"Because it was either her or Jade," I say bluntly. *Enough dancing around it. He's a big boy.* "Wrenn terrorized Jacey for years, forcing her to do whatever he asked of her. When she resisted, Jade had a few 'accidents' until Jacey acquiesced. If she refused any of his requests, Jade paid the price."

He's furious. I can see it in the narrowing of his eyes and the clenching of his hands. Much like me, he wishes Wrenn were still alive so *he* could kill him. He gets to his feet and walks to the glass wall behind my desk, staring into the darkness of the club as he processes. Finally, he says, "And you believe her?" It's not really a question, but I answer it anyway.

"Without reservation. The level of abject terror I witnessed not once but twice wasn't faked."

"Fuck," he murmurs softly. "It strangely makes sense. Her behavior at times was oddly inconsistent, even more so in the last year. I put it down to a late attack of conscience even though Jade has always defended her."

I move to stand next to him, silently lending my support. He's grappling to take it all in just as I was a short time ago. "Jacey said their mother told her many times that she had to take care of her sister."

"I'd say she fulfilled that," he replies, still appearing lost in thought.

"Agreed. But you cannot tell Jade. This is not your story to share. I feel like a piece of shit divulging her past with all of you, but something like this could destroy a woman as soft-hearted as your wife. Whether or not Jade knows is up to Jacey. And considering what she went through to protect her sister, if she ever does reveal it to Jade, she won't tell her why." *Because my woman is one of the strongest women I've ever known. And she killed the bastard who stole so much from her.*

Lee puts his hands in his pockets and rocks back on his heels. When he drops his head forward, I know he understands. "There is only one reason I'd ever keep anything from my wife, and that is to protect her. This would destroy her. She loves Jacey and longs to form a relationship with her despite what's happened between them." He's silent for a moment before clearing his throat, and saying, "Let's hear the rest." We return to where a silent Marco, Mike, and Nic sit waiting for us. Their solemn expressions tell me that hearing Jacey's story again is almost as hard for them as it is for me to disclose it. In a very short amount of time, they've grown fond of the woman who has stolen my heart.

How in the fuck did that happen?

I lay the facts of the previous night out for Lee. Due to the life he's lived, very little surprises him. *Jacey did.* "We think they may be—"

"They're connected," he mutters. "Caulder was a calling card. Collateral damage to get your attention. The murder isn't the most unsettling aspect here. It's the fact that someone knew you would go after the fucker. Answer the question of how that's even possible, and it leads you to the guilty party."

"Your house is compromised," Marco hisses in frustration. "There's either a bug there or someone's eavesdropping. You need to have it swept without telling anyone ahead of time. We also need to know everyone who was there when this was discussed."

Lee rubs a hand over his chin before looking at me. "I realize this is going to be hard for you, but we must assume that everyone is a suspect until we can exclude them. I know Lester and Cassandra have been with you for a long time, but the fucked-up truth is that everyone has a price. And often it has nothing to do with money. What happened to Jacey tells you that."

"He's correct," Mike concurs. "I've had similar thoughts, so I took the liberty of compiling a preliminary list. I realize you employ people there, but since this conversation took place after hours, that narrows down the suspects a bit. His fingers fly over his phone screen before he continues. "There's Lester and Cassandra, Dr. Atwell, four security guards, and a cook. Does that sound right?"

"Fuck me," I say as I attempt to deal with the ramifications of what Lee is suggesting. *He's right.* I should have thought of it myself but acknowledging that someone close to me might have betrayed me is a blow difficult to absorb. More so possibly than anyone else, Lester and Cassandra are in a power position within my inner circle, and I trust them with my life and the lives of those I love. A betrayal of that magnitude would be staggering. They hire and train my security detail for every aspect of my life. *Including hers.*

Nic, appearing unusually solemn, speaks up. "Tony, if it's any consolation, I don't think it's Lester or Cass. They've been privy to what we've been doing for a while now. I don't see them plotting to take you down and using this kind of obscure message to fuck with your head. That's not Lester's style. He'd go for the kill shot every time."

"Agreed," Marco pipes in. "That shit with Caulder was the work of a pussy. Someone without the balls for a head-on attack."

Then it hits me. I know what my next move must be, and no one here is going to like it. "That's right"—I nod— "which is why I'll go to Rutger and lay my cards on the table. He'll either kill me or help me. At this point, I'm not sure I give a good fuck."

"You're insane," Marco says incredulously. "Tony," he implores, "there must be another way. He's by the book. Draco's death still haunts him. There's no way he'll be a party to putting his son in danger."

Nic slides to the edge of his seat as he glances around the room before looking at me. *He gets it.* "That may well be why he'll agree to help." I might have been a teenager back then, but even I remember how he idolized Draco and Victor. He took their deaths hard. He took over as head of the family, and I don't believe it was a love of power that made him do it. He wanted to preserve what Draco started. He held the family together when everyone else was too busy fighting for position. If there is anyone that wants to see justice served, it's Rutger Moretti."

"I lean in that direction as well," Lee agrees. "I've known Rutger a long time. We're not best friends, but I'd count him as an ally if I needed one. He won't be happy that we've been digging into Draco's death without informing him—especially as we suspect it's someone within the family."

"What he'll be is fucking pissed at me." Marco sighs. "Then he'll probably tell my mother and let her have a go at me as well."

Nic shudders, giving his friend a sympathetic look. "I'd rather face your old man in a dark alley, than your mom. That woman is scary."

"Mrs. Moretti is a bit on the...intimidating side," Mike agrees. "But you've survived them thus far, so statistically, they're unlikely to kill you now."

"Why thanks for that, Einstein," Marco grumbles before giving me a nod. "I'm in. Whatever you think is best."

I brace myself for protests, knowing they'll be coming. "There is no reason any of you should fear the wrath of the family. As far as Rutger will know, I acted alone."

Marco begins laughing. "As if he'd believe we weren't involved in some way. My father's not a fool, Tony. He's fully aware of how close the three of us are to you. It's possible he might not include Lee in the equation, but yeah, that would simply insult his intelligence."

"The facts support his argument," Mike tosses out.

Well, fuck. "All right," I concede. "But I will not allow any of you to take the blame for this. If there is a price to pay, then it's all mine. In this, you cannot and will not protect me. Understood?"

There is general grumbling and objections, but in the end, I have their agreement. "I'll contact Rutger today and set up a meet for tomorrow if possible. I'll let you know as soon as I have the details."

Lee glances at his watch, and I know he needs to go. We've covered everything anyway. I hadn't expected him to accompany us to meet with Rutger, so I'm surprised when he says, "I'll expect to be notified as well. Rutger is less likely to make a move against you with me there." It isn't said out of conceit; it's simply the truth, and we all know it. The family does not want any trouble with Lee. His involvement will indeed add an extra layer of protection to our group.

"Thanks, brother." I clap him on the shoulder.

With his exit, everyone else gets to their feet and follows suit. Within a few moments, my office is blissfully quiet. I walk around my desk and take a seat, putting my feet up onto the corner of it. As uncertain as the days ahead are, I feel a strange kind of peace for the first time in months. Rutger will be angry, but with Lee's involvement, I think we can bring him over to our side.

As I stare at the ceiling, my thoughts go to her—my Duchess. She shocked the hell out of me last night. Taking the initiative and quite literally fucking me wasn't something I expected. I knew we'd sleep together eventually, but with shit blowing up all around us, I figured it might be later. It was as fucking amazing as it was unexpected. Underneath her bravado, she was sweetly shy, which only made me want her more. The look on her face when she came around me. God, the way she looked at me. *With awe.* She's so beautiful, and last night, I learned how incredibly sexy she is too. *And she has no clue. My goddess.* I thought I'd blow my load in an embarrassingly short amount of time, but an iron will—and some baseball statistics—meant I made it until she found her release. I planned to have a much more leisurely session this morning, but we overslept, and Clint woke us when he arrived to take Jacey to work. So, a hurried kiss was it. I knew she was as disappointed as well, but we'll have tonight. Jacey has never been with anyone who put her needs first, and I've never been with anyone I've wanted to make love to. I have no idea what tomorrow will bring, but tonight, I plan to give us both a first—several times.

JACEY

I'm deep in thought as I study the latest financial reports for the company. After selling every part of Wrenn with questionable ties, I expected the company to take a financial hit for a while, but that hasn't been the case. Our numbers remain strong and steady. *Why am I disappointed?* A part of me wanted Wrenn to fail so I could close the doors of the place I loathe so much and walk away. No one would question my decision to do just that if we were failing. But we're not, and I'm at a crossroads now. I want out so badly, yet I don't know how to leave. When the buzzer on the office phone sounds, I jump, having been so lost in my thoughts that I forgot where I was for a moment. "Ms. Wrenn, your sister is here to see you. You have your next appointment soon, though." I close my eyes briefly in self-loathing. I told Marsha months ago that if my sister came to see me, I was always to have an upcoming meeting. *I hate that I learned to be cruel to be kind.*

"It's fine, Marsha, you can send her in."

A few seconds later, my sister opens the door, giving me a bright smile. *She's nervous as always.* No matter how hard she tries to appear as if she's not, being around me makes her anxious. *Why does she keep doing it then?* I must give her credit for her tenacity. I'd have long since given up. "Sorry for dropping by unannounced. It's just that I was going through some stuff I had in storage, and I ran across a box of paper-work that belonged to Mom. I guess it got mixed in with my boxes when I moved into my apartment. Anyway, it appears to be some old financial information. Bank statements and such. I didn't want to throw it away without asking you." For the first time, I notice the bankers box at her feet.

"It's nice of you to check with me," I say carefully. "And I'm sure there's nothing there of value, but if you want to leave it, I'll glance through it when I get time and then have it shredded."

"Oh...okay," she says, obviously disappointed we aren't going to do it now—together. It's getting harder and harder to be around her. She's still so damn hopeful that I'll come around and be a real sister to her. *I can't.* She has no idea that I simply don't know how. Being the ice queen is the only thing that's kept me from cracking all these years. If I drop my shields and let her in, I'll simply break apart.

You let him in.

Tony is different. He knows what I've been through. I can be myself around him without fear. But Jade...I can never tell her what I did. It would devastate her, and I've protected her for too long to be the one to destroy her. She dons that overly bright smile once again as she asks, "How have you been? Are you still seeing Tony? I left you a few messages about having lunch, but I know you stay busy here. If you ever need me to help you—"

"Oh no, I've got it covered," I say before she can finish her offer. *Please leave. God, leave.*

"Sure, of course you do. I don't know what I was thinking. You have plenty of staff." She shocks me when she lowers her voice to add, "This place gives me the serious creeps. How can you stand being here now? Have you ever thought of relocating? Making a fresh start?"

Only every single day. "Sometimes," I admit. "But it's not as if a different address will give me a new life. Wherever I go, the memories will follow."

Her eyes fill with tears, and I want to slap myself. I've said too much. Revealed a weakness to her. *If she can't handle this, she'll never deal with the truth.* My hands are trembling as I stare helplessly at her. *Go. Go.*

She's on the verge of an emotional meltdown, and she's pulling me along with her.

Can't breathe.

Go, Jade, go.

Then one loud knock sounds on my door before it's pushed open. I look at him beseechingly and see him nod once. Tony steps inside and appears to read the situation in one glance. "Jade, great to see you again. I had lunch with your husband today."

I see her attempt to collect herself as she grabs a tissue from my desk and dabs at her eyes before turning to face him. "Tony, hi, it's good to see you as well. Lee mentioned he was meeting with you today. I forgot all about that. Do you two have plans?"

Before I can reply, Tony steps in. "We do. I'm going to take this beautiful lady out for dinner tonight if I can steal her away from the office. She works entirely too hard."

I have no idea if he came here for that reason or not, but his timely interruption is enough to have me smiling at him in relief. "You're one to talk, Moretti," I say lightly, attempting to shake off the somber mood of a moment ago.

"Touché, Duchess. So, it'll be good for both of us. I should have called first, but I didn't want to take the chance that you'd say no."

"As if she would." Jade winks at me. It appears we've both managed to regroup. If not for Tony, I fear we would be well into my box of Kleenex by now.

He looks from me to Jade before asking, "Can you leave now? I left my car double-parked, so you'll save me a bundle in parking tickets if you hurry."

I have a meeting in an hour, but I couldn't care less. That pretty much sums up my feelings toward Wrenn most of the time now. I open my bottom drawer and pull my purse from it. My hand hovers over my briefcase, but I don't pick it up. *Fuck it.* It feels surprisingly good to leave everything behind for once. I get to my feet and move to his side. His hand automatically goes to my waist, and I feel the warmth that only he can give me. "Fast enough?"

"Perfect." He grins, then turns to Jade. "Why don't you walk down with us? I recognized Lee's car and driver." *So that's why he hadn't appeared surprised to see her here.*

He motions for Jade to exit, then he moves his hand to the small of my back as we follow her. I let Marsha know I'm leaving for the day and ask her to cancel my meeting. Poor thing, she's practically speechless. I've never been one to leave work early or miss it altogether, and I've done both several times recently. I ask Jade how Victor is doing, and the elevator ride to the lobby is mercifully brief and light as we laugh over some of his antics. Lee's driver is already on the sidewalk and opening the door for Jade when we step outside. She turns and pulls me into a fierce hug that I return awkwardly. Her eyes are once again glassy when she looks at me, but luckily, Tony moves forward and takes her arm to help her in the car. "Call me," she says brightly, yet I hear the wistful note she's trying to hide.

When Tony returns to my side, he puts his arm around me and holds me close as we navigate the distance to his Range Rover. He opens the door for me and then crosses to his side when I'm settled in. He doesn't bother to start the vehicle. Instead, he looks at me with eyes full of concern. "I'm sorry, Duchess. You weren't answering your cell, so I called your office. Your secretary told me you were with your sister. I was planning to drop by later anyway, so I decided to come earlier, thinking you might need rescuing."

I rest my head against the cool glass of the window as I try to gather my composure. *Don't cry in front of him.* "Thank you," I whisper gratefully. "It was...harder than usual today. Every time I see her, she has that look of hope in her eyes as if she believes this time we'll turn a corner and be sisters in more than blood only. And I feel like such a cold, heartless bitch when I turn her away." I stare at him imploringly as I ask, "What else can I do? You know why I'm this way...why I've had to be like this. I love her, Tony, more than anything, but a part of me resents her as well, which is insane. She knows nothing of what I've been through. Even if our father gave her the opportunity to do his dirty work instead of me, I wouldn't have allowed it to happen. Don't get me wrong. It wasn't as if she lived a charmed life. Our father was nothing but a prick after our mother died. So not only did she draw his ire often, she had to deal with my insulting, condescending behavior as well. So yeah, it was no picnic."

Obviously, he notices that my hands are still trembling as they rest in my lap, because a moment later, he lays one of his on top of them. "She's happy now, and it's painful to watch." To my horror, the tears return, and this time, they refuse to stop.

"Ah baby, how could you not feel that way? The part of you that saved her is glad, and the part of you that sacrificed yourself for her is angry."

Startled at his intuitiveness, I turn to gawk at him. *How?* Shaking his head, he says, "Duchess, you'd have to be a fucking saint not to be. Even if you'd make the same choice again and again, it doesn't change the fact that you had no choice. And that is what really pisses you off. Your father was a fucking monster who took years of your life from you. Who forced you to do things that you hated to save someone you loved."

"You're right." I sigh. "And I want so much to put all that behind me and rescue what's still left of the love she has for me."

He sighs before running his hand through his hair as he always does when he's frustrated or upset. *God, what else? Can't handle much more today.* "Lee knows about...your past." *WHAT?*

My mouth drops open, and I hope I've heard him wrong. "Exactly what are you saying, Tony?"

"Trust me, I feel like the world's biggest bastard right now, Jacey. But how could I explain the situation with Caulder otherwise? I didn't think he'd buy into me wanting to take the guy out because of some bad construction work."

"God," I groan. "What's next, an ad in the paper? Jacey Wrenn, whore of Asheville. I bet those headlines will sell some fucking papers."

True to form, he never does what I expect him to in these situations. Instead of an apology, he matches my anger with some of his own. "I've about had enough of this whore business," he snaps. "You. Are. Not. A. Fucking. Whore. Are we clear?" Between the shouting and clipped enunciation, I can do nothing but nod.

Was a hug too much to ask for?

He sounds more like himself when he adds, "Good. I don't want to hear that again. I won't allow anyone to put you down and that includes yourself. Now put your damn seat belt on and let's go to dinner," he grumbles as he starts the vehicle. I buckle up and wisely keep my mouth shut. The bright side to his outburst? My tears have dried up.

I wipe my eyes with my hands before attempting to smooth my hair down. I probably look like a train wreck. "If it's all right with you, I think I'll take a rain check on dinner. I'm not really in the mood to sit in some crowded restaurant after the day I've had." For the first time since we left Wrenn, I check out our surroundings and do a double take. *We're in my neighborhood.*

"I feel the same way," Tony murmurs as he pulls into a space on the side of the street and stops the car. "That's why I made arrangements for something a bit less formal."

Does he expect me to cook? I can't think of any other reason we'd be this close to my building. Tony sent my clothing out to be dry-cleaned, so I'm not in immediate need of anything new yet. "I guess we can order takeout. I'm not much of a cook, so I don't keep a lot of food on hand."

He gets out of the car without replying and comes around to help me out. When I start toward the entrance of my place, he reaches out and catches my hand. "Our table is ready." *Is he high?* I turn uncertainly —and my eyes widen. The usual array of bistro tables is gone. Only one remains, and it's covered with a white tablecloth. *Weird.* There's a bottle of wine and two glasses as well as a candle in the center. *Don't cry—again.*

"Tony," I begin, trying to speak past the lump in my throat. "This is…no one's ever done anything like this for me before."

He raises the hand he's holding and presses a kiss to the top of it. "On the contrary, Duchess, I believe we had our first date here. I didn't even make you pay for half. You were so impressed that by the end of it, you offered to be my baby mama."

When he winks at me, I melt. My heart turns to a gooey puddle, and I'm surprised I don't dissolve at his feet. "Well, well, it's about time you got yourself down here, girlie," Edna calls out from the food truck. She raises the spatula in her hand and waves it in the direction of Tony. "If this one hadn't kept me updated, I'd have called the cops by now."

Wait—he did what?" I gape at Tony in shock. "You've been in contact with Edna?"

He appears a bit uncomfortable now, which is kind of adorable. "I stopped by a few times to check on your place. You know, to make sure everything was all right."

Edna gives him an approving smile, which lets me know that another female has fallen victim to the Moretti charm. Bring on the eye-roll. "Sure did. And he came right up to me and let me know you were with him. Gave me his cell phone number and he took mine. We've stayed in touch." She winks at me. "Got yourself a good one here, girlie. Don't screw it up. Now you two lovebirds sit, and I'll bring the food out in a minute. Mel is just finishing it."

Tony leads me to the small table and pulls out a chair for me then takes his own. He pours us both a glass of red wine, all the while looking everywhere except at me.

He's embarrassed?

"That is very nice of you." I put my hand on his leg and squeeze. "Thank you." His goes on top of mine, and we remain that way until Edna arrives with plates containing steak and a baked potato. "Wow, Edna. When did you start serving steak?"

"Since your young fella here requested it." She waves a finger before adding, "Now don't be getting used to this kind of finery. It won't happen again until you two get hitched. Then I'll cater your shindig."

Heat rushes into my cheeks at her words, but Tony doesn't appear bothered at all. In fact, he merely nods and says, "You have yourself a deal, Edna."

We both cut into our steak warily—not sure if Edna's talent with breakfast and burgers extends to everything—but to my delight, it's amazing. "This is good," Tony states appreciatively. I eat more than I have in years, finishing nearly all my steak and half the potato. As if by unspoken agreement, we keep our conversation light during the meal.

Edna is thrilled with our mostly clean plates when she comes back to take them. "He'll have you fattened up in no time, girlie."

I rub my stomach, groaning. "I'm glad you're happy about it. After all that, I'll be waddling back to the car."

Tony carries the wine and glasses for Edna, and I see him slip her some bills. She nods at whatever he says, then follows him back to where I'm now standing. "Don't be a stranger. And don't screw this up. You won't find another one like this." It's hard to be certain with his dark coloring, but it looks almost as if Tony is blushing. *God, the man is adorable. Sexy, confident, bossy, funny...honorable. How can I not love him?*

Shit.

I love him.

Oh fuck.

I'm in a daze for the entire trip back to the club. I don't know why thinking those three little words have freaked me out so badly. After all, I've had those very thoughts several times lately. Yet I've managed to discount it for various reasons. It's too soon. We don't know each other well enough. I am damaged goods, and surely, he'll never feel the same. And so forth. Yet it has been so clear this time. And I think what has shaken me most is the fact I haven't attempted to talk myself out of it. I've spent most of my life in denial for one reason or another, but it's no longer working. My walls are coming down, and with their collapse, my emotions are going haywire. Demanding to be heard and acknowledged. Tony parks, and we head through the club and upstairs to the apartment. As he closes the door, he leans back against it. "You were very quiet after we left dinner. Anything bothering you?"

You could say that. I'm in love with you.

"Not really," I lie as I lay my purse on the bar and take a bottle of water from the refrigerator. "I think I'm going to take a shower, though. It's been a long day, and I'm ready to get this suit off."

I'm surprised when he begins walking toward the bedroom. "Would you mind if I go first? I helped unload a truck here earlier, and I could use a shower."

I shrug. "I'll use the one in the other bathroom. Just let me get some clean clothes. Didn't you say they were dropped off earlier?"

I've only taken a couple of steps when he holds up his hand, stopping me in my tracks. "You're going to have to wait on me, Duchess.

There's a...plumbing issue in the other bathroom. Thanks to one of the guys, no doubt." He grimaces. "I promise I'll be quick. Have a seat and relax until I'm finished."

"Sure, okay. No problem." I didn't notice him smelling badly earlier, but it is his place. If he wants the bathroom first, then sure.

With him gone, I can finally relax. I lie on the sofa and allow my thoughts free rein. I am still slightly panicky at the realization that I'm in love with him. But it also feels good in a way. As if it's maybe a step toward being a normal person. Real people fall in love all the time. *Maybe I've been waiting for him.* I'm not sure if I believe such a romantic notion, but if it's possible for me to truly love any man, then it will be Tony. *You mean, it is Tony.* So, what now? When you're in love, do you just tell the other person? What if they don't feel the same? Is it okay to tell them via email or text? Uncertainty swirls in my head making me wonder why anyone would want to fall in love. As I lie there feeling much like a teenager with her first crush, I can't help but think that maybe it would be easier to live my entire life as a spinster. And that's still a distinct possibility because unless I find the courage to tell him, Tony Moretti will never know how I feel about him.

14

TONY

What a fucking idiot. I made a fool out of myself as I almost pushed Jacey to the side in my haste to get to the bathroom first. Part of this romantic night I planned was drawing a bubble bath. The rose petals and candles I picked up earlier are on the side of the sunken bathtub in the corner of the bathroom. I also bought bubble bath, thinking that women usually enjoy that. I have no idea why I even agreed to a bathtub in the apartment designs, and until now, it's essentially just taken up space. *But it seemed like something romantic, and I hope Jacey enjoys it.* I didn't expect her to go for the shower as soon as we arrived home, though, so thinking fast came up with a...*plumbing issue in the other bathroom? Idiot.* Hopefully, she doesn't decide to check.

When the bath is ready, I toss in the red petals and then light the candles. I put in a small amount of the bubble bath, then turn the jets on low to create a whirlpool effect. Even I'm impressed. Although rose petals *and* bubbles may not have been the best idea. Still, it looks amazing. I flip off the lights and frown. The candles aren't as bright as I thought they'd be, but after a few moments, my eyes adjust. I hesitate, feeling strangely nervous now. I've slept with my share of women through the years, but this is the first time I've ever gone to this type of effort to seduce one. And it has nothing to do with getting her into bed, but rather everything to do with showing her how special she is to me.

How much I love her.

Say what?

But isn't it true? As insane as it might sound to others, I knew the moment she passed out in my arms. I'd been riveted—spellbound. She was the girl from my dreams, grown up at last. I found the one I never thought existed in real life. And those two weeks she spent with me only strengthened that belief. I let her go, and I gave us both time to get our bearings. Yet there hasn't been a single moment in that time away from her when I seriously considered letting her go for good. She's mine. She has been since that very first dream, and I'm never going to let her go again.

With a renewed purpose, I stride through the apartment and hear her before I see her. She's fast asleep on the couch snoring with impressive intensity. *Fuck me, even that's cute.* Should I scrap the bath idea? But then she mumbles something under her breath and stirs. I move closer until I'm standing at her side. "Duchess, are you awake?" *Dumb question.*

She stares at me groggily before releasing a huge yawn. "Oh sorry," she murmurs as she puts a hand over her mouth. "I must have dozed off." She wrinkles her nose in confusion. "Did you take a shower and put on the same clothes?"

"Er...I decided to let you go first. I've already started it for you. So up you go." She's staring at me as if I've lost my mind. Maybe she's still half asleep. *Or maybe I'm just a dumbass.*

"Here, let me help you," I say as I lean down and slide an arm beneath her legs and another under her back.

Her eyes go wide. "Um, Tony, what are you doing?"

"I'm carrying you to the bathroom because you're too tired to walk." *Smooth, Moretti.* She says nothing more as I retrace my earlier steps to the bathroom. "So...surprise," I say grandly as I throw open the door.

"What the...?" Her words trail off.

It's much darker than I remember. "I drew a bath for you. Here let me sit you on the side of the tub until your eyes adjust." And then it happens. I slip on something and overcorrect. In almost slow motion, we pitch forward. Jacey squeals in shock as I literally toss her into the soapy water and end up on my knees on the floor. *What in the fuck?* Between the darkness and the fall, it takes me a moment to get my bearings before I begin trying to scramble up. *Why is the floor wet?* I hear gasping. *Fuck, is she drowning?* "Jacey, hang on, baby. I'm coming." It's pitch-black now; all the candles have obviously been washed out by water in our fall. I crawl on my hands and knees and manage to extend my arm enough to feel around for the light switch until I locate it. The glare of the overhead light blinds me, and I blink rapidly. Then I hear it again. The gasping. As my eyes adjust, I look at the bathtub, and my mouth drops open in shock. There are bubbles *everywhere*. On the floor, on the walls, and all over a laughing Jacey standing in the middle of them. "What...Duchess, I... are you okay?"

"Yes." She gasps, then dissolves into a fit of giggles. "Oh my God, we're so bad at this, Moretti. You were trying to do something sweet for me, and you...Tony, you blew up the bathroom with Mr. Bubble. Don't you know you can't put stuff like that in a whirlpool tub?"

She is the most beautiful thing I've ever seen.

The Duchess is nowhere in sight. Instead, this is possibly who Jacey would have had she never been forced to protect her sister. *To sacrifice herself.* And right there on the wet floor, surrounded by a sea of bubbles, I say, "I love you." She's still laughing, clearly not having heard me over the commotion. I consider letting it go but figure I might not be brave enough to say it again anytime soon, so I raise my voice and shout the words, "I love you!" Which just so happens to coincide with the exact moment she locates the switch for the whirlpool. My declaration seems to reverberate off the walls. If the way she's gaping at me now is any indication, she heard me quite clearly this time.

"Did you just say...?" she trails off uncertainly.

Do I take it back? She doesn't look happy. More like nauseous. I manage to get to my feet without busting my ass, which is nothing short of a miracle. I use the wall as support as I ease around to where she's stand-ing. *Man up. Don't be a pussy.* I clear my throat, then force myself to meet her wide eyes. "I said that I love you. Or maybe I'm in love with you is a better way to put it. Hell, I love Marco, but I'm not in love with him. So that's maybe...yeah, an important distinction."

She gives me a soft smile before shuffling to the edge of the bathtub. I reach out a hand to steady her as she climbs over the side. After dropping her earlier, I don't think it's a good idea to push my luck by picking her up again. She stops a few inches from me, and we're standing almost face to face thanks to her height. She rests her wet hands on my chest before saying, "I...think I love you too. I know I've never felt anything like this for anyone before. Thanks to my past, a part of me wonders if I even know what that is. But I do know this with certainty. There hasn't been a day in the past year when I haven't thought of you —longed to be with you. Regardless of the reasons behind it, these past few weeks with you have been the happiest of my life. This apartment feels like the home I've never had, but I don't think it's the walls that surround us that make it that way. It's you. You make me feel as if I'm finally home. Which I realize sounds insane. We hardly even know each other, but you've never felt like a stranger to me. A part of me recognized you from that very first day we met." *Thank fuck I'm not the only one feeling this. Never thought this would happen.*

"It doesn't sound crazy at all to me because I've felt much the same about you." *I'll tell her about the dream one day.* But for now, we gingerly make our way to the shower. We kick our shoes off and then step inside with our bubble-covered clothing on and let the spray wash us clean. We giggle like kids as we steal kisses and lingering touches. It takes both of us to remove my shirt. "We may have to cut the rest of our clothing off." The prediction ends up being a close call, but with a team effort, we're finally naked. *Why is this beautiful woman mine?* I finally understand the look of wonder that has crossed Lee's face more than once in the past fourteen months. I had no clue before now. Once we've washed and dried off, she becomes shy, crossing her arms over her chest and shifting uncertainly on her feet. *I hate the fuckers who caused her to doubt how fucking magnificent she is.* I take her face in both of my hands, tilting her head to look at me. "Do you have any idea how much I want to make love to you, Duchess? To take my time kissing, tasting, and touching every inch of your body?"

"I...please," she whispers. "I've never had that before. Never made love."

Me too, baby. I want to carry her to the bedroom, but the floor is still slick and dropping her again will certainly be a mood killer. Instead, I take one of her hands, threading our fingers together as we walk into the bedroom. The low lamplight creates an almost dreamlike setting as I lift and place her on the bed. I think for a moment that she's going to pull the covers over her naked body, but at the last moment, her fingers dig into the sheets instead. I move next to her, taking my time touching her body. "You're so unbelievably beautiful, baby," I murmur and mean every word. She is every fantasy I've ever had come to life. A low moan escapes her throat as my lips close around one rosy nipple, then the other. Teeth nipping the peaks into erect points. My tongue trails down her flat stomach to the apex of her thighs. My mouth is inches away from her sex when I feel her tense. "Relax, Duchess, let me love you." Then my tongue touches nirvana, and we're both lost. Her fingers dig into my hair, and she pulls and pushes as if undecided if she wants more or has had all she can stand. *I'll be the judge of that.* I bring her to orgasm three times with my fingers buried inside her while my mouth sucks on her clit. *Oh fuck, I love the sounds she makes.* She's trembling when I finally move over her. Missionary may not be adventurous, but it is one I consider the most intimate, which is why I've always tended to avoid it. But now, as I slide inside her tight, wet heat, I think it may well be my favorite. My mouth fuses to hers as our bodies move perfectly in sync. I put one hand under her ass, lifting her into my thrusts as I quicken my pace. Her legs are around my waist, and every inch of our bodies touch as we come together in an earth-shattering climax that has us both crying out. "Ah fuck," I hiss as my cock throbs inside her. *I've never come that fast in my life. Fuck.*

"I...wow." She sighs in wonder. "I had no idea—"

"That makes two of us," I agree as I regretfully separate our bodies before I crush her. She curls drowsily against my chest, and I wrap both my arms around her protectively. *Mine.* My world has just been rocked in more than one way. Not only is the girl of my dreams finally in my arms, but our love is real. There is nothing I won't do to protect this beautiful woman. Tomorrow, I will kick the game into a dangerous territory when I go to Rutger. But tonight, I'll lie awake and cherish every moment I have before the morning makes our future more uncertain than ever. *How the hell did I deserve this woman?* I don't. But I will love her how she needs to be loved.

Wholeheartedly.

Forever.

15

JACEY

I drifted around in one of those sappy glows all morning. Tony and I made love in the shower before Clint arrived to take me to the office. He even kissed me thoroughly in front of the other man, leaving me flustered, and I nearly face-planted on the way out his apartment door. *He loves me.* Although it seems that neither of us is the type to tell each other constantly. In fact, after his declaration the previous night and my own admission, we haven't said it again. It is so new that we both need time to get comfortable with it.

It's one of the rare days that I have no meetings, which is normally a good thing, but today I'm not in the mood to work. Instead, I wander around my office, resenting the gilded cage more than ever. *I'm selling Wrenn.*

And there it is.

What I've wanted to do since my father's death. I'll never be free of him while I'm tied to the business he created at the expense of others. *At the expense of me.* I need a fresh start, and I have no doubt Jade will agree with my decision. Remembering the box she dropped off yesterday, I take it to the seating area in the corner. I upend the contents on the coffee table and take a seat on the sofa.

There are stacks of receipts for deposits and reimbursements from

Wrenn Wear, the company she ran before Draco took it over. The rest appears to be bank statements—which hold no interest to me. I'm in the middle of putting everything back when a folded set of papers falls out from where they'd been wedged between the other paperwork. I almost toss it into the box without looking, but since I plan to have it all shredded, I double-check it's nothing of importance. An insurance policy? I scan the first page and am surprised to see that it's a life insurance policy for one million dollars in my mother's name. My mother died so long ago that I have no idea if my father even knew of this policy, much less claimed it. I quickly flip to the last page to look for the contact information of the company who issued it. With something this size, I should follow up on it. Then I see it—something that gives me a weird feeling in the pit of my stomach. I get to my feet to call Tony but am interrupted by a knock on the door. Clint sticks his head inside before saying, "Ms. Jacey, Tony wants me to take you to the compound."

"Now?" I frown, wondering what has him *summoning* me. *That's weird.* He planned to meet with the head of the family today, so did something go wrong? The house was swept for bugs yesterday and given the all clear, which means we still have no idea how whoever killed Caulder knew Tony would go after him. I'm surprised we're meeting there, considering the unknowns, but maybe there's new information. I grab my purse and stick the papers I've been clutching inside it. I let Marsha know on the way out that I'll be gone for the rest of the day. Even if I'm not at the compound long, I don't plan to return here afterward. I've been a slave to this company for far too long, and I'm amazed at how much lighter I feel simply from the decision to sell it. Surely things can only get better.

The ride to the compound is short thanks to the absence of rush-hour traffic. I don't see Tony's vehicle in the circular drive when we arrive, but given the estate is huge and he's likely parked elsewhere, I don't think much of it. Clint helps me from the car and escorts me to the door where he opens it for me. "Tony needs me to run an errand, so I'll drop you here, Ms. Jacey. He'll take you back to the city with him but go inside and wait in the study."

I nod, feeling a little unsettled as I return to the study. Both times

I've been to the compound, I haven't felt terribly comfortable. It's hard to imagine Tony growing up in this house. It's beautiful, but almost a little...lonely. I walk into the study, pondering what his life was like. Was he happy—

"Well, hello again, Jacey. Why don't you have a seat while we wait for the others to join us?" Marcel Moretti glances at his watch, a small frown pulling at the corners of his mouth. *What is he doing here?* The expression on his face is almost...snide, rather than the easygoing uncle I met a few weeks ago. *Odd.* "I do hope they're not late. I prize punctuality. It's a lost art."

"I...what's going on?" I ask nervously as my earlier unease returns. I put my hand over my purse, thinking of the documents I put inside it. He gives me a pleasant smile—but something's off. This feels all wrong. "It's rude to question your host, my dear. I believe I've told you that we're waiting on more guests. And I detest repeating myself, so if you'll please." He points toward the sofa, and I grudgingly perch on the edge.

It seems surreal when he asks, "Where are my manners? Can I offer you some refreshments while we wait?"

It's on the tip of my tongue to refuse, but it occurs to me that it might give me an opportunity to escape. Because even though he hasn't said it in so many words, I feel certain that leaving is not an option. "I'd love some water. I'd be happy to get it myself," I offer, getting to my feet.

"Stay where you are," he snaps. Then his face smooths out as he assumes the role of the perfect host. He crosses to a bar in the corner and steps behind it. "There is a bit of everything stocked here." He returns, handing me a chilled bottle.

I open it and take a small sip, which earns me an approving nod. "Um...how long until the...others arrive?" *Hurry, Tony.*

"Very soon. Tony was informed before you." He crosses his arms and stares at me as if fascinated. "You're very like her. Even with the hair color—which is hideous—the resemblance is striking. Your other sister wasn't so fortunate. I believe she looks more like Hunter. Such a pity."

I strive to make my voice as casual as possible, thinking he's more likely to keep talking if he believes this is idle chitchat. "How well did you know my mother?" *I don't know if she ever visited the compound or if they met...elsewhere.*

"Oh, my dear," he begins enthusiastically. "*I* introduced my brother to your beautiful mother, which turned out to be a tragic mistake for all involved."

My heartbeat quickens as I attempt to make sense of his words. *The insurance policy.* If my mother met Marcel while taking out the policy, then how had the relationship turned friendly enough for him to introduce her to Draco? By chance at Marcel's office? *No, that doesn't feel right. There's something more here.* "Yes, it was tragic that they both died so young." Even to my own ears, my response sounds forced, but I don't want to risk upsetting him by calling it murder.

A muscle clenches in his jaw, and I think I've gone too far, but he merely snorts indifferently. "There are no real tragedies in this world, my dear, only karma. Something none of us are immune to."

I hear what might be a car door slamming seconds before there is a sound in the foyer. Marcel doesn't bother to greet the new arrival; he simply stands waiting with that plastic smile plastered on his face. *He makes my skin crawl.* When Tony strolls in, he doesn't look surprised to see his uncle. But when his eyes land on me, there's confusion there, then wariness. He senses it too. Something is off. "Ah, my nephew"— Marcel actually claps his hands— "right on time. You've always had much better manners than your father." There's movement in the doorway, and I forget to breathe.

No.

Lee steps into the study with Jade at his side. *Oh, dear God. Why are they here?* "Lee, welcome," Marcel calls out. "And you brought your beautiful wife. I hoped you'd bring your son as well. It's been quite some time since I've seen Victor."

As always, Lee's expression gives little away. But not so for Jade. She looks pleased to see me, but I can tell she's picked up on the strange vibe in the room. "We came directly from the office," Lee replies as he walks Jade to take a seat next to me. He remains on his feet a few inches away with a look of inquiry on his face.

"Let me go ahead and dispense with the confusion so we can move past it. I'm the one who contacted each of you. Tony didn't summon you and Jade here, Lee, nor did he ask Jacey to come."

"Cass called me," Tony states. "Something about a fire in the kitchen. Lester was supposed to be waiting for me in the house."

"Yes, that's right," Marcel says. "I felt as if personal contact would be more likely to get you here with a minimum amount of questions. Fortunately, your relationship with Lee and Clint is such that a text was acceptable."

Tony's patience appears to have been exhausted. He puts his hands on his hips before asking, "What in the fuck is this all about? And since when have you resorted to trickery when you want to see me? I need to get to a meeting soon, Uncle."

"Oh yes, I know all about your meeting with Rutger. How you plan to ask for his help in flushing your father's murderer out. So very exciting, Anthony. I must admit, I've wondered if you'd ever reach that point. Oh, don't get me wrong, I know it's weighed on you. We've spoken of it many times. Yet you could never see what was right before you."

Oh, dear God. Jade slides one of her hands on top of mine and squeezes it hard enough to cut off the blood flow. I'm grateful for the discomfort, though, as it keeps me centered. Tony is clearly struggling to make sense of what Marcel is alluding to. "And what would that be, Uncle?" he asks softly.

I see Tony's fist clench when Marcel walks behind Draco's desk and takes a seat as if it's his rightful place. "Before I answer that question, Anthony, let me fill in a bit of background information. Otherwise, it will make no sense to you, and I very much want you to finally understand why things happened as they did. Marcel's eyes seem to drift off, and he's clearly somewhere else when he says, "Your father and I had a long history of falling in love with the same women. I'd find them first; then he'd swoop in and take them away. Claimed it was simply a game between brothers. My parents were certainly no help. They doted on their beloved Draco. I was simply the quiet one they didn't understand. I must say, I certainly didn't mourn their passing in that house fire. I don't think Draco did either since he benefited from the small insurance policy they left behind."

"My father never said anything about them dying in a fire. I mean, I knew they died young but—"

"Oh yes, dear old Dad died of a heart attack and Mom of a broken heart? Certainly, a better story and considering you never met them, probably easy to pass off. If you had known them, you would have realized that Mom's heart wouldn't have been in the least broken had the old man died first. She'd have been the first to celebrate. But I digress. Let's get back to Draco and me. We spent much of our youth and early adulthood in a kind of weird competition. Until two things happened. The first was he met your mother, and she ended up pregnant. He seemed to care about her, which of course required that I destroy that relationship. And truthfully, it was quite easy considering she was active military and surrounded by men daily. A few faked photos and eyewitness reports and his sweet little Cassandra became just another expendable whore. Only she had no family and no way to care for a child while deployed. So, the moment she had the baby, it was handed over to your father, and she was paid and threatened never to contact him again. Of course, as he gained fame and power as the head of the Moretti family, she would have been a fool to come anywhere near you. And she didn't...until his death."

"Cass," Tony murmurs in shock.

"Oh, yes." Marcel grins. "You've been kind enough to employ your own mother all these years."

"And Lester?" Tony asks appearing dazed.

"No, Lester doesn't know that you're her son. He isn't privy to any of this. Which has proved difficult, considering he's so good at his job. Had he worked for Draco, I'd never have been able to kill him without getting caught." There are indrawn breaths all around the room at Marcel's admission. Tony looks almost ashen as he stares at his uncle. "I realize that Hunter Wrenn took credit, but that fool could have never pulled it off."

"Why?" Tony hisses. "How could you possibly murder your own brother out of jealousy? What woman could have possibly been worth it?"

Marcel raises a brow, then pivots in his seat until his eyes land on

Jade and me. "Why, their mother, of course. Jasmine Wrenn, my soul mate. The woman I had an affair with for two years before I made the mistake of introducing her to your father."

"No," Jade whispers in horror, and I see Lee place a hand on her shoulder, lending his support.

"Yes, it's quite true. We met when she took out a life insurance policy with my company. Pretty standard when you're the head of a corporation. We just clicked from the first moment. We became friends, then more. She was miserable at home, longed to leave Hunter to be with me, but you girls were always in the way. Then my brother showed up at my place one evening unannounced and saw her." He appears on the verge of tears for a moment as he says, "From that day forward, it was the beginning of the end. Draco pursued her, and she succumbed to his charms as so many before her had. They were quite the happy little family. She came over here and brought either one or both of you and spent the afternoon at the pool with Draco and Anthony. I know you were all too young to remember, but you spent a lot of time together. Your mother told you it was playdates with her friends so if you slipped and said something in front of Hunter, he wouldn't be suspicious. After all, your mother was quite the social butterfly."

I'm shocked when Tony says, "I remember." He looks at me in wonder before adding, "I always thought it was a dream. Thought I loved you before I met you that night. But the little girl and boy, they were us. I can't believe it."

"Very good." Marcel nods approvingly. "She was going to leave Hunter for him but was simply biding her time. But something happened. Wrenn got wind of it and threatened you and your sister, said she could leave, but it would be alone. She'd never see you girls again. She panicked and ended it with my brother, and he lost his fucking mind. First, there was the drinking and depression. Until finally, with my prompting, of course, he wanted revenge." He points at Lee. "So you took Wrenn Wear and with it the last of her hope. She turned into as much of a drunk as my brother. Apparently, they actually loved each other, which wouldn't do. The funny part of this is that Hunter thought out their murders, hired someone to do both, and I'm the one who executed them. The bastard never knew." *Oh my God. I killed my father, thinking he killed my mother. But...he'd planned to, would have...so...he deserved to die. He was an evil man. Still, Marcel played us all. Will we never be free of monsters? Can no one be trusted? But for Tony...this will destroy him.*

"And Caulder?" I ask, finding my voice for the first time in a while. I have a bad feeling that none of us are meant to leave here alive, so our only hope may be to keep him talking until someone comes up with a plan. I hope to God Tony can regroup enough to do it.

He laughs, looking delighted at the question. "He was a dismal piece of humanity, wasn't he, my dear? I mean, I really had no idea about all the years you were forced to be your father's whore to protect your sister." I freeze in horror when his eyes go to Jade. "Apparently, your lovely sister had to fuck business associates and whatever else your monster of a father dreamed up or he threatened to make you do it instead. Do you realize how rare that type of sacrifice is?"

"Jacey." *Oh shit. Her pain. I can hear it.* I try so hard to keep my expression blank, but somehow, she sees the truth there anyway, and she breaks before me. There are no tears, no screams, she simply shuts down and stares at some point straight ahead.

Lee curses under his breath before turning his ire on Marcel. "What in the fuck is wrong with you?"

Marcel steeples his fingers as if giving Lee's question careful thought. "I believe you should recognize it well, my friend. It's called retribution after a lifetime of being kicked around. Isn't it very much what you did for Victor and for your daughter? Why is it acceptable for you, but not for me? You took Wrenn Wear for my brother. You interfered in things that were none of your business. Which is why I've returned the favor by telling your wife what the lot of you would have kept from her because you consider her too weak to handle the truth. It's a pity she won't live long enough to truly know how that type of thing eats away at you until you barely recognize yourself anymore."

"That doesn't answer the question of Caulder," Tony asks, sounding more focused. *Thank God.*

"Oh yes, sorry I got off course. Well, Cassandra was nice enough to record the conversation between you and Jacey for me. After all, if not for me, she never would have seen her son. That's right, I let her see you when Draco was off on one of his trips. No harm done. I even fixed her up with my old high school friend Lester, which worked out quite well for me later on. I'll admit, I killed Caulder simply for the shock value and because I could. I got a bit overzealous, but he was a mouthy bastard and brought it on himself."

"Marco and Nic will know I'm here by now. I told Mike to pass it along when he called to confirm my meeting with Rutger."

Marcel doesn't appear in the least concerned at Tony's words. In fact, he appears smug and vastly amused. And seconds later, I know why. Mike walks into the study as if nothing is amiss. "Ah son, there you are. Haven't we talked about how important it is to be punctual?" Marcel scolds lightly. *What the hell? Mike's his son?*

"Sorry, Dad. It took longer to get away from Nic than I planned on. Didn't want to make him suspicious."

"Dad?" Tony croaks out, once again shell-shocked. *When does this sideshow end?*

Mike has the audacity to clap Tony on the shoulder as if they're still the best of friends. "It's true. You know I was adopted at birth, right? Oh wait, my adoptive family didn't share that news with any of you. They also didn't impart the fact that they were paid very handsomely by my dad here to raise me."

Marcel looks like an eager kid at Christmas as he enjoys the stunned expressions on our faces. "I'm sure you're not aware of it, Anthony, but John and Carmen already had a child when he became an active member of the family. Why would anyone question the infant's parentage?"

Tony shoots Mike a look of utter contempt before staring at his uncle. "The better question here would be why you gave what I assume is your only son away?" He glances at Mike. "And you don't harbor any resentment that he never even acknowledged you as his? I can't imagine doing the dirty work for someone who tossed me aside at birth."

I cringe, expecting Marcel to lose it, but he doesn't. If anything, he acts as if this is going exactly as he wants it to, which makes me even more nervous. *There's more.* "You raise a valid point, Anthony. It does seem a bit odd. And I feel almost as if I'm neglecting Michael by not having a surprise for him." Marcel opens the desk drawer and pulls an envelope from inside it. He taps it against his other hand in a way that is like nails on a chalkboard. Mike is trying hard to feign indifference, but his eyes are riveted on the envelope. "Michael, as much as I've enjoyed being a father figure to you the past few years, it would be unfair of me to continue the charade when I've been so forthcoming with everyone else in this room. So, let me start by saying that you were born a twin. Granted you were the sickly of the two and weren't expected to survive. But your father believed you to be weak, and he had no respect or patience for what he perceived as a severe character flaw. Therefore, one son remained with him and arrangements were made for you to go to another family."

"What are you saying?" Mike smiles uncertainly, still believing this is part of the game Marcel is playing.

"Give your father credit. He did keep you close but not out of love. He wanted to make sure your identity was never discovered. He didn't like to leave things to chance and having you used against him at some point in the future was not an option."

"You're fucking insane," Tony snarls. "I could give a fuck about this traitor," he adds as he points a finger at Mike. "But enough with the fucking stories. The only proven fact so far is that you're a sadistic, lying son of a bitch."

Marcel narrows his eyes at Tony and then opens the envelope and pulls something out. He tosses it in Tony's direction, where it lands at his feet. "I think you'll recognize your father in that picture and possibly yourself as well, but the infant the nurse is holding is Michael. Your brother."

Jade comes out of her daze long enough to gasp, which mirrors my own reaction. Even Lee seems shaken, which scares me more than anything. Nothing perturbs him other than his wife's distress. Tony studies the photo in stunned disbelief. "Why?" he asks, clearly taken aback at the proof he's clutching in his hand.

Mike looks from Tony to Marcel. "This can't be true. I wouldn't... how could you ask me to...my brother?"

"Yes, yes," Marcel says grandly. "Let's save another ten minutes of denial and reassurances. Anthony is indeed your blood brother. Cassandra gave birth to twins. If it's any consolation to you, Michael, she left the hospital thinking you were dead. You were not expected to live, and Draco told her that you had not. He didn't want to deal with the unnecessary drama of her growing a conscience at the thought of you being given away. You know mothers and their bleeding hearts. A sick child could have made her change her mind about leaving. And really what did she have to offer? A career military officer with no family and two infants? She simply wasn't strong enough to deal with that emotionally or financially."

"But she came back." I speak up, having no idea why I'm defending a woman who sold her babies to a mafia king.

"She did." Marcel nods. "After all the dirty work was over. But I'm not going to quibble over it. She's been a great asset. Without her spying on her son, I'd never have stayed ahead of him, even with Michael's help."

"But why?" Tony asks. "Why would she supposedly come back because of me, then basically assist you in your attempt to kill me?"

"Oh, she thought she was keeping you safe. I may have filled her head with a bunch of nonsense about the family wanting to kill you because you were investigating your father's death. I told her I needed the information to protect you. And a mother would do most anything for their child...especially when there's a healthy dose of guilt involved for abandoning them."

As Tony visibly struggles to process this, Lee says skeptically, "So this whole elaborate web of lies, murder, and whatever the fuck else you've done was all because your brother scored more women than you did? Isn't that taking jealousy too far?"

Lee, shut up. I realize everyone wants answers while Marcel is so eager to talk, but I'm not sure that insulting a madman is exactly the way to go. For the first time, it dawns on me that we're all staying of our own free will, as he doesn't even have a gun. Or if he does, he hasn't shown it yet. But I also know Tony isn't likely to leave until he's heard everything Marcel has to say. There might never be another opportunity. Because either we'll be dead, or he will. There is very little hope that we'll come out of this alive. Marcel laughs, but there's a decided edge to it now. "Empires have been toppled, fortunes acquired and lost, and countless murders have been committed in the name of love. Ask yourself, Lee, what wouldn't you do for the woman at your side? Then imagine yourself loving not one woman, but several in your lifetime, and each time losing her to an arrogant man. Can you even fathom the gut-wrenching betrayal of overhearing the woman who you loved with every part of you laughing at the idea that she'd really have left her husband for you? And then discovering that the whore had packed her bags and was leaving everything behind, including her own children, for your brother, a man to which everything was expendable. He may have been infatuated with Jasmine Wrenn, but it would have burned out. He didn't know how to be faithful to anything other than the crime empire he'd built and the blood money he'd acquired through it."

"And what of Victor? Why was it necessary to murder him as well?" Lee asks softly. I can hear the pain in his voice as he speaks of his former mentor and the man who had been his only real father figure.

Marcel waves a hand indifferently. "Collateral damage. I had nothing against him. It was simply the fact that Draco let his guard down when he was with his best friend. He wasn't as paranoid after he'd had a few drinks and was goofing off with Victor. And there was the small fact that he possibly recognized me that day. I'm not sure why you're upset. You benefited handsomely from his death. If I hadn't taken him out, he'd still be alive, and there would have been no inheritance. You'd still be an active member of the Moretti family and the little family you prize so much would be in grave danger every moment of their lives."

"I've had enough of this shit," Tony snarls before turning to Mike. "If you want to continue being the lackey for this bastard, then more power to you. After the way you've betrayed our brotherhood, I don't even care." He glances at Lee before adding, "Let's get the fuck out of here."

Marcel clicks his tongue. "I'm afraid it's not that simple, kid. Why don't you look closely at the beautiful Wrenn sisters?" I see Tony's face go pale, then hear Lee's indrawn breath. *What?* I have no idea what has made Tony look so helpless, but it's then that I truly understand what the hell I've been through is nothing compared to the thoughts of losing the man who just hours earlier had declared his love for me. If those moments of happiness are all there is for me, then I'll die knowing I loved more in hours than some people do in their entire lives.

TONY

I swallow hard as I stare at the red points on light on the foreheads of Jacey and Jade. Lee has seen them as well, and he's livid. But he's also terrified. This entire thing is so surreal, and I feel as if I'm in the middle of a nightmare. My uncle murdered not only my father but also Jacey's mother. I have a twin brother, who enabled my uncle to spy on me. And I have a mother who has lived in my house for years under false pretenses. What the fuck else? I have just opened my mouth to ask my uncle where the guns are located that are trained on Jacey and her sister when I notice the bookcase behind the desk is ajar. *Has that been open this entire time?* I knew the panic room existed, but to my knowledge, it hasn't been accessed in years. The barrels of two pistols emerge first, then one of Jacey's guards, Bishop, appears carrying a pistol in each hand. *All that's missing here is fucking Santa Clause.* Cassandra's role in arranging my security has come back to haunt me in a big way. My own mother was privy to enough details in my life to literally bury me alive. Bishop doesn't appear contrite at all. He simply tilts one pistol slightly in greeting before saying, "Sorry about this, boss. Nothing personal; it's just business. Got a family to support and your uncle here pays better."

Marcel motions at Mike. "Please collect Tony's and Lee's guns. Gentlemen, don't insult my intelligence by denying that you're carrying. I'm fully aware you'd never leave home without." I bite back a curse as I pull my Glock from my ankle holster and hand it to Mike. He refuses to make eye contact and seems in a hurry to get away from me. Lee also has his gun in an ankle holster, and he narrows his eyes in anger as he gives it to Mike. Brother or no brother, he is our enemy. Mike tucks both guns in his waistband before dropping his shirt back down.

Marcel leans forward in his chair, and it strikes me again how much he looks like my father. Which seems to make this even worse somehow. *Distract him. Keep him talking.* My mind is desperately searching for a plan, and I know that Lee is as well. There are two guns and four of us. There is no way Bishop can take us all—but he doesn't have to. Marcel knows we'd never risk their lives by attacking. Right now, our hands are truly tied. A thought occurs to me. "I assume you poisoned Marco?"

"Actually, it was Mike, but yes, I'm indirectly responsible." *Indirectly, my ass.*

Mike has been quiet since Marcel broke the news of his *true* parentage to him. I steal a quick look his way and find him watching me as well. I have no idea what he's thinking, but I can't imagine it's good. "And the fact that he ended up being found by a Gavino. I've never bought into that being a coincidence."

"We couldn't fully ensure that would happen"—Marcel nods— "but we hedged the bets in our favor. You boys should really have learned something from Draco's death and stop being so predictable. You frequent the same restaurants quite often. In researching the Gavino family, I come across the lovely Nina—Franklin's stepdaughter. She seemed the easiest point to sow a seed of distrust between the two families. And as luck would have it, she lives in the city very close to one of Marco's favorite restaurants. Mike suggested eating there, then he canceled at the last minute. Luckily, Marco decided to eat alone since he was already there. Granted, he had passed out too far away from her place for her to find him, so we were forced to relocate him. We planned to leave him closer to her building, but it was simply too risky with the number of people around that evening. Walking that dog was a real lifesaver, especially for Marco."

"And what of Tommy and Frankie? Are they involved in this as well?" I ask. If I'm to die, then I fucking well want all the answers.

Marcels snorts. "The only thing they're guilty of is stupidity. According to Mike, they skim a bit off the top at times when they can, but it's nothing a lot of the other guys don't do as well. They had nothing to do with your father's death. They aren't smart enough for something of that scope."

Bishop shifts his hold on the pistols in his hands as he says, "This is dragging on for too long. I don't know how much longer Lester will be out. Trust me, you don't want him waking up; the dude's nuts."

"So where's Clint?" I ask, attempting to keep one of them talking.

Bishop rolls his eyes. "Clint's straight as an arrow. There's not enough money in the world worth him selling his honor. Unfortunately, I don't feel that way."

Marcel gets to his feet and pulls a gun from his lap. "Yes, well, as my associate has pointed out, it's time to wrap this up. I think I'll keep the Wrenns for a bit longer. After all, one does remind me so much of her mother, so it would be like stepping back in time. Perhaps young Jade can watch as her sister suffers for her one last time."

"Over my fucking dead body," Lee hisses. "You will stay away from my wife and her sister."

Marcel raises a brow, looking amused as he asks, "And who do you think will stop me, Jacks? With you and Tony out of the way, there really is no one left. I can promise you that I'll play the grieving uncle so well that the family will never question a few more disappearances. Hell, I'll be doing them a favor. I'll keep the Wrenns out of sight while I enjoy them, then they too will disappear. So, this is the end of the line for you, my friend. There is no one to save either of you."

At that moment, the unmistakable sound of a round being chambered has me turning toward the doorway. Cass...with her Glock in her hand. Her eyes are full of apology as she looks at first me, then Mike. *She knows.* She takes a few steps farther into the room until she's facing Marcel. "That's where you're wrong. I may be almost forty years late, but this time, I will save my boys." There are tears in her eyes as she comes to a stop between my brother and me. "I'm so sorry. I was young and alone. I didn't have any options." Turning to Mike, she adds, "And they told me that you were dead. I never knew any differently until I overheard it on the household intercom."

"This is so touching," Marcel utters as if he's bored by the whole ordeal. "But you're just as expendable as your offspring, Cass. You should have stayed away."

And then it starts. A moment of complete chaos much like the night Hunter Wrenn was killed. Gunshots are fired as I leap across the room, dragging Jacey onto the floor and falling on top of her. Lee does the same with Jade. There is so much noise that I have a hard time believing it's being made by only the people in this room. Finally, it is quiet. I raise my head but can see nothing through the smoke around us. "Stay down," I say to Jacey as I get to my knees and move at a crouch to survey the room.

"Don't go," she cries out in panic. "Please, just wait."

"Duchess, I need to see what we're up against." Lee has moved over while I've been talking to Jacey and is at my side on his knees as well.

"Don't know what the fuck just happened, but we need to get whoever the fuck is left before they get us."

Jacey moves over to Jade, and they link their arms together as we shift away. "I can't see shit," I whisper a second before bumping into something. Bishop is lying on the floor with his eyes open and lifeless. There is a bullet hole in his forehead but very little blood.

"That's one down," Lee murmurs, then gives a grunt of satisfaction as he finds one of the other man's guns on the floor nearby. He checks the clip, then pops it back in. "Still almost full."

"You can get up, Tony, you're clear," says a voice from behind me. I whirl around to find a very pale Lester with an assault rifle in his arms.

I hesitate, still not sure who to trust. Even though my uncle said Lester wasn't involved, who the fuck knows if that was yet another lie?"

Then a sound from near the doorway booms out, "Tony, Lee, you two all right?"

"Marco," I call out in relief. If there's anyone in the world that I still trust, it's him. Lee seems to be of the same mind because we both straighten and get our first good look at the area. The desk is overturned, and there are many bullet holes in the wood. The bottles on the bar are shattered, and liquid is leaking onto the floor. And there is another body facedown. This one obviously female. "Cassandra," I murmur, not really knowing how to feel. She was never a mother to me, but I've considered her a friend. And that is the person I will mourn the most.

"Marcel shot her just as I came into the room," Lester says as he too stares at her prone body.

"Where are Mike and Marcel? Fuck, please don't say they got away."

"Not exactly," Marco mutters. "Mike alerted me. He managed to dial my phone and leave his on speaker. I heard everything from the point just before Bishop showed himself until we arrived."

"He's a traitor," I spit out in contempt. "And apparently my fucking brother."

"I'm all those things, Tony, but for what it's worth, I was lied to maybe more than you were." I stiffen as my brother enters the room with Nic at his back and Marcel in front of him. But what has my attention is that Mike has a gun focused on an enraged Marcel. He's baring his teeth in more of a snarl.

"What in the fuck is this?" I hiss in anger.

I stand my ground when Mike stops a few feet away and extends his gun by the handle to me. "You were denied your right of retribution once before against the man you thought killed your father. Now you know who was responsible. I could have easily taken the shot myself, but this is yours. Pay this bastard back for what he's done to so many people."

I'm shocked speechless. I see nothing but sincerity and sadness in Mike's eyes as he nods. Marcel's hands are tied behind his back. There's nowhere for him to run. I glance at Jacey and Jade, who are now on their feet holding hands. Jacey returns my look, giving me a nod of understanding and showing me that she supports me. I shift my gaze to Lee, who understands what I want perfectly. He walks to his wife and puts one hand on her elbow before putting his other one on Jacey's. Neither woman protests as he leads them from the room before returning alone. Marcel glares at me with hate-filled eyes before spitting in my face. "You don't have the balls, kid. You never have. You're a coward just like your father. He always wanted everyone else to do his dirty work. So why don't you follow behind the women and let someone else take care of this?"

I'm calm, not in the least rattled by his taunts. My focus is solely on him, and no amount of his bullshit will shake that. He's opened his mouth, ready for another blast of bullshit, when I calmly raise the gun and shoot him at such close range that it removes half of his head. There is zero chance he's still alive, so only one shot is necessary. Marco crosses to me and takes the gun, dropping it into a bag and pocketing it. "Go on home with your lady. I'll handle this from here."

"And what of him?" I ask, pointing at Mike.

Marco claps me on the shoulder. "That's up to you. He'll go into lockup until you've decided."

"That won't be necessary. I've been through enough and so have you. I'm ready for it to be over." When we all turn to stare at him, Mike pulls a gun from his waistband, and before anyone can stop him, he puts it in his mouth and pulls the trigger.

"Fucking hell." I stagger backward.

Lee puts a hand on my back, keeping me steady. "Let's get out of here. I think we've seen enough for tonight. I'll drop you and Jacey off at the club."

And with that, I feel the shutters coming down over my mind as I lock down. I've lost both friends and family tonight, and I have to process my grief before I lose my mind. Jacey takes my arm as we walk to where they're waiting in the foyer. She studies my face, then takes charge. Before I know it, Clint meets us at the entrance of the club and assures us he's checked every inch of the building including the apartment. He advises that he'll be staying until I tell him differently. Jacey thanks him and leads me through the apartment and into the bathroom. She undresses first herself and then me. I step into the shower and simply stand there while she washes us both. I know she's worried, but she doesn't say anything. Instead, she helps me out, dries me off, and then finds me a pair of shorts to slip on before helping me into bed. Then she turns on the light on her side of the bed and turns mine off.

She stops at my side and drops a kiss onto my forehead. "I know you need time. I'll be in the living room when you're ready or if you need me." She pauses before adding softly, "I love you." Strangely, even with everything going on inside my head, it touches me that she understands my need for time alone to process. And with that, she closes the door behind her, and I zone out completely. I have no idea what I'll feel later, but for now, I give myself up to the blessed oblivion of darkness, hoping that somewhere inside it, I'll find not only some answers but peace as well.

16

JACEY

I checked on Tony several times during the past twelve hours, but he's still sound asleep. Marco and Nic have been by, but they've known him a long time, so they're not concerned about his behavior. In fact, Marco explained that Tony has been that way for as long as he could remember. Lee called once, and I asked him how Jade was. He paused before admitting that she was very depressed over what she learned from Marcel. I didn't know what to say after that. I have no idea how to deal with my sister any more than I have for the past ten years.

When I hear a sound in the next room, I freeze, listening intently. I'm almost certain the shower is running. I hurry into the kitchen and take out some eggs and bacon to make a quick breakfast. He must be hungry.

The food is ready, and I'm dividing it onto two plates when he walks up behind me and nuzzles my neck. "Hey there," I say softly as I put the food on the bar and turn around to face him. He's freshly shaven and smells amazing. There are dark circles under his eyes, but he appears alert and relaxed. "How are you?" *Stupid question.*

He smiles, but there's no real humor behind it. "I'm okay, Duchess. Tired of trying to make sense out of something that can't possibly be explained away rationally. I officially give up." He kisses me lightly on the lips before taking a seat. I pull out a stool beside him, and we eat in silence for several minutes.

"You know," I say casually, "I had to accept long ago that not everything can be fit into a neat box with a logical explanation attached to it. Simply put, sometimes life fucks us over out of the blue. And we have no control over it. But we can control how we choose to see it and react to it." This next part is going to be tricky, but at this point, I don't think there's anything to lose by trying. "I've been thinking of all the players involved in your uncle's games. Your mother made a bad decision not once, but twice, but both times, she thought she was protecting you. She couldn't take care of you, so she let your father, who had the financial means, raise you. And you've said many times that he loved you... was good to you. Your upbringing may not have been the most conventional, but you were happy. And she helped Marcel, thinking she was saving you. Yes, she was misguided, but in her defense, I believe she was so desperate to make up for giving you away that her judgment was impaired. Imagine for a moment the intense grief she must have felt at discovering that not only had she assisted the man who killed your father but who was also planning to kill you. Then to make matters worse, she also learns that her other son didn't die as she was told but was given to another family. She threw herself in front of Bishop and took a bullet that was meant for Mike. Marco said Mike was in shock over it. But at least she died in peace, knowing she saved a son she thought dead all these years."

I see him mull my words over, his food long since forgotten. "I had a brother all along, Duchess. I spent so many hours around him and never knew it. I could have...saved him...if I'd known. How he must have hated me in those moments when Marcel told him of what our father had done. I lived a good life as you've pointed out, but he was tossed away."

"Were John and Carmen, his parents, good to him?" I ask, hoping to God they were.

He nods slowly. "Yeah, they were. They doted on him. Hell, I was even jealous of the time John spent taking him fishing and hunting. Those were things my own father didn't really have a lot of time for.

And now they've probably already been informed that Mike is dead—in whatever way Marco decided to make it look."

"My heart breaks for them," I say softly. "Marcel is to blame. Marcel poisoned Mike with lies. But Mike saved all of us, Tony. If not for him calling Marco, we'd all probably be dead right now. It's as if he couldn't have lived with what he'd done on his conscience."

He rubs his hands over his face. "Fuck, I know. It's just...too many tragedies have plagued this family. And I want that to be the end of them. I want to live my life in peace. I want to have a family with you and grow old with you. I want us to run my clubs and spend so much time together that we're sick of each other."

"Are you asking me to marry you, Mr. Moretti?" And amazingly enough, the thought of that doesn't panic me at all.

"Um. I was thinking more of living in sin...but I guess I can put a ring on it if I must." I punch him in the side as he continues to tease me. Suddenly serious, he pulls my hand to his lips and kisses the fingers. "I'm serious, Jacey. I do want all that with you. I've been in love with you since we were kids. I've always thought the dreams were nothing more than that until my uncle admitted we spent time together as children. I knew the moment you fell into my arms that I'd never be the same. You were the adult version of the girl I've always loved."

"Oh, Tony," I whisper as tears spill down my cheeks. "I never thought I'd have this. Someone who loves me, knowing all the bad things I've done. Even if they were for the right reasons. But you've always seen past the ice queen to the woman inside. I firmly believe I was meant to find you, because like you, I knew the first moment I saw you. I love you with all my heart, Mr. Moretti, and yes, I'd very much like for you to make an honest woman out of me."

He gets to his feet suddenly and picks me up in his arms. I squeal as he bounces me lightly before turning toward the bedroom. "You drive a hard bargain, Duchess. But if it's okay with you, I think we should go ahead and start practicing for this baby-making bargain we made. After all, I'm a man of my word, and I agreed to make you my baby mama."

"You certainly did." I grin. "So, let's get to it. I figure if you're walking around in the club with our six kids, then maybe, just maybe, you might not be such a hot commodity."

"Oh please," he huffs out as he tosses me on the bed. "I'll always be hot, but only for you, Duchess." As our laughter dies away and our passion rises, I can't help but marvel that we've survived what would have killed most people. Instead of giving up and walking away, we're now firmly on the path to our future together. He fell in love with me almost thirty years ago, and even though I have no memory of it, I feel certain that we gave our hearts to each other back then for safekeeping until the time came for us to reclaim them and each other again. How that was possible is a mystery I'm sure I'll never solve. In this case, I have to thank my mother. Had she not been so incredibly vain and self-ish, Tony and I never would have had the chance to love. He would have had unfulfilled dreams, and I would have stayed alone and bereft of one of life's greatest gifts. Tony will continue to grieve his unimagin-able losses; of that, I have no doubt. But we will grieve together. And over time, we'll heal together too. Because that's what true love is.

Hope...and never being alone.

The End

EPILOGUE

TONY

It's almost like the dream I had of us as adults. I stare at my beautiful wife as she walks out of the pool at the compound with a baby held securely at her hip. Her newly restored blond hair glistens in the sun as she drops a kiss onto the baby's soft curls. My heart turns the now familiar flip that it always does when she's near. If anyone had told me a year ago that Jacey and I would go through something akin to a horror story and come out on the other side stronger than ever, I would have laughed. Don't get me wrong, I knew she'd be important to me from that first moment we met, but I had no idea I'd be capable of loving another in this capacity. It's different to anything I've ever experienced. We married right here in a poolside wedding a month after we were rocked by so much tragedy. When Jacey suggested having our wedding here, I balked until she explained that she wanted us to have a happy memory here to hopefully lessen some of the pain from what happened.

Life slowly returned to normal after that night. We ended up telling Rutger everything, knowing he deserved the closure as well. He arranged for John and Carmen to be informed that Mike had died in the line of duty. None of us could see any benefit in taking their good memories of their son away from them. My uncle quit his job and moved away, or at least that's what his employers were led to believe via email. And Lester still works for me although I know he struggles with not only Cass's death but her deceit as well. Bishop disappeared but was kind enough to leave his family enough money to take care of anything they might need in the future.

She turns to face me as if sensing my eyes on her and waves at me with little LeeAnn's hand snuggled in her own. "Damn, I feel old," Lee drawls at he drops down into a chair next to me.

"You should; you have two little kids now. Leave it to you to knock your wife up immediately after a shootout. I mean, I admire your concentration and all, but couldn't you have waited for at least a week? It's kind of tacky."

Lee glances around to make sure no one is near before flipping me off. Apparently little Victor is imitating his father now, and Jade wasn't too happy the first time he gave her the finger. "Don't sulk because you're less of a man," Lee mocks. "Luckily for you, Jacey is quite taken with our kids, so there's no pressure for you to reproduce."

I watch Jacey as she hands LeeAnn to her mother, then swings little Victor around in a circle. By mutual agreement, we decided to put our own baby-making plans on hold. Jacey realized the reasons she wanted a child were not the right ones. And she no longer needed a baby to love her unconditionally, because she had me for that, as well as her family. Right now, we were enjoying it being just us. She sold Wrenn about six months ago, and we're running my clubs together. She has an amazing head for business and has handled most all the details for the new club we're opening next year. "That's true. And I'm not gonna lie, man. I like buying them loud shit and sending them home with it."

"That fucking flute was pure evil," he grouses, shaking his head. "Don't worry, though, I'll pay you back."

I incline my head toward where Jade is standing with her sister. "How's she doing? I know the therapy has really helped Jacey. She still has her moments, but she's getting more comfortable with who she is."

Lee watches his wife for a moment before turning back to me. "She's doing better. Like Jacey, there are better days than others. I was worried when she found out she was pregnant so soon after discovering what Jacey had been through. But I think the distraction was a good thing. I believe the joint therapy sessions with Jacey along with her individual ones have been a big help in her learning to cope with what is almost a form of survivor's guilt. Even though Jacey didn't die, Jade blames herself for Jacey losing part of her life."

"I'm glad they've been able to form a relationship. I know it's still awkward at times, but they're finding their way. And no matter how much she denied it, Jacey needs that just as much as Jade."

"I still feel like a bit of dick over the way I treated Jacey in the beginning," Lee admits. "But I had no reason to believe that things were anything other than how they seemed."

"She understands that, Lee, and she's finally stopped making those voodoo dolls of you," I say with a straight face.

He grins. "Fucker."

"What's a fucker, Daddy?" We both freeze when little Victor steps into view. Neither of us noticed him slipping behind our chairs at some point.

Lee casts a nervous glance in Jade's direction before picking his son up and sitting him beside him on the chair. "It's nothing, Victor. I was just paying your uncle Tony a big compliment."

His little brow scrunches up before he stubbornly shakes his head. "That's weird—"

"Oh look, Jacey has some ice cream," I interrupt before the kid digs in his heels and starts with the rapid-fire questions. If he doesn't grow up to be a lawyer or a judge, he's missed his calling.

"Thanks." Lee sighs. "That was a close one. I swear that boy slips around so quietly it's unsettling. After a few awkward moments, we make sure our bedroom door is locked at certain times, if you get my meaning."

I pick up my beer and tap it against his. "Loud and clear."

"Where are Marco and Nic?" he asks as if their absence has just occurred to him.

"The big cook-off is coming up, so Nic is frantically trying to perfect his recipe. I swear if Tommy beats him this year I'm fucking moving to another state. He whines like a little bitch. And Marco is probably stalking Nina Gavino as usual. He's asked her out repeatedly, but she doesn't want anything to do with him. Says she wants a normal guy and not a mobster."

"That's harsh." Lee grimaces.

Jade and Jacey join us with Victor trailing behind them. Jade hands LeeAnn to Lee, then perches on the end of his chair. "What are you boys over here gossiping about?" she teases as she swats Lee's leg.

"If we told you, we'd have to kill you," I quip, then roll my eyes when both women cringe. "Too soon?"

"You could say that," Jacey mutters as she slides backward until she's sitting between my legs with her head on my chest. Victor hands her his Popsicle, and she removes the wrapper for him. "Here you go, sweetie."

"Thank you, fucker," he deadpans, and there is complete and utter silence.

Jade turns to Lee with narrowed eyes while Jacey whirls around to stare at me. "Which one of you?" she asks. But we've been down this road before, so Lee and I keep our mouths shut, presenting a united front. As she huffs and lectures me under my breath, I know I'm actually the luckiest *fucker* in the world.

Once upon a time, I had a dream that would one day change my life. The woman in my arms isn't the same girl I dreamed of, because she's better in every way. She's a warrior, a lover, a friend, my equal, and most importantly, she's mine. Forever.

Coming Fall 2018
MARCO

I sit in my car outside of Nina Gavino's apartment as I've done so often in the past year. Only this time, things are different. There is unrest akin to panic in the Gavino organization, and it's no longer safe for Nina to be on her own. I have been fixated on the beautiful little minx since she quite literally rescued me from a pile of dog shit after I'd been poisoned. I've pursued her to no avail, but she wants nothing to do with the mafia. She had enough of that as the stepdaughter of the recently deceased, Franklin Gavino—head of the Gavino Family. And considering I am the son of the head of the Moretti Family, I'm completely entangled in the life she is so determined to avoid.

But none of that matters any longer. Franklin and his son, Frankie Jr., were murdered last night, and now no one is safe or above suspicion. The Morettis might be allies of the Gavinos, but my word alone will not stop them from harming Nina should they decide to. And thanks to Frankie Jr's obsession with his step-sister, there are many in the organization who know her name all too well.

The only way I can ensure her safety is to claim her publicly. And that is exactly what I intend to do. It's a drastic step to take for someone who is essentially a stranger. Especially one who wants nothing to do with me. *Why* you might ask, would I do something like that for her when there are so many willing women out there? *Because* I want her more than I've ever wanted another woman. And...I feel responsible for the predicament she could well find herself in. After all, I killed Franklin and his son. Did I forget to mention that?

ACKNOWLEDGMENTS

My amazing editors: Marion Archer and Jenny Sims with Editing4Indies. Love you ladies!

Melissa Gill for my beautiful cover.

And to my blogger friends, Elizabeth Swain, Catherine Crook with A Reader Lives a Thousand Lives, Jennifer Harried with Book Bitches Blog, Christine with Books and Beyond, Jenn with SMI Book Club, Chloe with Smart Mouth Smut, Shelly with Sexy Bibliophiles, Amanda and Heather with Crazy Cajun Book Addicts, Stacia with Three Girls & A Book Obsession, Lisa Salvary and Confessions of a Book Lovin Junkie.